The Witch's Daughter

LEIGH ANN EDWARDS

The Irish Witch Series
(Book Two)

Suite 300 – 990 Fort Street
Victoria, BC, Canada V8V 3K2
www.friesenpress.com

Copyright © 2015 by Leigh Ann Edwards
First Edition – 2015

All rights reserved.

No part of this publication may be reproduced in any form, or by any means, electronic or mechanical, including photocopying, recording, or any information browsing, storage, or retrieval system, without permission in writing from the publisher.

ISBN
978-1-4602-6460-7 (Hardcover)
978-1-4602-6461-4 (Paperback)
978-1-4602-6462-1 (eBook)

1. Fiction, Romance, Paranormal

Distributed to the trade by The Ingram Book Company

Dedication

My second novel, *The Witch's Daughter*, is dedicated to three amazing people who are wonderful blessings in my life.

To my husband, Mark; your quiet, calm, steadfast demeanor and willingness to adapt to most any situation, is exactly what I need to ground me, even during the most difficult times. The courage you showed in pursuing your dream, by moving to Canada from the UK, definitely inspired me to continue with following my own lifelong dream to become a published author. Your unquestionable support and unwavering belief that I must continue to keep writing and publishing my novels, even on the days when I have my doubts, are immeasurably important to me, my love.

I would also like to dedicate my book to my two daughters, who are vastly different, but equally special and precious in my heart. I love you both, and absolutely cherish the relationship I have with each of you.

To Katrina, my first-born; I appreciate your warmth, sense of humor and gentleness, your ability to accept change, along with your support in my writing and my life. Thanks for reading every single one of my books even though at one time you were probably a bit too young to do so. Your never-ending encouragement and assistance with marketing my novel has been so helpful, and welcomed more than I could ever tell you. It means a lot to me that you enjoy my books, and wish for me to be keep writing; that you realize it will always be my passion. I am extremely proud to call you my daughter and so happy you are my friend, Katrina!

To Jerilyn, my baby; you are my feisty, strong-willed daughter, who has often been compared to my sister, Darla, and I agree, your temperament is much like hers. Although parenting a headstrong child is not always an easy task, I must tell you I sometimes envy your great determination, and ability to speak your mind. I am exceedingly thankful you value keeping family close, and that you always take the time to make holidays and celebrations extra special for everyone. I look forward to your daily phone calls and our lengthy conversations. Even though you haven't read my books, and find it a little "weird" that your mother writes novels and especially "love scenes", I am grateful to you for helping to promote my book and truly wanting me to succeed. I am very proud of you and adore our friendship, Jerilyn!

My heroines, Alainn and Arianna (who is found in the latter part of the series) are both largely based on the important women in my life. Their personalities are a combination of the many strengths and characteristic traits of both my daughters, my Mum and my sister, Darla.

Acknowledgments

Once again, I would like to thank Pip Wallace, my author account manager at FriesenPress. I appreciate your quick replies to my emails and phone calls, and always being able to answer my numerous questions. Thanks for being genuinely excited for me and encouraging me through each step of the publishing process. It was great to finally meet you. I would also like to acknowledge the editorial and design teams at FriesenPress who worked with me to make the "The Witch's Daughter" visually and literarily appealing.

As mentioned in the dedication, thanks always to my husband, Mark and my daughters, Katrina and Jerilyn.

Thank-you to my four wonderful grandchildren: Darien for your humor and quick wit. Daniella for your beautiful smile and amazing hugs, Grayson for your infectious laugh and keeping me entertained, Novak, for your mischievous grin and affectionate manner. Thanks to each of you for making me feel special and always being happy to spend time with me. You are all precious to me; you warm my heart and bring me unequivocal joy and unconditional love. You make my world a brighter and more meaningful place.

Thanks to my two son-in-laws, Roy and Shane for that you do and for the many ways you have helped me through the years. I do appreciate it!

I would like to thank my brother, Kerry for your continued support, your ability to make most any situation humorous, and for your help with promoting my book. Though in our younger years we may not have been the closest of siblings (that might be a bit of an understatement since we did fight a lot)! I now treasure having you as a brother, and a friend.

Thanks to my sister-in-law, and good friend, Tannis for being such a big supporter and definitely my champion when it comes to boasting about my book and marketing. You have hands down sold more copies than any individual. Thanks for all your help, and you may just learn the ending after all!

Thanks to my cousin, Andy, you have been a close second in the area of promotions, bragging about my novels and selling copies for me. I appreciate it very much. Thanks for your encouragement, Andy, for being such a lovely person and great cousin.

Thank-you to my nephews Grant and Matthew for being so important in my life, because of the two of you, I will always have a part of your mum with me.

Thanks to Darla and Mum for your much appreciated signs from above that reaffirm, you will *always* watch over us and send love and heavenly support.

I wish to acknowledge my many great friends who have been very supportive, and to those who attended my book launch and library visits. I appreciate all the votes of confidence and well wishes.

To my valued fans who have fallen in love with Alainn and Killian, and their world, thanks for supporting my writing. With your ongoing support, I hope to publish many, many more novels in the Irish Witch Series.

Please know I couldn't accomplish any of this without all of you!

BOOK TWO

The Witch's Daughter
IRELAND 1536

Chapter one

In a state nearing exhaustion, Alainn dodged the horse and cart trundling into her path and hurried along the crowded street. Her feet throbbed painfully in her thin slippers, already bruised from the uneven cobblestones. Weaving in and out of the scattered vendor stalls, pushing through the crowds, she paused but a moment to catch her breath and inhaled deeply. The fetid scents of the city swamped her senses, and she felt her stomach lurch queasily. She set off once more on aching feet.

Hoping to find somewhere to hide for a time, Alainn rounded the corner of a narrow alleyway only to pull up short. Pierce stood before her, exasperation clear on his young face. She met his stare with disdain.

"Pierce MacArthur, my patience wears thin!" she rasped angrily. "I've told you no less than a dozen times. I've absolutely no intention of returning to Castle O'Brien!"

"Aye, 'tis true, you've told me," he protested with ever-thinning lips, "but I cannot in good conscience leave you here alone in this city. I have promised Killian I will watch over you in his stead, and I intend to keep my word on that count. I am here to protect you!"

"I do not desire your presence nor require your protection, so be gone with you. Sure, Cookson must be nearly ready to set off for the castle. Join him now and be off!"

Pierce narrowed his eyes, crossed his arms, and set his jaw in defiance. In a flash, she turned and sprang away from him, but his strong hand reached out and clamped on her arm. He began dragging her toward the din of the market and, though she struggled, she was no match for his strength.

"Sorry I am, Pierce, but 'tis you who have you forced my hand." He looked back sharply, eyebrows knitting in question. "Truly," she spat out, trying to wrench free her arm, "You would have been wise to respect my decision and heed my words!"

Pierce glanced up as a tall stack of crates came loose from their ropes and flew at him erratically. He jumped back in alarm, though each crate seemed to pass narrowly by without hitting him. They crashed at his feet, smashing open, spewing their contents before him and capably blocking his path. Alainn ran. She thought she felt his accusing glare on her back long after he was lost from sight.

After a fair distance, Alainn darted through the back doorway of a building. She found herself in a crowded ale-house surrounded by a rowdy group of bleary-eyed men. They had obviously been partaking of the wares for a goodly while. Hoping not to have been noticed, she turned back to the door when a patron lurched in front of her, blocking her exit. He eyed her up and down.

"You can't simply turn up here givin' us a wee glimpse of yer beauty and then expect to leave without even an introduction," he slurred, his breath sour. Alainn glanced toward the door with growing impatience as he continued to speak. "But you don't seem so very friendly. Why'd you even bother comin' in here then?"

Trying to ignore the foul odor permeating the air around him, Alainn looked up at the huge man who dwarfed her. Never gifted in deception, she struggled to come up with a response until he leaned in, his lips pursing.

She backed up and stammered, "I-I beg your pardon, sir, I seem to have made a grave error. I'd thought this was the alchemist's shop. I'm in need... I'm in need of an elixir, yes...an elixir to aid my family for I fear they may, they may...be stricken with the pox!"

He stopped advancing, his face uncertain, then his eyes grew wide with obvious fear.

"The pox," he hissed. He slowly backed away as did the men nearby. "Two doors down," he managed, covering his nose and mouth with his hands. Alainn turned and made haste.

Relieved, she fled back down the alleyway, nearly smacking into two sailors on the verge of a confrontation involving knives.

"Give it back!" the taller man demanded, a knife fisted in his hand.

"I don't have yer damn coin! I've told you before and I will tell ye again! I did not take it!"

"I saw ye eyeing it last night after we were handed our pay!"

The men started to circle each other, knives gripped and ready for slashing, knees bent, ready to spring. Alainn moved into the shadows, hoping to remain unseen as she inched her way along the stone building. When the first blade swept through the air she was certain they would be too intent on their quarrel to pay attention to her. However, when she narrowly missed stepping upon a huge rat as it scurried before her, she could not stop the startled shriek that escaped her lips.

Momentarily distracted, they looked at Alainn. She could see thoughts of lascivious activities with a young maiden replacing their current feud. They lunged toward her.

"'Twas Conelly!" she blurted, dancing away from their hands.

"What?" they asked in unison, trying to grab for her.

"Fergal Conelly, he stole your coin."

This clearly got their attention. They looked first at each other and then at the golden-haired girl who stood before them, the sheer picture of innocence.

"He has it in his boot," she insisted, "but sure he'll be spendin' it this night if you don't get to him straightaway!"

"How can she know?" one man hissed, the forgotten knife now slack in his hand.

"She's got the gift," whispered the other, crossing himself. The men stood unsure, assessing the situation and the possibility that this odd young woman might possess the gift of second sight. They stepped carefully away from her, and the one who had lost his coin turned and ran to find the accused Conelly. The other stared at her with some doubt, but soon followed his mate.

Alainn made her way back to the safety of the crowded street, shaking her head. The sights and sounds of the city surrounded her, and affronted her senses. She had read of cities before, had tried to imagine them. But, imagining and actually being there were vastly different things. She was beginning to regret her hasty decision to escape Castle O'Brien, even though it had seemed her only option.

Trying to form a plan, she walked on, deep in thought.

"I want your hair."

A man walked just behind her, so close she could feel his hot breath upon the nape of her neck. He snarled, his lips curling back to reveal a mouth nearly black with rotted teeth.

"I want your hair," he repeated.

"My hair?"

"Aye, 'tis a most unusual shade, a lovely golden color. The tresses would be much in demand."

The man was by no means destitute. His garment suggested he was a merchant of sorts, though a dirty one. There was a large broadsword in his scabbard, and she reasoned, by the size of his upper arms, that he had the strength to wield it well.

"What would you do with my hair?" she quizzed as he began fingering the ends of her locks.

"Ah," he leaned in and sniffed her hair. "There are men and women alike who would be most pleased to have your locks made into a fine wig."

The man unsheathed a small knife from his belt. It glinted in the sunlight.

"Shall I see you parted from your golden tresses?" he murmured almost lovingly.

Whether he intended to reward her in coin for her locks or simply meant to shear them and be done with it, she did not fancy either option, though losing her hair would clearly be preferential to losing her life.

"I am rather fond of it, myself," she protested trying to calmly release her hair from his possessive grip. He grinned once more, and Alainn caught the repugnant stench of his foul breath.

"I'll be takin' more than your hair should you cause me any hardship," he drawled.

Her eyes skirted the area in an attempt to find help.

"You'd be wise to think twice about disturbing my hair or any part of me," she cautioned.

"Do you have a man about somewhere nearby?" he sneered. "I wouldn't have left someone so lovely alone in a city, myself. Something most unfortunate could happen to her."

"Not a man. I have something far more powerful and effective than a mere man." She added in a whisper, "I am protected by fairies."

He smirked and guffawed.

"You should not take this lightly, good sir," she chided, her face solemn. "Interfering with anyone under fairy protection is a most grievous matter."

"Are you addle-minded, woman?" he muttered impatiently, but nonetheless looked around nervously.

"Do not rile them," she warned. She, too, glanced around as though she saw fairies surrounding her. Smiling wickedly, she concentrated on the knife and willed it from his hand. It flew free, whizzing through the air, and lodged itself in a nearby signpost.

He reached for his sword, but it too was torn from his grasp. It clanged to the cobblestone street, echoing unnaturally. His face paled, and he bent to retrieve it. Alainn took advantage of the moment and darted behind a nearby cart. Sword in hand, the man stood up uncertainly, obviously deeply confused. He scanned the area, trying to locate the woman who had only now stood before him. When he turned his back, Alainn set off in the opposite direction, her feet fairly flying on the cobblestones.

Certain she had surely given the man the slip, she dared cast a glance back. Her heart raced in fear to see he still followed. She set out running at full speed, blocking his path with whatever objects she passed, Killian's voice fresh in her mind. "You may not look for trouble, Alainn, but it seems to find you nonetheless."

The loud footsteps seemed too close. The man was gaining ground. Her burning lungs felt as though they would surely burst. Her stomach reminded her it was still queasy. She searched for a doorway through which to escape but could see no place to hide. Cursing under her breath, she wondered how she always managed to find herself in such dire circumstances.

As she rounded a corner, she heard the clomping of a horse nearby. Carefully envisioning the face of the man, she called upon her magic. It happened all at once. She heard the horse neigh and rear, the man cry as he leapt out of the way, and his curses as he slipped on a fresh pile of horse dung and fell face first into another.

"Protected by fairies," she softly whispered and sent the message off on the wind.

Chapter Two

Alainn cried out as her head was slammed against the table. She was pinned down; her skirts, pushed up. Hands squeezed her tender breasts, and the man positioned himself above her. Her stomach lurched as he roughly prodded her. She screamed in pain and protest. His disturbing laughter rose above her noise. He shoved her knees apart, holding her arms high above her head till her shoulders ached. Her wrists burned with the deep bruises he was causing. She looked with hatred into the contorted face of her attacker, Chieftain Hugh O'Brien. She screamed once more and awoke.

A small child clasped Alainn's wrist. She glanced down at her arms. They were riddled with bruises that remained no less painful than when they were inflicted, only days before she'd fled Castle O'Brien. The young boy quickly pulled his hand away, but Alainn gently patted the wee hand and smiled reassuringly. She glanced around and breathed. As seabirds cried and waves crashed gently against the shore, she relaxed, remembering where she was and how she'd gotten there. She stood and took the child's hand. A warm smile crossed his tiny face.

He pulled her to a large group of children who immediately surrounded her, chattering and dancing while the sun shone brightly, warming the sea breeze. Her long, sun-kissed locks fell freely down her back, and she squished warm sand between her bare toes. She lifted the small child and swung him onto her back. He laughed, clinging tightly to her neck as she carted him around.

Alainn recalled the glorious afternoon they had spent in the bright sunshine before it had lulled her to sleep. They had played on the beach, collected shells and spent hours wading in the waves of the Atlantic Ocean. She reveled in the scent of the salty ocean breezes and gazed admiringly at the beauty of Galway Bay. After all the many mishaps she had faced earlier this day, she welcomed the chance to feel carefree for a time. But too soon, thoughts of Castle O'Brien intruded in her mind.

She had spent all of her ten and seven years at the castle, being raised by the old healer, Morag. She had learned the craft well from the aged woman and become healer to the O'Briens and their clan. Though she had not led a life of privilege, she had been given many opportunities denied those of lowly birth. She could read and write as she had been allowed time with a scholar, which was a most unusual occurrence for a girl-child of any station. Throughout her life, she had spent much time with the Chieftain's family, his wife, Lady Siobhan, and his twin sons, Rory and Riley.

She had also fallen hopelessly in love with the chieftain's nephew, Killian O'Brien. It was certain that many a maiden before her had lost their heart to him, the handsome, stalwart, and courageous champion. His grandness was inescapable, and his charm and appeal unmatched by any man in and around Castle O'Brien. And Killian was deeply in love with Alainn.

They had been friends as children. She had healed him after his father's castle had been invaded and he had been gravely injured, not expected to live. Their love and admiration had grown through the years, and they began a relationship that she had known well enough could not end without heartache. But, she'd felt Killian's love was worth it.

It was Killian who had begun to desire unrealistic possibilities, who wanted to spend his life with her. Although she wanted nothing more than to be with him forever, she knew he must fulfill his destiny. He was expected to follow in his father's footsteps, to become chieftain to his mother's clan. It had always been enormously important to him.

He revealed to his uncle, the O'Brien, his intention to abdicate his rights to the chieftainship to marry a commoner. After learning her identity, the infuriated earl lashed out in response, attempting to rape her. It was then, in her great state of fear and uncertainty, she revealed her supernatural powers. The chieftain's priest, a man far from holy and without a conscience, had also been witness to her abilities. It was a most grievous occurrence, and now her time at Castle O'Brien would never be peaceful again.

Knowing their continued relationship could only cause Killian pain, she had chosen to leave. She could not allow him to lose his birthright or put himself in danger by going against his uncle's wishes. It was not a risk she would take.

The children's laughter pulled Alainn from her worrisome thoughts, and a child splashed her. She lifted her foot and kicked the water, spraying the slender girl, leaving them all nearly breathless with laughter. Alainn shifted the small boy on her back, and her mind returned to her troubles.

Recently Alainn had discovered she was not the farrier's daughter, as she had always believed, but the daughter of Mara, the Glade Witch, a woman who had cursed the entire O'Brien line. Years earlier, the witch had been brutally raped by Hugh O'Brien's father, and in retaliation, she placed a curse upon him, a hex so powerful that the wretched man's entire line would soon die out. No further children survived their birth to any of the old man's six sons after the curse was uttered. Babies were stillborn or lived mere hours.

The witch had caused great hardship and tragedy for the O'Briens, and she was despised by the lot of them, Killian included. If he should ever learn the truth of Alainn's parentage, he would surely abhor her as well.

Mara had revealed it might be reversed if the conditions of the curse were met and Alainn accepted as nobility. But, she held little hope. Her mother claimed she was the daughter of an important chieftain, that the amulet Alainn was given at birth had once belonged to him. Mara had hidden a part of it in the walls of the dungeon many months before Alainn's birth. If she could locate it, it would be proof enough, for it bore the crest of her father's family.

Although Alainn did not trust Mara completely, she would have little to gain by creating such an elaborate falsehood. Alainn had ventured near the doorway of the dungeon to see if her powers of perception could help locate the missing piece, but to no avail. The dungeon was undoubtedly an unpleasant location that held many gruesome and disparaging memories. As she started down the dimly lit winding steps, she had sensed a presence truly dark and nefarious. Perhaps an unsettled spirit that had met its cruel fate there. Never before had she felt pure evil. Her heart began beating unnaturally fast. Her skin became clammy. She could go no further. How was she to locate her father's family crest in the dungeon if such a malevolent being dwelled within its depths?

And now, Alainn carried Killian's child; a child surely ill-fated by her own mother's curse. For the sake of the child, she must prove her paternity, but she was uncertain how to begin. If she could protect herself from the threats of Hugh O'Brien and his malicious priest, she might find a way to end the curse. If she distanced herself from Killian, her head might be able to think more clearly. Her magical powers might become manageable.

Yet, the mere thought of spending time apart from Killian caused her heart to ache. And, at present he was off collecting the woman who was to become his wife.

Alainn roused herself from her memories and glanced at the sweet faces of the children around her. The warm waves licked her ankles, and the sea breeze gently consoled her. As the children's laughter and pleasant chatter lulled her, she fell back into her thoughts.

Chapter three

"Would you have me sleep on the street, then?"

"Alainn, I have only coin for one room," Cookson complained. "Sure, ye can't be intendin' to stay with Pierce and me. Not in the same room!"

When she'd seen Cookson leaving Castle O'Brien in the cart to collect supplies in the city that day, she'd taken the opportunity to escape and jumped into the back of the wagon. Cookson and Pierce, the captain of the guard's son, had attempted to discourage her, but she would not be dissuaded. Once they arrived in Galway, they were reluctant to share a room with her.

"I suppose it would please you if we were to sleep out on the street?" Pierce snapped impatiently.

"At the moment, Pierce, I shouldn't care if I sleep on the floor or in the same bed as the two of you. I simply wish for a place to lay my weary head."

They realized there would be no reasoning with the young woman. Once settled in the small bedchamber, however, the two young men remained ill at ease, their faces ruddy with uncertainty and embarrassment at sharing a room with her.

"You can both stop acting so confoundedly awkward. I have known you lads all my life and consider you to be my valued friends. On the morrow, when I am warmed and rested, when my mind is clearer, I will seek employment and shelter."

"And what of Killian?" Pierce asked brusquely.

"What of him? He's off fetching his intended."

"So you will simply disappear from his life without explanation? He will surely search for you."

"Aye, Killian is a determined man, and he well loves you," Cookson agreed.

"I will write a letter of farewell to him. I shall tell him I am most pleased he will soon marry a noble woman, someone who is his equal. I shall insist he has my blessing and my good wishes. I will encourage him to leave Castle O'Brien and go off to rule as chieftain of his mother's clan. And I will explain I have ambitions of my own. It will surely dissuade him from searching for me. You'll deliver the letter for me, won't you, Cookson?"

"I am not certain I care for that task, Alainn. But, aye, I will do so."

Her deep sigh was audible. She retrieved a small portion of paper and a quill pen from within the pocket of her frock, sat down on the bed, and began composing the letter.

"What are these ambitions you speak of?" Pierce demanded, interrupting her.

"Perhaps I will set off by ship to a far-off land," she mused.

"You couldn't!" Cookson blurted. "It wouldn't be safe!"

"An unmarried woman cannot travel alone, it is unheard of! You couldn't board a ship unaccompanied, a young…beautiful…woman," Pierce stammered. "You would be accosted, violated. Would that not be considerably less appealing than being forced to wed someone you don't care for?"

"But it's to be the swine handler or the aged Widower McLean," Cookson reminded him. "They are the O'Brien's choices for her."

"Well, you could marry her then, Cookson. Or I—" his young face flushed deep red. He cleared his throat and tried to avert his eyes from the bed.

Perhaps if she had been feeling less miserable, she would have found humor or gratefulness in the young man's offer, but she felt neither.

"Though your generously charitable offer is very much appreciated, Pierce," she said, her voice chilly, "I will not be marrying anyone. Only when or if I should ever desire it."

They left her to her dark mood and the unpleasant task of inking Killian's letter, and hovered near the doorway. Tears slid slowly down her cheeks as she wrote the words of farewell to her only love. She dabbed at her eyes, neatly folded the paper, and handed it to Cookson. He kindly passed her his handkerchief.

"But in seriousness, Alainn, where will you go?" he asked, his voice tender with concern. "We'll all miss you. What shall we do without our healer?" Alainn affectionately patted his round cheek.

"I am confident the chieftain's new physician will be most adequate in his abilities." Cookson's face told her he believed otherwise.

"I shall worry much regarding your safety, Alainn."

"Sure I will find employment in an alchemist's shop. I am told there are more than a few here. My knowledge of herbs, potions, and remedies is vast. I am confident I will manage to provide for myself, should I choose to stay in this city."

"It is my understanding that many young women alone in a city are forced to seek shelter and employment in a brothel," Pierce cautioned.

She did not respond, nor glance at the two men, but wearily chose a pillow and blanket from the bed, and slowly lowered herself down on the chair, hoping to finally rest. The young men insisted she take the bed and pulled their chairs near the window. She might well have offered them the bed, for she slept not a wink, weeping every time she allowed herself to dwell on being forever parted from Killian.

She thought even now, as she stood on the beach, her swollen eyes bore the evidence of her many tears. She hoped Pierce had finally given up his search for her and gone to meet Cookson. Surely they would have left the city by now.

The sun was moving westward, and it was time for the children to think about going home. Two parents came to fetch their children and offered her coins for keeping them occupied all day. She had not known where she would spend this night and thought there may now be enough coin to pay for a room at an inn. Her mood suddenly lighter, she hummed a tune as she and the children skipped their way toward the wharf.

As they got closer, Alainn saw a cluster of people on the docks surveying the fishing vessels in the harbor. They were finely dressed and obviously of wealth and position. A middle-aged man and woman walked arm in arm. Upon seeing the remainder of the crowd, Alainn turned abruptly, lowered her head, and began walking in the other direction. The children followed her without breaking stride, clearly thinking it was a new game. Her heart beat at an unhealthy rate, and she quickened her pace. Finally she was clear of the group and looked up. Pierce was heading straight toward her, his face dark with anger and frustration.

"Pierce!" she hissed. "Why have you not left with Cookson?"

"He has not set off yet! He's awaiting our return!" he shouted.

"Shhh!" she shushed loudly, moving toward him and lowering her voice. "I told you I have no intention of returning with you. Go to where you are to meet him and be gone. Sure your father and Cook will be fit to be tied."

"We have agreed we cannot leave you here in this city alone. 'Tis a dangerous place for anyone, most especially a woman."

"I am not alone, Pierce. I will be kept safe."

"And you believe these wee wains are going to keep you safe from harm then?" he demanded, his voice rising with his anger.

He looked past her to the docks, and his face softened with relief. Alainn lunged for his hand, but it was too late. He waved enthusiastically and called out to them. Alainn started walking quickly away from him, but he grabbed her arm and pulled her toward the docks, the young boy still clamped to her back.

When she resisted, he became most displeased and snarled, "Alainn McCreary, we are taking this matter to Killian. You know well enough what his opinion will be. You'll not be stayin' here in the city alone!"

Alainn had never heard Pierce use such a sharp, demanding tone with anyone before, and certainly not with her since he'd taken a fancy to her years ago. The children immediately came to her defense. One of the young boys kicked him hard in the shin with his bare foot. Two others joined in. Another leapt upon his back punching him in earnest, while a small girl grabbed hold of his hair with both hands and pulled with a mighty fury. Pierce let go of Alainn's arm, yelping in pain, trying to dislodge the children.

"You wee buggers, what are you about?"

"Don't you hurt our Lainna!" one child lisped. Alainn closed her eyes. Only Killian had ever referred to her by that fond name.

As the children continued their attack on Pierce, the young boy on Alainn's back leaned over and threw himself at Pierce. His legs, still tucked safely in place, unbalanced him. He missed Pierce altogether and pulled Alainn to the ground with him. They landed with a thud as a sizeable wave crashed over them. Alainn held onto the boy as the wave tried to pull them back into its depths, her scream drowning in a mouthful of briny water. She came up coughing and sputtering, spitting sand and seawater. The child shook off her hands and scampered onto the beach as Alainn finally managed to stand.

She glared at Pierce and flushed with anger. She picked up a large handful of the wet sand and threw it at him. The children delighted in this and amid peals of laughter, splashed the young man with feet and hands, hurling fistfuls of sand and pushing him farther into the water.

"Stop it, ye wee hooligans!" Pierce ordered, but his fury was clearly directed toward Alainn. "Make them stop this at once!" In reply, Alainn grabbed more sand and aimed for his face. Pierce swept her legs out from under her.

"Pierce? Alainn? Whatever are you doing?"

It was Rory, one of the chieftain's sons. He was crouched at the end of the pier, looking down on them with amusement. "Children, that's enough," he said with authority. The children stopped their splashing and ran to stand behind Alainn and Pierce.

Alainn managed to get to her feet again with little dignity and half-heartedly brushed dirt from her sodden garments. Her hair was dripping wet and matted with sand. She gingerly removed a piece of seaweed from across her face and attempted to smile. Her teeth were caked with grit. She coughed and spit sand from her mouth.

"My word, the wee urchins are filthy! And the entire lot of them wears no shoes, not even that young woman!"

Alainn looked past Rory and her face flamed red at the sight before her. Rory was not alone. Behind, at a safer distance on the pier, stood the older couple with a young woman. They watched her with unhidden disapproval. Riley was with them, accompanying another young woman. Both women had bright red hair and matching snooty expressions. As they leaned in to whisper to each other, Killian was revealed, his betrothed on his arm. It was the woman from Alainn's dreams.

She was tall, willowy in form, with lovely dark curly hair, and she was indisputably beautiful. Alainn met Killian's eyes and found she could no longer breathe. She turned swiftly toward the children. Pierce had yet to answer Rory's query.

One of the redheads made a sound of disgust as she glanced at the children. "Look at their clothes; they are scarcely better than rags!" Her sister giggled nastily.

Alainn turned back, stepping forward to give her opinion of their rudeness, when Killian's intended walked closer. Alainn looked down in embarrassment.

"That looks most enjoyable, walking on the sandy seashore with no shoes," the woman said in a thick Scottish brogue. "Why, I haven't done that since I was a wee child! How I would love to do so again. Or maybe even a swim, the water looks lovely and appealing."

"Sure no one will stop you if you wish to join us." The impulsive words were out of Alainn's mouth before she had thought them through. She began to untangle her lengthy locks, eyes lowered.

"You wouldn't dare think of it, Mary. You would ruin your dress!"

"Och, I've at least a dozen just like this one."

"Don't you dare consider it, Mary MacDonald! I forbid it!"

"Oh, Aunt Ida, it looks like great fun."

The young woman had reached the edge of the pier and was clearly thinking of jumping off into the sand. Killian took her hand and gently guided her as she lifted her long rich skirts. His eyes met Alainn's once more. They held a hint of guilt.

"Robert, really, you must stop her. She intends to interact with these vile creatures."

"Aye well, she's always been a spirited lass. With only brothers in her family, my sister and her husband have allowed her to cavort about with them, I suspect. She'll be a handful for you to be sure, lad."

Killian nodded without taking his eyes off Alainn.

"Do you know these people?" one redhead asked with great disdain.

"Aye," said Riley, "they are from our castle."

"They're servants then?"

"Aye, we've come to collect supplies for the celebrations," Pierce finally managed.

"And you allow your servants time to frolic freely about on the seashore?" the older woman asked, obviously most taken aback.

Alainn's eyes remained helplessly locked with Killian's as he approached with Mary.

"You have verra long hair," the woman said to her. "And och look at what a beautiful shade it is, even when it's wet."

"Aye, you might say it is the color of sand!" the older redhead tittered.

Mary walked closer, and Alainn was startled to see her long flowing skirts drag into the water. The woman seemed not to care.

"Truly, I've never viewed such a lovely golden color." She reached out and helped to rid seaweed from the back of her hair. Alainn fought the urge to knock her hand away. "And your eyes! They are surely as blue as the sea near the coast of Antrim."

"Th-th-thank you," Alainn stuttered, her teeth beginning to chatter as the cool ocean breeze blew across the bay, sending a chill through her. Pierce stood quietly at her side, trying to still his own trembles.

The woman continued to assist her with brushing away the sand and then thoughtfully passed Alainn her shawl. She was reluctant to take it and shook her head.

"No, I insist, you take it, for you appear to be verra cold. You'll catch your death standing here soaking wet." She draped the fine garment over Alainn's shoulders and smiled encouragingly at her.

Killian moved in so close that Alainn could feel warmth from his body. He dared graze her hand and an electric charge spiked through her. Alainn moved away.

"How could you give her your lovely shawl, Mary? She's sure to get it filthy. That's probably the first water she has seen in months," complained the redhead on Riley's arm. "Stay away from her, Mary. You're sure to catch something!"

"Alainn is much valued at Castle O'Brien," Rory chastised. "She is a gifted healer and a great asset to our clan and kin."

"Why would a gifted healer be so far from your castle if she is so important? And why would she be seeking supplies from Galway?"

"Seaweed is most beneficial for many maladies," Alainn answered, her jaw clenched. "A great cure for a bitter tongue and a haughty temperament.

Perhaps you might try a hearty mouthful." Alainn picked a slimy piece from her hair and held it out.

"Did you hear that, Father! She insulted me. This meager servant has just insulted me!"

Mary stifled a giggle. Alainn frowned, for she wanted to despise this woman.

"How many of these filthy wee imps belong to you?" the older woman asked, holding a cloth to her nose.

Alainn's eyes flashed with anger. She took Pierce's arm most possessively, smiling at him and batting her eyelashes. He looked down at her warily. "Only three thus far," she said brightly. "But sure we intend to have an enormous family, don't we my darlin'?" She leaned into him affectionately while he looked on with mortification. She stood on tiptoe and planted a lengthy kiss upon his equally sandy lips. His cheeks blushed scarlet. Rory and Riley guffawed. Killian did not appear so amused.

"Alainn, is it then?" Mary inquired.

"Aye, my name is Alainn McCreary," she sniffed.

"Mary MacDonald of Ayrshire Scotland." She curtsied to Alainn. "I am sincerely pleased to make your acquaintance."

"You most certainly will not become friends with a chieftain's servant!" the older redhead scolded, horrified.

"I will if I choose, Iona. My dearest friend in the entire world was my maidservant. She has married and is now with child, so she could not make the journey with me. But I am searching for another. Should you find yourself interested, Alainn, I would welcome you to come live with Killian and me once we are wed."

Pierce coughed loudly.

"Alainn is much needed by my uncle and our kin," Killian declared gruffly. "She is far too valuable for my uncle to permit her to leave Castle O'Brien."

"Then why has she been given leave from her duties to procure supplies?" asked the younger redhead.

"Aye, I was wondering that myself." His eyes burned into Alainn.

" Milord." She bowed her head and curtsied very low. "Your uncle has recently employed the services of a physician, so I have made the journey to the city, in search of…in search of…seaside herbs."

"Might I speak with you, Milord, before we leave to meet Cookson?" Pierce asked, his eyes pleading. Killian nodded.

"Chieftain McDonnel, I have business with our captain's son. Would you escort Maiden MacDonald, back to the inn while I attend to this matter, sir?"

"Och Killian, I think you might refer to me as Mary. We are promised to one another, after all. I think it isn't necessary for us to be so formal." She touched his arm with affection.

Alainn curtsied once more, turned swiftly, and fairly ran down the beach, the horde of children following close behind.

Chapter Four

Pierce and Killian trudged down the beach away from the group at the wharf. When they were out of earshot, Pierce could contain himself no longer.

"I am done with this impossible task you have handed me," he snapped, furiously shaking sand from his hair. "She will listen to absolutely nothin' I say, and 'twas not my notion to travel to Galway. She persuaded Cookson she was coming, wouldn't listen to me, simply would not be dissuaded. She does not respect my words, nor my opinions, has decided she is staying here and not returning to the castle. We both spent half the night trying to make her see reason, but she is the most stubborn female I have ever had the misfortune to be acquainted with!" His voice rose as he related his frustrations. "I must meet Cookson, for he will surely be most displeased we are to leave so late. Cook will have his head, and my father mine." Almost as an afterthought, he added, "And this very morning Alainn visited an alchemist's shop and a brothel."

"You allowed her to go to a brothel!" Killian roared. He grabbed Pierce by the tunic.

"I allowed her to do nothin'!" he shouted, batting at the hand. "She simply does whatever she pleases!"

"Aye," said Killian coming to his senses. He removed his hand and straightened Pierce's dirty, rumpled tunic. "Well I do appreciate your attempts to keep her safe." He chuckled. Pierce scowled.

"I will see to her safety now," Killian assured him. "You may return to the castle with Cookson for you are right in assuming your father will be sorely aggrieved. I will speak to him and to Cook as well on your behalves when I return to the castle." They both turned and looked with grim faces down the beach where Alainn and her young followers grew smaller in the distance.

Alainn was delivering the children to their parents in a noisy crowded street when the two men finally caught up with her. She did not look their way. Instead, Alainn warmly embraced each of the youngsters and told them she hoped to see them again soon. When she heard Killian bidding Pierce farewell, she turned and spoke to the younger man.

"God speed, Pierce. I apologize for making your task a difficult one. Tell Cookson my farewells. I will miss the two of you most assuredly."

"Aye, keep you safe, Alainn," Pierce mumbled. He nodded to her and, despite all the grief she had caused him, could not help smiling sheepishly.

"And, Pierce," she said, her eyes twinkling, "You might decide to turn your eyes toward Molly. She is my dearest friend and a lovely, demure young woman. She has been smitten with you for quite some time and dearly loves to hear poetry."

Clearly flustered, Pierce did not respond. He waved to Alainn, nodded to Killian, and hurried off down a street. He was soon lost in the crowds.

Alainn started down the street herself, ignoring Killian who kept pace beside her. She picked up the pace until she was nearly running. He grasped her elbow and swung her around.

"Alainn, we must talk."

"There is naught to be said, Milord," she said without looking at him. "You ought to go now to your betrothed. I am certain she wonders what might be keeping you." She tried to step away, but he held her firmly.

"By Christ, woman! Look at me!" Killian demanded.

"I have no desire to look at you or to be in your company. Go to her, and I will be off."

"Off to where exactly? Where do you intend to go?"

"I will stay here in the city for a time. I quite like it here."

"Because you have had a time romping with some children at the seaside, you think you know what it is to live in a city? 'Tis a dangerous place for any woman, and most especially a young woman on her own. Do you not realize what thievery, rapes, and murders occur each night in a city?"

"I am not your concern, Milord, not any longer. So take your leave from me. There is no need for you to tarry in getting to your dearest Mary."

"Alainn, you must allow me to explain the situation."

"I am not a fool, Killian O'Brien! I understand the situation quite sufficiently. Your uncle has chosen a wife for you, and that is the end of what we shared. In truth, I am much relieved. I had dreaded the day it would happen, have fretted over it far more than I care to admit to you, but now that day is here, I feel entirely liberated. 'Tis a marvelous freedom. Henceforth, I shall be accountable to no one, not ever."

She had yet to look at him, and he was growing steadily more perturbed. He took her arm possessively and pulled her toward a large stone building, grasping her by the shoulders and staring down into her lovely blue eyes, now filled with deep sadness. Alainn closed her eyes, and tears began sliding down her cheeks. He drew her close to comfort her, but she pushed at his chest and stiffened in his arms.

"Let me go," she said, her voice breaking. "Please, just leave me. Take your intended back to your uncle, for I am certain he will be most delighted to see what a handsome, noble couple you make. Forget you ever knew me. I intend to do the same in regards to you."

"Alainn, I am in love with you." His voice dropped to a near whisper. "And that has not changed because my uncle feels he has chosen me a good political match."

"She is most taken by you and not nearly so offensive as the rest of them. You will be most happy together, I am certain."

"I will be happy with no one, bar you, Alainn. You well know that," he insisted.

"There is nothing further to discuss, Killian. I intend to remain here in Galway. There is nothing you can do about it."

"Aye, there most certainly is. I can take you back to Castle O'Brien."

"For what purpose? Would you expect me to be her servant as she suggested, or your mistress?"

"I would expect neither. It is not a certainty that she and I will wed. My uncle knows I have no intention of going through with this marriage."

"Why bother to protest? Your uncle will not allow you to defy him. It will be as he desires. Embrace your destiny, Killian O'Brien. It is what you have dreamed of all your life."

"You will travel back with Robert McDonnel and his family. There is room in the coach." He seemed to pay no attention to Alainn's words. She erupted in anger and stamped her foot.

"Aye, I suspect there is room in hell, as well! I'd as soon go to the devil as spend the better part of a day trapped in a wee coach with that loathsome, arrogant, wretched woman and her horrid daughters, not to mention your betrothed! And nay, you have entirely no say in what I do!"

Killian shook her with impatience. "Why would Morag allow you to leave the castle? Did you go without telling her?"

"Morag is dead!" she cried. His face fell.

"Sorry I am, to hear of your great loss, Alainn. Please forgive me for not being there for you."

"Killian O'Brien, I do not require your pity." Alainn sounded suddenly tired. "And I no longer care to be in your company, so if you would kindly remove your hands from me, Milord, we might both be on our way."

"I will not allow you to stay here."

"You have no claim on me, or I on you, so unhand me or I swear I will scream."

"And what purpose would that serve?"

"It would cause a scene and perhaps your promised will be suspicious should she catch wind of your indiscretions."

"Alainn, I do not consider you an indiscretion, and at the moment your causing a scene is perhaps the least of my concerns."

"You are only prolonging our parting. Can you not see this will benefit us in no way? Do me this kindness and depart swiftly."

Killian let go of her, and they stepped back from each other. He clasped his hands together as if to keep from touching her.

"Alainn, this has been the longest week of my life, being parted from you. How do you expect me to live without you? It is not within my capabilities to simply say farewell and turn away from you. Please come with me where we might speak more privately."

"You are to meet your Mary and her kin. I shall not stand in the way of your plans with your intended."

"I need to be alone with you, Alainn. I need to hold you and kiss you and remove all doubt from your mind that it is you I love, and only you I want to spend my life with."

"I am aware you love me, Killian. And truly, I shall treasure that knowledge for as long as I live, but it changes nothing. Our love is not enough to stand up to your uncle's power." She looked into his eyes as she spoke these words and could not hide the depth of her pain.

"Come with me, Alainn, allow me to get you some food. I will find a place for you to stay this night. Nothing need be decided this moment. You look pale and tired, and you are thin. Pierce tells me you have scarcely eaten in these days he has been with you. Are you unwell?"

"Pierce had no need to divulge that to you. I am not ill, 'tis only my heart that is ailing, and I doubt food will be an adequate cure for a forlorn heart."

He squeezed her wrist in deep concern. She winced and pulled away.

"What has happened to you?"

He lifted back first one sleeve then the other to reveal many deep bruises.

"What in hell happened to you!" His face darkened, and in his fury, he inadvertently squeezed her wounded wrists.

Her face crumpled with pain, then drained of all color. Killian swore and caught her as she fell in a dead faint. He gathered her to him and swiftly carried her to a nearby inn.

* * *

Alainn awoke to find Killian holding her hand and another man she did not recognize peering closely at her. She looked around the room at the rich furnishings and the enormous bed upon which she lay. The nape of her dress was open, and her hand immediately went to the bruises there. Killian's eyes were filled with intense despair. The other man summoned Killian to the door, and he reluctantly let go of her hand to speak with him before he left the room.

Alainn straightened her damp dress and attempted to determine whether the physician had learned of her condition. Killian returned to the chair by the bed and sat down, staring at her with great concern.

"Who did this to you, Alainn?"

"It could have been much worse, Killian. I might have been lashed or possibly even hanged."

"What are you talking about? Tell me who did this to you, and I shall go cut his throat where he stands."

"I stole your uncle's horse."

"You…what?"

"Well, in truth, I borrowed it from the stables, but your uncle assumed it to be stolen."

"My uncle did this to you?"

"I suppose I should consider myself fortunate, for I know well enough the punishment for horse thievery."

"He beat you? He did not have his enforcer do it for him?"

"No…"

"Christ, I shall kill him! I promise you this, I shall run him through with my blade!" he seethed. He jumped up, his body rigid. His fists were clenched, his jaw tensed. He began pacing as he spoke. "This was not about the taking of a horse. It was to get back at me for telling him I was in love with someone who was not a noble. He must surely have discovered it was you. Was that why you left the castle? Did he threaten you as well?"

"He told me you were betrothed. He did not know of my intention to leave the castle."

"He will be made to pay for this, Alainn. I will vindicate the wrongdoings done to you. I promise you that!"

"You cannot threaten him or harm him in any way, Killian. He is the chieftain, and you know well enough he could have had me hanged for taking the horse. You would only be in jeopardy yourself if you avenge me in any way, for no one would think he was unjustified in beating me when he might have had me hanged or beheaded."

Killian appeared deep in thought.

"Why did you need the horse, Alainn? Why didn't Pierce find a horse for you if you needed one that desperately? He was to stay with you at all times."

"And he made a valiant effort to do so, Killian. You must not place fault on him for any part of this. He was unaware I took the horse."

"But you have not told me why you needed it."

"I went to see Mara."

"Christ, Alainn! Was going to see the witch so cursedly important that you needed to steal a horse and suffer the punishment of a beating at the hands of my uncle?"

"I thought so at the time!" He raked his hand through his thick hair and continued pacing the floor. "Killian, you must give no further thought to this," she warned. She slowly got off the bed, though still light-headed, removed slippers from her pocket, and put them on her feet.

"Where do you think you are going?"

"I am going to find a place to spend the night, for daylight dwindles and I doubt the coins I possess will be adequate for a room such as this."

"You are going nowhere. I have made payment for the room, Alainn. You must stay and sleep. I have arranged for food and a warm bath for you. The physician tells me you are undernourished and in much need of rest."

"A lot he knows. 'Tis a wonder he didn't attempt to bleed me dry for 'tis their solution for everything. I possess herbs that will be far more beneficial than anything he might have suggested," she groused. "You owe me nothing, Killian," she said, holding onto the bed frame as her head swam, "and any mention of the unpleasantness between your uncle and me would cause more dissention between the two of you."

"Aye well, there's a good deal of dissention between us, and you can rest assured he will hear my opinion on how he handles women with so little regard. Sit back down, Alainn!"

"Please discuss this matter not with him, Killian. I beg you, leave well enough alone. Allow me to stay here in Galway."

He stood beside her now, looking down into azure eyes that pleaded with him so desperately.

"You don't believe what we share is worth fighting for?" he asked, his voice wavering with emotion.

"If there was a way to win the fight, aye, I would fight for our love and for the right to be together. But I see no way. His word is to be unchallenged. He means for you to be wed to the Scot, and so therefore it shall be so."

"I am not without title or influence, Alainn. There are those that would stand by me. And there have been chieftains who marry commoners."

"Aye, 'tis true enough, they may not be daughters of earls or chieftains, but even still, they have some wealth or position, at the very least a suitable dowry to offer. I have nothing. And I know well enough you possess much influence, Killian, and the respect of many. But you would surely lose your title and relinquish your right to be chieftain if you chose to wed me. Your uncle would perceive it as defiance or perhaps treason. He would think it a slight to him and your clan."

"Perhaps, but 'twould be worth all of it if it meant I could live out my life with you."

"So you say now. But one day, you would grow to resent me for it, Killian. And that would be a greater pain for me to bear."

"I would never resent you, Alainn." He stepped forward and took her hands before she could stop him. "Please say you will come back to the castle with me. Somehow we will find a means to be together. We must find a way. Perhaps your magic could be employed."

"'Tis a dangerous consideration, for my powers steadily grow and I am not always able to control them as I once was. Killian, I truly fear them at times. Today when your Mary touched your arm, I wanted to harm her even though I do not dislike her. She seems most amiable, but I have a deep jealousy and possessiveness toward you." She linked her fingers with his. "I am unsure if I would be able to control my rage toward her or toward your uncle should he choose to harm you. I have thought on this much, Killian. It is best for everyone if I simply stay here."

"And you intended to do so without even alerting me? If we hadn't met you today on the wharf, you would not have bid me farewell." He stepped closer.

"I have sent a letter with Cookson. He was to give it to you upon your return to the castle. I thought it would be simpler for both of us if we didn't see each other again. I explained all my reasons in the letter."

"So you decided for the both of us what is best?" She did not respond but turned away from his accusing gaze. "Well, I will not have it, Alainn! This will not be the end of what we share." He kissed her fingers and then reluctantly released them. "I must go now to meet with the McConnels as I've given my word I would do so, but we will continue this discussion when I return."

"I will not be here, Killian."

"Aye, but you will!"

He pulled the large key from his pocket and headed toward the door.

"You intend to keep me prisoner?" she asked, her eyes wide with disbelief.

"Aye, I will do whatever it takes to ensure I finish what I have to say on this matter." She ran to the window and pulled back the thick coverings. There were bars upon the windows. "It is to ensure the patrons are kept safe, but I suppose they will serve my purpose as well."

"I have abilities even you are not aware of, Killian. You cannot keep me here."

"Then don't make me resort to such drastic measures, Alainn. Stay until I return. Promise me you will do me that courtesy. Please! I shall beg you if you force me."

She saw his determination had not dimmed, but there was also a profound desperation in his bold green eyes. It wrapped around her heart and squeezed until she felt unable to breathe.

"I will not leave, not until I have spoken further with you. I promise you, Killian. I will be here when you return. But, you will not sway me."

A glimmer of hope filled his eyes, and he smiled sadly.

"We shall see, Lainna. We shall see."

Chapter Five

She was soaking in a large wooden tub that had been brought to the bedchamber, enjoying the sensation of warm water against her bruised and weary body, when a key turned in the lock. She reached for the wrap beside the tub and held it in front of her, sinking lower into the deep water. Killian stood in the doorway.

"Is the bath to your liking, Alainn?" He smiled as he spoke, but Alainn noted how melancholy he appeared.

"Aye, 'tis lovely, Killian."

Though he seemed drawn to gaze at her, he turned his back, and she stood, the wrap held tightly to her as she and moved from the tub to dry herself. When she had cloaked herself in a blanket from the bed, he turned.

"Do you have any notion how much I want you, Alainn? I can think of nothing but for how much I want to carry you to that bed and love you 'til sunrise."

She swallowed deeply and looked away from his captivating stare. He went to her and touched his hand to her cheek, tenderly running his fingers over her full lips.

"Killian, no. You must not. I…we—"

He stopped her words with a kiss. Her knees buckled, and he lifted her easily, and effortlessly carried her to the bed. The candles across the room flickered as he removed his overcoat, his sword, and its sheath, and lay down beside her. She felt his body harden as he pulled her to him. His hands slipped beneath the blanket that covered her, and her body arched at his touch. She gently removed his hands. With all the will she could find within her, she moved away from him, wrapping the blanket tighter around herself as she stood.

"No Killian. We cannot allow this to occur."

"I need you, Alainn," he said, his voice ragged with passion. "Surely more than ever before. I must be with you this night. Tell me your need is as great as mine." He went to her and pressed against her, his lips gently caressing the bruises on her throat. She gasped.

"Killian, it will only prove to make our parting more difficult if we spend this night together."

"Aye, well," he whispered, "I do not intend to ever be parted from you, so it will only be the beginning of many."

"And how will you explain that to Mary MacDonald, and your uncle?" she asked, closing her eyes.

"I do not wish to speak of this at the moment." He gently grabbed hold of her hips and tugged them forward.

"But we were simply to discuss matters further when you returned."

"Alainn, I want to make love to you. This moment, there is need for lovemaking, not unpleasant discussion."

She felt his heightening arousal through the thin fabric of her blanket. His mouth captured her lips again, and they responded of their own accord. Her hands betrayed her, slipping beneath his tunic to touch his broad, muscular chest. Her hips leaned in and wantonly moved against his trews.

He growled with passion at her waning resolve, and his kiss grew more demanding. She felt the blanket drop to the floor. Briefly ending the kiss, he stood back to gaze at her alluring loveliness. His strong hands reached out to caress her shoulders as his gaze consumed her body; it hummed with a great desire to be pleasured. He moved his hands softly up and down her arms until she ached to have him. She tugged at his tunic with clumsy hands, and he assisted her, pulling it roughly over his head and tossing it to the nearby chair. Their eyes met, and he chuckled.

His chest felt hot with fire where it brushed against her breasts, her nipples peaking instantly. She groaned as he rubbed their rose colored peaks. His mouth replaced his hands, and she pulled his head tighter to her breasts. His hand moved seductively down her thighs until he found her womanly treasure. She could scarcely contain her passion as he caressed her.

Alainn stroked the rigid form beneath his trews and fought with the fastenings, impatiently pushing the trews down over his impressively muscular hips and thighs. Her womanly triangle brushed against him, and he grew larger and firmer. Their eyes locked. She placed her hand on his manhood.

"I need you, Alainn!" His voice was rough with passion. "I have missed you these long days."

"And I, you, Killian."

He sucked in his breath and moaned deeply as she continued stroking him. Then, he gently pushed her back onto the bed. Sensing his great need, she parted her knees, but he knelt by the bed and placed his mouth upon her. Her hips bucked and quivered as waves of pleasure pulsed through her. Killian continued until she cried out in ecstasy, then positioned himself atop her. He paused for a moment, lingered in completing the joining.

"Tell me you want me to love you, Alainn. Tell me your need matches mine."

"And has my body not shown you such?"

"Aye," he whispered raggedly, showing unparalleled restraint. "But I need to know your mind and your heart want me as well." She caressed him, and he moaned.

"Aye, Killian O'Brien, every part of me from the top of my head to the tip of my toes wants you. Now!" she demanded and pulled him into her. The swiftness of the penetration startled them both. Her hips rose to meet his, and they rode the waves of passion together until she once more reached her crest, calling out his name. His lips claimed hers hungrily and with a guttural cry, his body became rigid with desire and slipped over the edge to fulfillment.

They lay trembling and breathless in each other's arms until sleep claimed them.

***

When Killian awoke, he found himself alone in the bed. Alainn was gone. She had left behind the new gowns he had purchased for her, taking only the garments she had come with. His heart grieved as though pierced through.

After the night they had spent loving each other, holding each other, he thought she'd seen how right they were together. But still, she had gone. The room seemed unnaturally quiet and empty without her beauty and spirit.

He would not allow his uncle to keep them apart. No matter what the cost, he would find a way for them to be together. He could still smell the sweet scent of her on his pillow, could still feel the sensation of her hair on his chest, the warmth of her when they joined. He gathered his garments, strewn haphazardly about the floor, and dressed. He would speak with Rory and Riley and the others, explain that business would keep him longer in Galway, insist they go on without him. Then, he would begin his search for Alainn. Thanks to young Pierce, he thought he had a notion where she might be.

* * *

Hours later, he found her behind the counter in an alchemist's shop. She did not seem surprised to see him, though not entirely pleased. A small, peculiar-looking old man stood beside Alainn, transfixed, watching her mix an elixir. He barely seemed to notice Killian.

"And you say it is a cure for the ague?"

"Aye, if you heat it before you add the final ingredient, I assure you, it will cure the highest fever."

"If this proves to be true, you may begin employment in my shop straightaway."

"Aye, 'twould be agreeable to me."

Killian smacked his hand on the counter, and the alchemist started.

"I regret to inform you that our healer is needed back at Castle O'Brien."

"You did not mention you are already employed by an earl!" the little man squeaked, noting the O'Brien pin on Killian's overcoat.

"Because I no longer wish to be in said employ," she snapped.

"My dear lass," the old man said nervously backing away from the counter, "I suggest you and your lord discuss this matter, for I'd not want to cause discord between myself and Hugh O'Brien. He is a valued patron. But, get you back to me if you'll be sharing any of your secret potions with me." As he stared at Alainn, he licked his lips and rubbed his unusually small hands together.

Alainn slammed down the bowl and walked out the door, her lips pursed and chin held high. Killian followed close behind her.

"So last night meant nothing to you then!" he roared.

"Wait until we are clear of these people," she hissed. They moved into the shadows of an alleyway, and she turned on him furiously. "Aye! It proved we continue to burn for each other, that our bodies still thrill at being together, that I am capable of no restraint when it comes to you."

"And that displeases you!"

"It changes nothing, Killian!" She put her hand out to stop him from moving close. "And how did you know where to find me?"

"Pierce told me you had been to the alchemist's yesterday. And to a brothel. Why did you visit a brothel yesterday!"

"I was curious."

"And was your curiosity sated?" he asked grimly.

"I was offered shelter, and food…and employment."

"Aye, I'm certain you were."

"Killian…"

"Let us not quarrel. Come, break fast with me."

"I have no appetite for food, Killian. And are you not to meet your Mary and her kin for the morning meal?"

"They have left for Castle O'Brien. I saw them off earlier."

Her face registered surprise.

"And how did you explain your reason for staying on in Galway?"

"I said I had further business."

"And do you suppose your Mary suspects your business is that of another woman?"

"She is not my Mary, Alainn, and I doubt she knows I have a lover."

"She is most eager to begin such activities with you. I read her mind." She looked down and studied her hands. "Though she is virginal, she finds you most appealing."

"Alainn, it is surely most intrusive to read someone's mind!"

"I can hardly stop thoughts from coming to me. You think I would choose to know how another woman anticipates becoming your lover, when she will soon be your wife and share your bed! Have you imagined what it will be like with her, to take her to your bed?"

"Alainn, of course I have not. I can't keep thoughts of bedding you out of my head for more than minutes at a time. Why would that notion even enter my mind?"

"You are a man!" she snapped. "And she's quite lovely. Tell me, how many virgins have you been with, Killian O'Brien?"

"Christ, Alainn. What is the purpose of this interrogation?"

"Do you prefer to be with virtuous women or experienced harlots?"

"I prefer to be with no one, bar you, and if you're intent on discussing this subject I'll take you back to the inn straightaway and show you exactly what it is I prefer."

"So it arouses you to discuss such subjects?"

"What are you about this day?"

"I am only about learning what might be valuable information should I decide to take the alternate offer of employment. The coin is entirely better than at the alchemist's shop."

"Are you attempting to make me jealous, as you did when you kissed Pierce?"

She smiled impishly.

"That was mostly to disturb that dreadful woman and her inconsiderate daughter. The younger, Brigid, seems salvageable if she's separated from her mother and sister. I think she and Rory could be happy together, but Riley and his intended will be no heavenly match, I'll tell you that straightaway. She is neither virginal nor eager to marry him, for she prefers older men."

"You know all this from reading their minds?"

"Aye, I hear their thoughts."

"Then why do you doubt me? If you can hear my thoughts why do you not know how deeply in love with you I am?" He gently clasped her hands.

"I cannot hear your thoughts often," she said, wrinkling her brow. "It is so with some people. I could not always hear Morag's thoughts, or Molly's, or Lady Siobhan's. Perhaps it is the people I care about the most whose thoughts escape me."

Chapter six

They reached an inn with many outdoor tables and she was thankful she would not have to suffer the smell of food being prepared. The herbs in her apron pocket were helping with the putrid stomach, but she still was prone to dizziness. The odor of meat would most certainly cause her stomach to heave.

Killian pulled out a chair for her and signaled to the serving boy, scowling when the young man could scarcely keep his eyes off Alainn. He looked around, glaring, until the other men near them found something else to interest them.

"What is it you are thinking about, Killian?"

"You really can't hear my thoughts?" he asked. She shook her head, and a half-smile crossed her rosy lips.

"Only some of the time. When we are together." She leaned in and whispered, "When we are joined intimately. Then, I am able."

"That is somewhat unsettling." His cheeks reddened slightly. "You must think me lecherous."

"No more so than I," she murmured.

Their food arrived, and she grimaced. But, as they sat together, not speaking of the tribulations before them, Alainn realized her appetite had returned. They broke bread, ate cheese and drank warm cider, and she felt a slight trickle of hope creep into her heart. It was a foolish consideration to allow within.

Later, when they had finished their food and were strolling along the cobblestone street, they passed a church that appeared quite ancient. Its pointed spire seemed to reach up to the heavens. Killian stopped to consider it, then gazed at her with an expression of longing.

"Marry me, Alainn," he said quietly. "Marry me this very day. We shall find a priest and be married."

"Do not taunt me, Killian," she whispered. "You know it's not possible."

"Why not? My uncle cannot deny what has already been done."

"Aye, but he could. He would simply not recognize our marriage as legal. He would surely have it annulled. Then, I am sure he would kill me and hurt you."

"You truly fear him."

"I know what he is capable of. I do not share his blood or his station. I am able to see his flaws."

"I do not believe him to be without flaws, Alainn. But, I don't believe he would harm me, and though I will not soon forgive him for causing you pain, I am certain he would not wish you ill will."

"Then we are of opposing opinions, Killian, and it is simply another reason why I cannot return to the castle."

"If we are wed, the marriage legal and performed in a church by a priest, if it is consummated, he would have no grounds to annul it. Tell me you'll become my wife. Make me the happiest man in all of Eire."

She looked at the peaceful church and felt pain in her heart as if it were truly breaking.

"No Killian," she said simply. "'Tis not possible. And there are things about me of which you are unaware."

"Nonsense, Alainn. I know you as well as I know myself."

"There are always secrets hidden deep within, and I have more than my share, I fear."

"Alainn, if you speak of these powers you possess, I have known about them from the first day we spoke. I do not fear them." He smiled encouragingly. "Show me your powers, then. If they have become so great, show—"

The church bell pealed from the bell tower with a deafening noise, drowning his words. Alainn tilted her chin, concentrating on the tower, and the enormous bell silenced mid-peal. All around them, people stopped to stare and mutter, clearly disturbed by the occurrence.

"That was your doing?" His voice was skeptical.

"Aye."

"Show me more," he ordered.

She turned her head to a flock of seagulls gathered by the harbor. They were squawking loudly, attacking one another over a thick crust of bread. She showed them her palm, and they immediately settled, sitting quietly and staring at her. She swept her hand through the air and they all flew away, except one, on whom she kept her eyes trained. He flew over and perched on her shoulder.

"You have power over animals?"

"It has been so for some time now."

"Can you control…people?" he asked, as if reluctant to learn the answer.

"I've not tried. I think it would surely be considered evil to attempt it."

"Could you change the way my uncle feels?"

"I'm not certain." She stroked the feathers of the bird's chest.

"Try it with me."

"I won't!" The bird screeched and flew off as if insulted. She watched it grow smaller in the sky, being too disturbed to look at Killian.

"When you use these powers, Alainn, it requires much strength? It leaves you weakened." He gathered her close, and she leaned against him, feeling his warmth.

"Aye. It is as though I become weary and must sleep, especially if my mind is filled with other quandaries."

"I would not have asked you to show me if I'd known." With that, he lifted her into his arms as though she were as light as a feather.

"Killian put me down. I am perfectly capable of walking." He ignored her and kept his pace. "Where are you taking me?"

"Back to the inn."

"You know well enough, if we go back to the inn together, we will neither rest nor sleep."

"Aye." His seductive smile made him undeniably charming, but she resisted.

"Killian, I am most serious, put me down. I will not go back to the inn with you. You must go back to your uncle's castle. The celebrations will begin in mere days, and you are your uncle's champion in the games of skill and strength. He will not take kindly to your absence."

"Do you believe my heart would be in jousting and swordfights if you are here alone in Galway? I would probably suffer a sword through my heart. And if you truly believe we will never be together, then I am not so certain I wouldn't welcome the blade."

"She seems a lovely girl. You have a chance at happiness with Mary."

He stopped walking and dropped her roughly onto her feet. "I will not accept you truly believe that. If your powers are so vast then surely we can think of a way to be together."

"Would you have me kill your uncle?"

His eyes narrowed at her question.

"It won't come to that, Alainn."

"Would you have me kill him?"

"No! I don't wish him dead."

"Then, there is no way we can be together, for as long as he lives, he will never agree to our marriage or allow us to live in peace."

"I will join the bonnachts. There are many nobles who would welcome my knowledge and skill with weaponry. It could hardly be considered treasonous to my uncle if I fight for Ireland against the English."

"And so we would be wed, and you would leave to fight and die in battle. I would rather you wed Mary than see you dead. I will not be your widow if that is the price I must pay to be your wife."

He breathed a heavy sigh, for she was correct that the life span of a soldier in the Irish army was short.

"Then, marry me, and we'll find a small parcel of land somewhere hidden far away from my uncle."

"There is nowhere in all of Ireland where he would not find us, Killian. Is that how you picture our marriage? Hidden away, worrying that one day he will find us, then attempting to flee his army and his wrath?"

"We will go to another country! You've often spoken of wanting to see the Americas, and I have sufficient coin to secure passage on any number of ships. There are more people leaving for the Americas every day."

"I cannot leave Ireland. There is the curse to contend with."

"And how do you plan to contend with it if you remain in Galway?" he asked with growing impatience.

"After you and Mary are wed and have gone to your castle, I will return to see what might be done. My m...Mara believes there is a way if we work together."

"Your Mara," he spat. "She has become so endeared to you that you refer to her as yours!"

"She thinks there may be a way to reverse the spell, but I believe there will be consequences. Mara and her descendants might die."

"And where is the problem within that? Her son is dead, and he surely fathered no children. She clearly deserves to die in retribution for her abhorrent curse."

"I did not say she has not committed terrible sins. Her curse has devastated many, including Lady Siobhan, who is very dear to me."

"Yet, you hesitate. You would risk the entire future of all the O'Brien clan to save a witch who has brought about death and heartache to my kin."

"Mara was wrong in cursing the entire O'Brien family, but she was justified in cursing your grandfather. I would have cursed him myself for what he did to her."

"So, she finally told you what prompted the curse?"

"She did not tell me. I witnessed it. I saw it... I heard it within the walls of the room where the crime was committed. I watched him rape her, knowing full well she carried a child. He beat her unmercifully and took her beloved from her."

"You saw it, heard it? How is that possible? It was years ago."

"Nearly ten and eight. I saw an echo in time. I do not welcome this new magical power."

"She cursed my family, Alainn," he said, his jaw tight. "Perhaps if you were to go to the bedchamber where my aunt lay in childbed five or six times, only to have the children born lifeless or die within hours. Perhaps if you heard the echo of her weeping and grieving while she held her stillborn babes, or clutched them close, agonizing over how long it would be before they were taken, surely then the thought of the death of one accursed witch would not seem such an unreasonably high price to pay." He was furious.

"I did not say I would not go through with it," she muttered.

"But, 'tis obvious it pains you greatly to consider it, even knowing what ill she has caused!" he roared. His green eyes were blazing.

Alainn turned away from him and strode toward the seashore. This solution he was so eager to attempt might claim her life and that of their unborn child. Yet, if she did not attempt it, the child would die. Either way, their child was surely doomed. She had barely allowed the thought to cross her mind when she felt a flutter, liken to butterfly wings, within her belly.

She longed to cry out in joy, to reveal the truth to Killian. Instead, she pressed her hand lightly to her abdomen as her child moved once more, and tears swam in her eyes. She knew she must fight for this child as she'd never fought for anything before in her life.

"Alainn, you must come back, we have much more to discuss!"

"Go to Castle O'Brien, Killian!" she cried without turning.

"Aye, if you are so damn eager to drive me away, so be it. I'll oblige you, woman! I have paid for the room at the inn for this night. You may have it. I assure you I won't come near you again."

She kept her face to the sea as seemingly endless tears spilled down her cheeks. Nodding without speaking, she listened as the echoes of his stomping boots on cobblestones became fainter and fainter

Chapter seven

Alainn found herself nearing the docks once more. She had spent most of the day wandering aimlessly through the streets, so deep in thought she seemed scarcely aware of the people and noise, the clamber of the city around her.

The day had grown late when she glanced at the skyline; the golden-red ball was sinking low over the western horizon. She walked along the beach, allowing herself time to gaze at the tranquil beauty of the sunset. Water quietly brushed her bare feet, grazed her ankles, the cool waves trying to still the tumultuousness within her.

It was then that Alainn felt the presence. It made her skin prickle, the hairs on the back of her neck stand on end. She was not alone. But as she glanced around, she could see no one near. Fishing vessels were pulling into harbor and several people remained on the nearby docks. The presence was surely not human. It was liken to what she had experienced in the dungeon of Castle O'Brien.

Taking a deep breath, she closed her eyes and concentrated on her abilities. When Alainn was a child, increasingly disturbed by the presence of the many spirits around her, she had learned how to block the other world. The spirits were no longer visible to her unless she allowed herself to see them. She took another deep breath and opened her eyes.

An elderly spectral couple strolling hand in hand smiled warmly at Alainn. A young woman sat on a large rock, weeping mournfully, silver tears pouring down her pale ghostly face as she waited for her lover to come back. Alainn knew without question that he had met his fate on a downed ship and the weeping woman had walked out into the depths to join him. She wondered why they were not together in the afterlife. Sometimes death was no more fair than life.

Alainn spotted another young spirit sitting on the sand with her knees pulled up to her chest. She moved nearer, feeling drawn to her. The girl spoke without looking up.

"You should not be here, 'tis not safe."

"This is where you met your fate?"

"Aye, I was murdered on this very spot, not by a sailor filled with too much drink or a lustful suitor, but by my very own father. I intended to marry a man not of his choosing, and so he chose to end my life. You must leave this place now, young witch. There is no time to waste."

"Who is it I should be fearful of?"

"No one you can see," the spirit answered ominously.

The damp air grew cold, and the sun disappeared from sight. Alainn moved quickly onto the docks but felt no safer in the presence of the men. A few looked at her suspiciously, the odd one lasciviously, and she pulled the hood of her cloak over her unbound hair. The chill within her grew.

For as long as Alainn could remember, she'd had the ability to detect auras. She could see a colored glow surrounding each person, could often detect what lay within their souls. She had only ever known two people with unusually dark auras. One was Richard McGilvary, the steward's son. He had been a horrid child and was now a loathsome young man. He tortured animals, and violated and abused many women. Killian had nearly beaten him to death on more than one occasion for his unconscionable acts. He did not yet know that Richard and his older brother, Henry, had tried to rape her and nearly succeeded.

If not for Pierce's protection and her own magic, they may well have accomplished the feat that was ordered, she later learned, by Chieftain O'Brien himself. However, they were more than pleased to oblige him. Henry was a very nasty sort, but Alainn thought Richard harbored within him a depth of malevolence that was purely evil.

The other dark soul was the chieftain's priest. She had felt great unease ever since she was a child because of his ever-darkening aura.

Morag, the old wise woman who raised her, had talked of dark spirits and creatures more menacing than the spirits. Humans who delved into the black arts who dared conjure demons and creatures from the Unseelie Court, the realm of evil that lives between worlds. It could be in part why Morag had always tried to have Alainn keep her powers at bay, lest someone with malevolent intentions learned of them.

The fairies in the glade had also warned her of entities filled with abhorrent darkness, those who enforced their powers with evil. Alainn shivered again and picked up her pace until she was nearly running.

"Young and powerful witch, come to me, reveal your many powers!" She gasped, for the voice was speaking inside her head. Then, the words of old Morag filled her mind.

"When darkness approaches and threatens, do not simply call upon your powers. Face your fear and create your own light. Let only goodness shine through."

Alainn stopped running, inhaled several slow deep breaths, and imagined herself sitting in the tiny chapel of Castle O'Brien. She pictured the holiness of the place, the innocence and sweetness of newborn babies, the warmth of kittens and lambs, the soothing beauty of Irish harps, the goodness of Lady Siobhan, the power of the many glade fairies, and the strength of Morag. She envisioned sunlight pouring through the windows of the chapel and at once she could feel warmth and light radiating from within her, swirling around her, surrounding her in its ethereal glow. She looked down and could see light shining through her. The darkness shrank back and receded entirely, but not before she heard the unearthly voice once more.

"One day, we will meet again, young witch. I shall learn what great powers you possess and take them for my own!"

Chapter eight

It had been another night without sleep. At first Alainn was undeniably unnerved by the dark presence. But, once back in the warmth and safety of the inn, she could almost believe she'd simply imagined the entire unpleasant experience.

Now, she hid behind the curtain of the bedchamber window, watching Killian. He stood by his large grey stallion, had been there for nearly an hour since the sun had risen, but he had not yet looked up toward the window of the inn. She had not been able to lie upon the bed for she could still detect the musky scent upon the sheets from their recent lovemaking. She stifled a sob, as the memory of it filled her senses entirely and she realized they would never be together in that manner again.

She sat down heavily upon a chair and waited for the sudden uneasiness in her stomach to settle. The herbs did not seem capable of stopping her queasiness this day. A new sharp pain sliced through her head, and she was overcome with a revulsion so intense she barely made it to the basin before her emesis erupted in earnest. She was blinded by a vision so clear and disturbing, she cried out in protest. Killian lay dead upon a battlefield. Beside him, lay Rory and Riley, both bloodied and lifeless. The entire moor was littered with bodies, and beyond the hills stood men in the red uniform of the English army. As quickly as it came, the vision went, leaving her sweaty and weak.

She ran toward the window, but Killian was no longer there. Collecting just a few of her possessions, the treasured combs he gave her, her dagger, and herbs, she raced down the steps and onto the street. His horse, Storm, was a swift steed; she would never catch them on foot. She would surely need to find a stable and locate a horse. But, the meager coins in her pocket would not pay for even a lame nag. Would she be driven to procure a horse by way of her magic?

"You took your sweet time, Lainna."

"Killian!" she screamed and ran to him, throwing her arms around his neck. Tears flowed down her cheeks, and she could not stifle her sobs. Her body trembled with relief at seeing him safe and well, holding him in her arms.

"Shhh, there's no need to weep so, my sweet Lainna. We are together now, and that's all that truly matters."

"I thought you'd left."

"I tried to leave. I couldn't manage it." He gently touched his fingers to her swollen eyes. "Have you wept all night, my sweet Lainna?" She didn't answer for her sobs would not subside. He bent over and kissed each eyelid, and the tenderness within his touch only proved to increase her tears. She laid her head to his chest and listened to his steady heartbeat, inhaled his masculine scent until her tears finally ebbed.

He lifted her upon the horse, swung himself up behind her, and pulled her close. She leaned against him, still hiccupping and trembling. He placed a soft kiss upon the top of her head and buried his face in her lovely tresses.

"Thank you," he murmured.

***

Alainn jerked awake and, for an instant, could not recollect where she was.

It was only a dream, she thought, stiffening in a panic.

"You've slept the day away, Lainna," a deep voice rumbled in her ear as muscular arms tightened around her. The horse swayed beneath her. She leaned back against Killian and looked to the darkening sky. The sun had nearly sunk beneath the western horizon.

"Should we not have reached Castle O'Brien by now?" she asked.

"Aye, but I decided to take you to another location this night. And before you protest, I assure you we will be back to Castle O'Brien before my uncle has to forfeit any of my bouts. I suspect I should not rile him further if we intend to have him see things our way."

She sighed deeply.

"Where are we off to, then?"

"To my father's castle. I promised to take you there one day."

"I was only a child when you promised me that. I would not hold you to it."

"Aye well, I once told you I'd take you to see the sea and you managed that one without me. I do not intend to renege on this promise."

"How long has it been, Killian, since you've been back?"

"Nearly two years."

"They won't be expecting you. Does your mother's cousin live in your castle?"

"No, he has a castle of his own, but he manages affairs for my family and has agreed to do so until I take over."

"Will there be others there? Is it kept?"

"Aye, there is still a full staff of servants. My father was a wealthy chieftain, and the land is unusually rich for being so near the sea."

"You must be exhausted."

"It was not a night I care to repeat."

She squeezed his hand and felt his arms tighten possessively.

"Are you hungry, Alainn? You seemed so weary I thought I would not wake you."

They stopped and dismounted. He passed her a pouch filled with bread and cheese, and a waterskin. She drank heartily.

"Are we near to where your castle is situated?" she asked, taking a bite of the bread.

"Aye, perhaps an hour away."

She finished the food as they walked to stretch their legs. He held her free hand as if afraid to let her go.

"How will you explain me to your servants?"

"They will require no explanation."

"But even if they haven't seen you in almost two years, they will surely know you have not yet married. Will they not wonder why a woman travels with you unaccompanied by a chaperone?"

"They may wonder all they want. I doubt they will inquire about it."

"Where will I sleep this night?"

"Wherever you desire. There are many rooms to choose from."

"Where will you sleep?"

Killian sighed and kissed her fingers.

"Lainna, if you're wondering whether we will spend this night together, that is entirely up to you. There are many adjoining rooms if you are concerned about prying eyes and the whispers of servants. I will not ask you to share my bed, but you know if I'd had my way we'd be in our marriage bed this night."

"You will not need to ask me, Killian. I will share your bed and try not to think of Mary MacDonald."

"If you're in my bed, you can be certain no thoughts of any other woman will cross my mind."

* * *

Alainn lay upon an enormous bed, freshly bathed and feeling most content. The sheets were soft and inviting; the pillow cool and comfortable. Killian had been correct in assuming the servants would welcome him, and no had one questioned the fact that he'd brought a woman with him. They were all most polite and entirely accommodating. He had told them she was the woman he loved and intended to marry, and that was apparently all the information they required.

The servants had seemed very pleased to see him, and several had asked if he was here to stay. *Soon*, he had said. His mother's cousin had been sent for, and now Killian was in the castle's great hall, speaking with the man.

The castle was as grand and spectacular as Killian had always boasted. It was larger than Castle O'Brien and nearly twice as wide; the turrets more massive, and the parapets higher. The evening breeze blew in lightly through the open window, tickling her. She left the comfort of the bed and stepped onto the open balcony.

The gentle wind caressed her bare shoulders. She was wearing a new chemise that Killian had purchased for her. It was a soft pink color with feminine lace, and it made her feel lovely and desirable. There was also a dress in a lovely pale shade of green. Killian told her he had another garment for her but was most secretive about it, insisting it would be saved for a grand occasion.

She heard the door open in the chamber that adjoined hers. Her heart quickened knowing he would be with her soon. Hugh O'Brien would not be pleased at her attempts thus far in discouraging Killian's attention toward her. She'd shared his bed once and was fully intending to do so again.

Her thoughts went to the Scottish girl who was promised to Killian, and she shook her head as if to dispel the unpleasantness. They would have this night with no guilt and no regret, for she did not know what lay ahead of them. In her vision she had seen her man dead, and she would do anything possible to prevent that from happening. Tonight, there would be no room for discord, only love and passion.

The door opened between the two rooms and he called her name softly. She smiled and entered his room.

She walked through the doorway and her beauty took his breath away. The moonlight caught her hair as it fell in soft, beautiful waves down her back. She must have used the brush he'd set out for her. It had been his mother's. She would have liked Alainn.

Killian could almost hear his parents, and his brother and sister. He remembered how Alainn had spoken of rooms containing echoes, and he wondered if she could hear his family even now. Alainn had been his family since his own had gone, even more so than his uncle and his kin.

He went to her and placed his hands lightly on her shoulders, slowly caressing her arms down to the wrists until he found her hands. He kissed them, and she touched his cheek, pulled her hand through his thick mane.

"Your brow is creased, Killian. The meeting with your kin did not go well?"

"No, it went well enough, Alainn. But let us not speak of anything but you and me this night."

"So it shall be, Milord." She began removing his tunic, and her soft touch on his bare skin set him afire. "Sit down here on the bed, Killian. I will ease your tired body."

She climbed onto the bed and knelt behind him, her fingers kneading the taut muscles in his back and shoulders, strained from the lengthy journey on horseback.

"You must be employing your magic," he murmured, feeling his body relax. When she leaned closer and placed her lips on his neck, he felt himself sinking into a realm of complete pleasure. She slid off the bed to stand before him.

As her lips kissed every inch of the long scar he bore on his chest, she unhooked his belt and laid his sheathed sword upon the floor. Then, she slowly unfastened his trews and released his manhood. He moaned in appreciation of her actions.

He closed his eyes as her kisses continued downward and breathed in sharply when she placed her mouth upon that part of him. He opened his eyes to watch. She had never before been so bold, never pleasured him in this manner, and he could scarcely contain his great need. When she sensed his mounting passion, she moved from him, deliberately pushing him back onto the bed with an eagerness that intensified his arousal. She finished removing his trews and mounted him. He lay back, watching her lovely form as she rode him.

He rubbed her firm breasts through the soft fabric of her chemise and felt the nipples peak and harden. She emitted a soft mewling sound that made his aching masculinity throb with a searing need for her. The heat of her enveloped him, and he thrust again and again as she took them to the epitome of pleasure, and beyond.

She collapsed on top of him, her forehead damp against his bare chest. Her breathing was labored, and he chuckled.

"You've not had enough riding this day?"

She opened her clear blue eyes and smiled at him.

"I slept through the first ride, 'twas not nearly as invigorating as this one. And besides, you managed the long journey today. I thought I might save you exerting yourself further."

"And you did so most capably, and it was not all that you did most capably!" he smiled as he spoke.

"It was adequate then?"

"Aye, more than adequate, my Lainna."

"The women at the brothel seemed to believe that above all other requests that manner of pleasure is most in demand by men and that it was a certain remedy to cure whatever might be broken between a man and woman."

He did not respond.

"And is it so?" she pressed.

His cheeks colored with embarrassment.

"Well it's most arousing and most pleasurable, I'll not deny it, but no more than lying with you, Alainn. Come to it, just kissin' you and holdin' you creates a desperate fire within me. Even lookin' upon you makes me ache with the need of havin' you. Touchin' your flawless silken skin and hearin' your lovely voice. The scent of your lustrous hair. Your sweet laugh. You heighten every sense I possess, Lainna."

"You are either very sweet or very wise."

They remained locked in a lovers' embrace, but her eyes still held a glint of passion.

"Are you overtired, Killian? Too weary to love me again?"

He was stunned at her request.

"Never too weary for my Lainna," he said, flipping her onto her back to gaze down into her eyes. And he proved true to his word.

This time, the lovemaking was slow and tender. When their release came it was so overwhelming they fell asleep still intimately joined. Yet, sometime in the middle of the night, Alainn was aware of him removing her garment, of his soft caresses, and she gasped as he entered her, yet again.

* * *

The chatter of magpies, the trill of songbirds, and the deep cries of gulls woke her. The bedcovers lay twisted at their feet and the morning sun was already radiating through the arched window. The scent of the morning freshness filled her nostrils as she lay watching him sleep.

He was a grand form of a man. His body, firm and muscular; his chest expansive, his arms filled with unquestionable strength. If only they could remain here together, live out their lives in this place so dear to him.

He stirred beside her, but did not wake. She knew they must leave soon to ensure they reached Castle O'Brien before nightfall, but she feared the wrath Hugh O'Brien when he learned she had not lived up to his demands. And she could only imagine Killian's reaction if he learned of her true parentage or what had transpired between her and his uncle.

Her mind once more went to Mary MacDonald. She was a likeable young woman, and she truly meant her no disrespect or humiliation. Her eyes trailed down Killian's uncovered body and fell upon that part of him she was often too unnerved to look at. That part of him, even when not in a state of arousal, was no less impressive or grand. His thighs were long and as powerful as any sculpted warrior. His skin was golden brown and much darker than her own pale complexion.

She looked down at her own body. The bruises on her breasts were only barely noticeable. Killian had not mentioned them. She tried to detect if her body had begun to change in accommodation of the child that grew within her. Her belly was still flat enough. Once again, she felt him move within her and smiled.

A boy child. She instantly knew she carried Killian's son. Her breasts were larger and tender. She dared wonder how many times her wee son would be allowed to suckle at her breast before being taken by Mara's curse, if he was allowed to take breath at all. She shivered and moved closer to Killian's warmth.

Her hand traced the long white scar upon his chest, and she sensed his body become firm as he pressed closer to her. His eyes opened.

"It must have been a sensual dream you were engaged in," she murmured.

A smile crossed his broad lips, and his eyes revealed his contentment.

"'Tis not uncommon for men to awake in a state of arousal, but the fact I awaken in the company of a goddess might contribute to my present condition."

His hands slid down her back, and her skin tingled at his touch. He grasped her buttocks firmly and thrust himself toward her as she most willingly arched her hips to meet him. "Killian O'Brien, I will be incapable of walking if you continue with your present actions." The hands caressing her inner thighs and the soft mound above her womanhood, stilled.

"I have hurt you then, Lainna. You should have warned me for I forget myself with you. You always return my passion so unquestionably. 'Tis rare for a woman to require the coupling as much as a man. But, you must alert me if it is too frequently, or too intense."

"You haven't hurt me, Killian. My womanly parts are tender, to be certain, but I am not damaged in any manner. Although I admit 'tis a powerful and mighty asset you possess."

His cheeks colored at her mention of the proportions of his manhood. Her hand went to it and fondled the object of their conversation. He moved from her touch.

"You must not continue this if I cannot have you. It leaves a man in an unenviable state, and in truth it is not only uncomfortable but actually most painful."

"It hurts you to be aroused?" she appeared taken aback by this.

"Aye, if there is no release, there is a great discomfort and a fierce aching below."

"Ah." Her hand moved from his swollen manhood to the firm objects beneath. "'Tis your ballocks that ache so fiercely, then?"

He moaned in pain and pleasure.

"Christ, Alainn, I am most serious, 'tis a cruelty to keep touching me if I've no way to relieve my mounting need."

"And if I were not here, how would that need be relieved? Would you find a servant girl to accommodate you?"

"No, perhaps at one time," he rasped in a passion-filled tone, "but not since I have come to love you so entirely, certainly not since we have become intimate." He moaned. "Alainn, 'tis quite enough." He half-heartedly attempted to move her hand away again, but she only continued more fervently.

He moaned loudly, and she felt him tremble beneath her touch. She continued until he was still. His handsome face was ruddy with embarrassment.

"Why do you feel shame in this, Killian?"

"'Tis not a proud way to behave with the woman I love. You control my body so entirely. It appears it is not within my capabilities to contain my lust for you."

"And I would much rather pleasure you in this manner than have you seek out services elsewhere."

"I suppose you have the answer to your question. 'Tis only by my own hand the deed is achieved when my need is so great and I am unable to be with you."

"Even if the priests do consider it to be a sin, Morag always insisted it is a most common practice among many men used to relieving their primal male urges. It does not offend me, Killian."

"You are a rare woman, Lainna. I have always been able to discuss any subject with you. That is as important to me as the physical love we share."

"Aye, to me as well," she whispered and kissed his lips. A disconcerting look crossed his face, and she stopped. "Something disturbs you, Killian. I can see it in your eyes. There is an uncommon intensity within those deep green eyes that I know so well."

"You have spoken of the jealousy you feel toward me, but I must tell you," he said, staring into her eyes, "I feel it as well. For after what we have shared, the very thought of you ever being with another man like this, disturbs and enrages me so I cannot bear it. I know how you thrill to my touch and demand to be pleasured as well. Because you have only ever been with me, I suppose I dwell on whether another man could make you feel what you feel with me. You have an extremely rare affinity for physical love, Alainn. 'Tis not common. I swear, if I ever learned you had been intimate with another man, I would kill him without question, perhaps you as well."

"You…do not… trust me, Killian? You could actually believe because I take great pleasure in the act of physical love that one day I might be driven to be unfaithful to you?"

"'Tis not that. Truly, 'tis not that I do not trust you. I should not have spoken of this. It was wrong of me to speak of this with you."

She moved away from him, pulling the blanket around her as she rose to go within the water closet. He noticed the wounded look she wore and wanted to flay himself for revealing his insecurities.

The sun's position through the window told him they had tarried long enough. They would need to make haste to arrive at his uncle's castle before the celebrations began. He dressed and fastened the belt that held his sword and scabbard. When she still had not come out of the tiny chamber, he went to the door and called to her.

"Alainn, please come speak with me. I must apologize to you for it was most certainly not my intention to make you think I doubt your fidelity."

When she finally stepped out, her blue eyes flashed with anger. She raised her chin as she always did when she was about to lay a tongue-lashing on him.

"Let me have it then, Alainn, for I deserve it."

"Aye, you do!" she began. "You dare to question my fidelity! Why? Simply because I truly enjoy the act? Would it please you more if I was frigid, or if I only allowed you to be with me because I knew you wanted me? Am I not to achieve pleasure from our joining? Is that not what is intended between a man and a woman who share such a love as ours? Or do you doubt me because I fairly begged you to deflower me? Do you expect I will be wanton with any man?"

"'Tis not that. nay, Not at all, Alainn. I am filled with uncertainty! Can you not see that? You are as beautiful a woman as God ever created. I lust for you so entirely, and you do not belong to me. Though I feel it within my soul that you are mine, you refuse to marry me."

"And you believe marriage ensures fidelity? You've obviously not taken a good long look around Castle O'Brien, for the secret affairs and scandalous deceit found within would surely startle even you, Killian O'Brien!"

"Even me, now what precisely does that indicate?" He felt his own hackles being raised.

"You've not led the life of a monk. What is the point of becoming a gifted lover if you don't want your partner to be pleasured by your actions? Did you question the fidelity of the miller's daughter, for she certainly appeared to be enjoying the coupling when I found you two mid-coitus. Or the cobbler's daughter, the tailor's. Need I go on?"

"I did not know you knew about—" he began but then thought better of it. "Alainn, how might I undo this unpleasantness I have caused? Certainly I want you to feel pleasure during our lovemaking. There is perhaps no greater feeling to a man than to know he can make his woman reach fulfillment, to know he can satisfy her needs. I most certainly would not want you frigid. I cannot find the words to tell you how much I cherish what passes between us when we share a physical love. And I have never felt a greater satisfaction with any other woman, Alainn. I swear to you!"

"When you are wed to Mary MacDonald, when you spend each night with her here in this castle, will you still demand my fidelity?" she asked, her face crimson with anger. "Would you sentence me to a life of celibacy, expect me to remain unmarried?"

"I will not marry her, Alainn. How could I when I burn for you, when I love only you? And no, I'll not allow you to wed another. The day you take a husband will be the day he meets my sword." He pulled her to him, though she tried pushing him away for he had been pressed as far as he would allow. "So you are able to admit your jealousy in my regards, but I am not to be allowed the same freedom? You have told me you fear for Mary MacDonald, that you feel you might use your powers to harm her. Am I not simply stating the same? I do not possess the abilities you have, but my sword does not miss its target. Are you being any less unreasonable than you now see me?"

Still quivering from her deep emotion and burst of temper, Alainn put her arms around his neck. He held her for a moment before she spoke.

"Killian, I must tell you a truth that each and every man alive would be wise to learn and to heed. Though a man may be almost entirely ruled by his body and many often allow their body rather than their mind to think for them, 'tis not usually the way with women. Aye, to be sure, there are women who simply seek out men for physical pleasure, but most often a woman's desires are led by her mind and her heart. It is when she truly loves a man that she derives the greatest physical attraction and satisfaction. Heed these words, remember them well and know with no uncertainty, my heart is yours and therefore so too is my body. Only yours."

"Please forgive me, Lainna. I want no quarrels. There is too much uncertainty before us; we must remain united in our love. Don't be angry with me for I cannot bear when you pull away from me. And tell me that what I have said will not affect how it is between us when we are one."

"I should not have become so ill-tempered, for I know only too well what jealousy does to a soul. Please do not doubt my faithfulness to you, Killian. I promise you I will not lie with another man unless he is my husband. Not willingly. But should your uncle choose a husband for me, we would undoubtedly need to abide by his wishes or face the consequences, for he is still the chieftain and his word is still law. You are not above reproach. You may be his nephew, but you too will surely be made to bend to his will."

"'Tis high time I leave my uncle's rule, for 'tis a good many subjects we no longer agree upon." Anxious to begin their day's journey, Killian changed the subject entirely. "I will have the servants fill the tub with warm water for you, for a short soak will surely ease your tenderness. A day on horseback may not be so pleasant if you are hurting in such a manner. Perhaps you might attempt riding sidesaddle?"

"I tried once when I was a girl, it was most uncomfortable. And one has so little control of the horse."

"Aye well, 'tis to be hoped the ride won't be too disagreeable for you. We will break fast before we leave. There are many horses within the stables; you may choose whatever one you desire, for we will make better time if we ride separately."

She only nodded as he headed for the door.

Chapter nine

As they left the castle grounds, Killian upon Storm and Alainn on a horse selected from the expansive stables, Killian showed off his home. He pointed out the view of the sea from the edge of his land, the boundless rich fields, and rolling hills dotted with sheep. Servants and field workers bowed to him or waved as they passed by. He had a warm smile for all, and Alainn knew what a well-respected and well-liked chieftain he would one day become.

Once past the borders of Killian's land, they approached a castle of immense proportions. It was by far the largest, grandest stone building Alainn had ever seen. Even the fields surrounding it boasted of many workers and teams of oxen. But, it was the castle itself that Alainn could not keep from staring upon.

"What clan lies claim to that giant?" she asked, sitting high on the dark brown mare she'd chosen.

"'Tis Castle O'Rorke. Lady Siobhan's parents' castle. Niall O'Rorke is the most powerful and wealthy chieftain in all of Ireland. His clan and my mother's have been alleged since the forming of the clans centuries ago. Their alliance has withstood many battles and wars between the clans and the English."

"I knew Lady Siobhan was from the same area of Ireland as your mother's kin, but I had no notion their lands bordered one another. Riley and Rory's kin are most influential, then?"

"Aye, the word of Niall O'Rorke is questioned by no one. He is the descendant of a once great Irish king. A druid king."

"So 'tis the paternal side of the family that were druids?"

"No, both sides apparently. Niall's wife was a Fitzgerald."

"Of the Kildare Fitzgerald's? The Fitzgeralds who once held the lordship of all of Ireland?"

Killian nodded. "Aye, they still remain most prominent and influential. And 'tis said they plan to defy the English once more if they continue their attempts to rule."

As they drew nearer to the enormous castle, Alainn asked, "Will you stop to pay your respects to the O'Rorke?"

"I had thought to, but I am certain he would have left to attend Rory and Riley's birthday celebrations. He and his wife are of an advancing age and would need a goodly time to make the journey."

"And what children do they have besides Lady Siobhan? I know of a sister she lost when she was younger, but are there sons and other daughters as well?"

"Lady Siobhan does not speak of her family often. Though she has lived at Castle O'Brien longer than she lived with her parents, she misses them terribly and longs to return home."

"Aye, I sensed that as well."

"There were four sons and two daughters born to the O'Rorkes. The eldest son, Conn, died in a battle of the clans. It was with Clan Kavanagh. My own mother lost two brothers in that battle. And two of the O'Rorke's sons, Collum and Finn, died the same day my father's castle was attacked, the same day my own brother died."

"Your clans are not only alleged politically, but in tragedy as well."

"Aye, and there is a deep friendship and respect toward one another. My mother and Lady Siobhan were childhood friends. And when my father came to rule as chieftain of my mother's clan, he was accepted without question by Niall O'Rorke and his family."

"And the fourth son?"

"His name was Teige. He was once a valued friend to my father. 'Tis uncertain what became of him, but there was an apparent quarrel between him and his father. He had already been named joint chieftain with Niall and stood to inherit all of this land, the castle, and the many possessions, but the disagreement was so great between them, the son left and has not been heard of since. To the best of my knowledge, there is no one left to inherit the castle or the land. I know Niall has spoken to both Rory and Riley. If they desired it, one of them would become earl of all this should Teige never return."

"'Tis sad to think a rift could be so severe it could not be mended."

"Aye, it has left the elderly couple grieving still. I think they never recovered entirely from the loss of their youngest child, their daughter Shylie."

"How did she die? Was it an illness that took her life?"

"No, a far more tragic and violent death befell her. Lady Siobhan seldom speaks of the events surrounding her younger sister's death. She fell victim to a demented soul, for she was found murdered, strangled in a wooded area on their property. I am told she was very beautiful and angelic in disposition, and loved by all who met her, was said to be the favorite child of both her parents. She was but ten and three when she taken."

"How tragic for them! I thought Lady Siobhan's sister was much younger, the way your aunt spoke of her."

"Aye, she always referred to her as her wee baby sister. She possibly remembered her more clearly as a youngster, for she had already married my uncle and was living at Castle O'Brien at the time of her sister's death. She was ripe with child, carrying my cousins, when she received the news of her sister's murder. My uncle said she nearly lost them, her pain and despair were so great. She spent the last two months of her term in bed, barely able to move for fear she'd miscarry. 'Twas most fortunate she did not lose them," he said bitterly, "for she was never able to see another child live past a few hours time. She bore a daughter, I'm told, who lived only moments, and she wanted one so desperately. That loathsome curse!"

They rode in silence toward the castle gates. Killian called out to one of the guards who recognized him.

"Killian O'Brien, 'tis good to see you, lad!" the guard shouted, coming to meet them. "Have you come to secure your position as chieftain of your father's land?"

"Not as yet, Michael, but it will be truth soon enough."

"And is this your lady? I have heard through the O'Rorke that your uncle has found a suitable match. Your lady's a Scot if I've managed the information correctly?"

"Aye well, this is my lady, but she's as Irish as you and me, Michael. I fear my uncle and I disagree on what woman would suit me best. 'Tis Lady Alainn before you."

The man bowed in reverence to Alainn, and she felt her cheeks grow warm as she nodded to the man. She'd never been addressed as a lady before, and certainly no one had ever bowed to her. She was not entirely in agreement with Killian's deception.

"So, this is your wife, sir?"

"That too will be a certainty soon enough, and we will return to my lands and my castle when the celebrations of my cousins have concluded. Speaking of which, have Niall and Katherine left for Castle O'Brien?"

"Aye, two days previous. Lady Katherine has been of failing health of late. Her mind wanders often back to the time when all her children still lived. 'Tis a sad state and a great encumbrance to our chieftain, for their great love and devotion have always been evident."

"I will meet him then, when we get back to my uncle's lands."

Alainn removed her cap to refasten the knot in her golden hair when the man glanced her way. He grew pale and staggered backward.

"Michael are you quite well? You look as though you are ailing."

"'Tis like lookin' into the face of a spirit," he whispered. "She resembles Maiden Shylie so. You would not remember her," he said louder, managing to compose himself, "for you would have been a wee infant when she met her misfortune. But I'd wager much if you'd known her, you'd agree."

"Lady Siobhan has also spoken of the resemblance."

"Aye, 'tis uncanny, and in truth the eeriest of sensations has overcome me. Milord and Milady will surely be unnerved by the resemblance if they have never met your lady."

"I don't believe they have."

Alainn shook her head and said softly, "No, I have never met Lady Siobhan's kin."

The man's eyes widened.

"The voice is identical. Are you kin of the O'Rorke's, Milady?"

"Alainn's kin are from the lands near Castle 'O'Brien, nowhere near the Clan O'Rorke."

The man continued to shake his head in disbelief as they rode away.

"That was most certainly odd for Michael to be so unsettled by the mere sight of you," Killian said, frowning slightly. "I have seen the man in battle with my father the day our castle was in siege. Even though he was injured, he was dauntless."

Alainn did not respond. They rode on quietly, each deep in their own thoughts.

They spent the entire day pushing onward, speaking at times, and at other times enjoying a comfortable silence. They stopped once to sit upon the soft green hillside overlooking a scenic valley and partake in food the castle's cook sent with them. Alainn delighted in the solitude they shared, knowing that by this time tomorrow they would be dealing with the O'Brien's temper. They sat close together, bodies touching, allowing themselves a few precious moments of affection. Alainn touched the amulet that still hung from Killian's neck. He reached as if to remove it from his neck.

"No!" she cried, deeply disturbed. "You must never allow this to leave your neck, not even to bathe." She smoothed it back into place on his chest. "You must promise me that, Killian. Make a solemn vow to me that you will not remove it. I must charm it again," she murmured, "to be certain it protects you."

"What have you seen, Alainn?" When she turned her head away, he insisted, "You must tell me." He wrapped his arms around her tightly, and she looked up at him with fearful eyes. "Please tell me, Alainn. Whatever it is, surely 'twould be more beneficial to know what lies before me."

Her chin trembled as she whispered, "I have seen you dead, Killian. You, and Rory and Riley as well. In a battle with the English. But I know not when or where."

Realization dawned on his handsome face. "Sure 'twas not your love that brought you back to me that morning in Galway. You would have allowed me to leave! Your vision forced your hand."

"Aye, but it was not the whole of it. My love for you would never allow harm to befall you. For then, I would surely die as well."

"That was why you were so desperate when you thought I had left. You felt obligated to warn me."

"It would kill me to see you die, Killian. I have already seen it within my mind, and my heart shall never heal from the sight of it! Please, promise me you will not remove the amulet, and if I see more details, you must heed my word without question. Do I have your word on it?" She leaned in toward him, but he rose abruptly and went to ready his horse.

"Aye, I'll heed you well, Alainn," he said in a chilly tone.

She crossed the distance between them and put her arms around his waist, leaned her head against his back. He stiffened in her embrace.

"It was not simply obligation that made me come to you, Killian. You are everything to me. My love for you is so great, so all-consuming it frightens me. How am I to allow you to marry another, to be parted from you forever, when being across a room from you feels like an impossible distance?"

He turned and looked into her eyes, recognizing the torment in their depths, and kissed her with a desperation and possessiveness she returned without hesitation.

"You must allow me to charm your amulet once more before we go on any further," she insisted.

Killian knew it was pointless to argue when she had her mind made up. If she believed he was in peril, her magic may truly be his only hope. Even during the charming process, she did not remove the amulet, so he concluded he was surely in grave danger.

When their blood had been mixed and the metal singed, Alainn blew on it until it was cool enough to sit against his skin. She traced the scar upon his chest as though it belonged to her.

"This mark does not repulse you, Alainn?"

"No, I adore it."

"You adore this gruesome reminder of my ordeal?"

"'Tis a proud battle scar you bear, Killian O'Brien." They both smiled as she repeated the words she had used when they were just children. "I helped heal you. I feel a great possessiveness."

"I burn for you, Alainn. When will this fire be sated? I can think of little else when I am near you."

She impulsively reached for the fastenings of his trews, but remembering their rift from the morning, let her hands fall to her sides.

"Alainn do not allow my cross words this morning deter your desire. I would be greatly grieved if it hampered your eagerness to love me. But the hour grows late, and you have admitted you are tender from our previous joining."

"Then we will make time, for I feel the horses could run wildly for a time."

"And what of your tenderness?"

"You will be cautious and gentle with me this time, but next time," she added saucily, "I will not ask for gentleness."

Chapter ten

They were within a few hours ride of Castle O'Brien when Killian began steering his horse off course.

"Where are you headed, Killian?"

"'Tis not a great distance to the most spectacular sight you'll ever see, Alainn. I will show you something so extraordinary, you will be truly stunned."

She found herself growing excited with anticipation as the land grew steadily rockier, the rolling hills more craggy and steep, the trees sparser. Finally, Killian stopped and dismounted, and lifted her from her horse. He found a tree and tethered the horses, then took her hand. Together, they walked up the steady slope.

The sun was just beginning to set, and the ball hung low in a sky made lovely with pinks, crimsons, and gold. When they'd walked a short distance, he placed his hands over her eyes and she laughed but allowed him to lead her. Finally, he stopped and removed his hands.

"Oh Killian!" she cried, finding no other words. "Oh Killian." Five immense cliffs rose up from the sea in marvelous grandeur. They were as tall and craggy and enormous as any mountains she'd seen in paintings. The layers of rock were varied in color and the radiant sunset playing against them only added to the enchantment of the location. She watched as waves crashed against the monumental stone walls.

She stood on tiptoe, fairly bouncing, so elated was she. Killian gave a hearty laugh, and she smiled back at him.

"You have not done that since you were a child, Alainn, that wee bouncing motion. Rory, Riley, and I used to see who could cause you the greatest amount of glee, for we liked to see your wee dance."

"You taunted me unmercifully about it, Killian, the three of you."

Her eyes had still not turned from the spectacular view. "They take my breath away, Killian. How grand and marvelous, how utterly magnificent they are. I have never beheld such an astounding, impressive sight. Apart from seeing you unclothed, of course," she added.

"Aye, the cliffs are a good second choice, I suppose." He chuckled.

He held her until the sun had sunk far beneath the horizon and the cliffs were barely visible in the twilight.

"This is such a beautiful country, Killian. I adore it all so much. I have just recently seen the great Atlantic Ocean, with its rocky burren and sandy beaches, and now these miraculous cliffs. I love it all the more. 'Tis no wonder whoever touches Ireland's shores wants to claim it for their own. The Norse, the Normans, the English. But they are never so very kind to the Irish people."

"Aye, they've not dealt us many kindnesses to be certain. They want to claim our land but change everything about the people, from our customs and traditions to what we eat, how we dress and wear our hair, what music we make, what musical instruments we play. They even alter our manner of speaking."

"The English are the worst of the lot, Killian. There is so much heartache ahead for the Irish people. It makes my own heart ache to know how much tragedy still lies ahead."

Her tone had grown so sad and ominous he attempted to change the subject.

"So you are well-pleased with our grand cliffs, Lainna?"

"Aye, I adore them as I do all of this beautiful land. But what are they called, these cliffs?"

"They are called many names. The Cliffs of Mhothair in Gaelic. We shall come back one day by moonlight or at first light when the puffins and seahawks scatter from the top and plunge downward to the sea. But now, the hour grows late."

She placed her hand to his cheek and whispered lovingly, "Whatever happens between us, Killian, know that I am happy. At this precise moment, I am truly happy. Thank you for sharing this with me, and for what we have shared these weeks and, in truth, all the years we have been together."

"Christ, Alainn, you sound as though you are bidding me farewell."

"Well if it is to be our farewell, it would be best done here in a place of such beauty with no one around us, and only the wind and the seabirds to hear my weeping."

"'Tis not a farewell, Alainn. We will find a way."

She was so filled with dread a chill descended upon her, and the wind accelerated and grew cold. The waves below the cliffs peaked white and began to crash forcefully against the rock. The air filled with the rumbling of thunderclouds, and lightning illuminated the sky. Cold, hard rain began to pelt down upon them.

"Jesus, Mary, and Joseph, the weather in this area changes quickly. But, I've never seen such a violent storm brew so quickly. We must find shelter, yet there is surely little to be found here."

"Just hold me, Killian!"

"Alainn, we must move away from these cliffs before the gale throws us over the edge!" he shouted above the screaming of the forceful wind. "The lightning is bound to hit us or the horses, for there are few trees." "Hold me, Killian, if you trust me, hold me but for a moment!"

"You are sounding addled!" But he held her tightly against his chest. Before the moment had passed, the wind died, the sea grew quiet, and the thunder and lightning stopped as quickly as it had begun.

"'Twas me," she whispered in a broken voice.

"What are you sayin', Alainn?"

"'Twas me!"

"You're talkin' nonsense and sounding whirled."

"I caused the storm."

"That's impossible. Even with your powers. No one but our God can control the weather."

"There is a prophecy," she said in a tight voice. "Morag and Mara have both spoken of it to me. There will be a witch capable of conquering all around her. She will have the ability to control objects, then flora and fauna, the weather, the seasons. A being able to cross the realms of fairies and druids, capable of seeing into the past and looking into the future. Capable of spanning the portals of time. Able to both heal ill and inflict pain. And that creature will be the first of a line of many with such powers."

"Alainn, 'tis surely just superstitious legend. There are dozens of such stories that have not a thimble of truth to them."

"Killian, you must think on this. I have moved objects and been a seer all my life. I can heal, you know that well. I am able to enter the fairy glade and surely able to go through the portals within. I can control animals, and you've said for a long while how unusual it is I am able to grow plants others cannot. I've suspected for a time that my moods could change the weather."

"It cannot be true!" he said angrily.

"If you want to turn and run away, I'll understand. I will not make you suffer because of what I am."

"Even if this were a certainty—"

"It is a certainty, Killian. I have no doubt."

She walked away, into the darkness of the night. He did not try to stop her, but followed some distance behind. When she was halfway down the trail, she crossed the open pasture land.

"Alainn, what is it you're doing?"

"Finding holy ground."

"What by God's nails are you talkin' about?"

"This was a burial ground for an ancient people," she said, gesturing toward an ancient pile of stones, "so surely 'tis holy. Do you believe it is so, Killian?"

"I have no way of knowing, Alainn, but aye, perhaps you are correct."

"Come sit here with me, Killian."

He sighed deeply, but appeased her and sat down on the damp ground beside her.

"You have the amulet safe around your neck?"

"Aye. I promised you I wouldn't remove it."

"Good, now stay here. Do not move from my side, for it will be dangerous for a time."

She closed her eyes, and he watched as a huge ring of fire began to burn around them. He swallowed hard but did not move. The flames were immense, as tall as a round tower. When he believed he could be no more stunned by what was happening, enormous stones fell from the sky, framing the ring of fire and forming a perfect circle. Thirteen massive stones in all, tall and pointed, like grave-markers, only considerably larger.

Alainn began chanting in the language he'd heard her use at the fairy glade. Then he noticed the dagger in her hand and almost attempted to stop her, for he was not completely sure she would not harm herself. But she only nicked her thumb with the tip of the blade, and red droplets fell to the ground. Without being asked, Killian offered his hand.

She gently poked his thumb and squeezed the drops so they fell and mingled with her own. They burst into flames, and she spoke once more, this time in English.

Forever more through all eternity, the powers that rise from within me,
Shall never be capable of causing ill to those whose hearts remain joined still.
Not by fire, nor water, air or earth, not by my hand or of those I birth,
Nor any descendants of mine; however far down my line.
By the forging of blood that flows through my veins,
And his whom I've given my heart free reign,
As I've declared it, so shall it be, forever more through eternity.

With those words, fire leapt up, and the flames seemed to encompass them entirely. Killian could feel the heat, but the flames did not touch his skin. A wind began to howl eerily over the nearest hill, and a heavy rain fell, extinguishing the fire, yet not one drop landed upon them.

"'Tis done," Alainn said calmly, rubbing her hands together. Her tone was matter-of-fact, as if she'd just put together an ointment or potted some herbs. She stood and shook the grass from her skirts while Killian sat, unable to move.

"I will rest easier this night knowing my powers shall never bring you harm. No matter how angry or displeased I may be with you at any time, you will be safe from my magic. Immune to my supernatural abilities, except those that will benefit you."

"How?" was the only thing that managed to escape his lips. Her eyes held a wild quality, and he wasn't certain he didn't feel fear. She noticed.

"I'll tell you once more, Killian," she said in a stiff voice. "If you wish to go back to the castle without me, I will go to the fairy glade. I shall remain there this night, and then go to Mara on the morrow to see what can be done to end the curse."

"You've unnerved me, I'll admit it full well, Alainn, but it has not changed my feelings for you. And though you have still not agreed to marry me, I think, whatever just happened, whatever ceremony you performed, we are joined just the same."

"Aye, we are joined by the laws of nature. By druid and fairy ritual, we are one."

"How can you know all this, Alainn? You were not raised in druidism."

"It just comes to me," she shrugged, "as if from a long suppressed memory. More knowledge comes to me each day and with it more power, I fear."

Killian drew close and took her hand, but the sound of the horses' hooves behind them caused him to turn his head sharply. Two tiny dots of light shone in the distance. He put his hand to his sword.

"'Tis Riley and MacKenzie MacArthur, your uncle's captain. They search for you."

He did not ask her how she knew. She stood on tiptoe and softly kissed his lips.

"You must go back with them, Killian. Your uncle is surely concerned about your whereabouts. He's sent out many men this night to search for you."

" I will not leave without you."

"A family of musicians in a large wagon will round the bend by the time Riley and MacArthur reach us. They come as part of your uncle's entertainment for the celebrations. I will accompany them to the castle and take the horse if you allow it."

"It is yours, Alainn, to keep for as long as you desire it."

"You know your uncle will not permit a servant to own such a possession."

"Perhaps, but it is yours just the same. He will soon have no say over us, for he cannot deny my wife anything I choose to give her."

His lips sought hers in a desperate kiss. She brushed the rich dark brown hair from his eyes and stepped away.

"Sleep well, my love, for tomorrow you will surely be involved in many bouts and challenges. I will not come watch, for I become too unnerved knowing you risk life and limb for such frivolous games."

"You are not so confident of my skills, Lainna?"

"Oh, I know well enough you are the most skilled at all weaponry and games of brawn. But the other competitors will want to take away your many titles and revel in defeating your uncle's champion. Even Riley, and he loves you well." She stepped into the shadows under a tree as Riley and the captain rode up.

"We thought you were attacked and surely dead when you did not return from Galway," Riley said with some relief. He peered into the shadows. "By God's bones, Killian!" he crowed upon seeing Alainn. "Now I see the reason for your delay!"

"I'll escort the lass back to the castle," Mac suggested, "for I think it unwise if you arrive back together. The O'Brien would surely not approve. He has already announced to his guests that you are promised to the MacDonald lass."

Killian looked at Alainn with concern.

"No storm clouds, thus far," she said with a hint of humor.

"What is this you speak of, Alainn?" asked Riley.

"Nothing of importance."

"We saw flames and thought the trees must be on fire, though I know of very few trees near the cliffs. We came to investigate. 'Tis the reason we found you here."

At that moment, a wagon filled with people playing musical instruments rounded the bend and came rolling to a halt. It was accompanied by a lone soldier, a young man, perhaps not as old as Alainn. She thought it most peculiar that she had not seen him in her vision, only the musicians.

"Good evenin' to all of you!" shouted an old man.

"Good evening!" Mac called back. "And where are the lot of you headed!"

"To Castle O'Brien. We are to entertain the chieftain and his kin. I hope we are headed in the correct direction. We were not plannin' to be out travelin' in complete darkness, ye understand, but we had an unfortunate mishap with our wagon some miles back and had to replace a spoke on the wheel. It was the oddest occurrence, for they were right as rain when we checked them this morning."

Killian glanced over at Alainn. She smiled mischievously.

"Fortunately we have three strong sons who were able to fix it in little time. And this fine young soldier assisted most graciously."

It did not escape Killian that all three sons were staring intently at Alainn. Nor did he miss how the young soldier gazed at her. It disturbed him even more, for he wasn't openly ogling at her. There was something else about how he looked at her.

"Might I accompany your family back to the castle?" asked Alainn. All three sons jumped off the wagon to assist her.

"Aye, to be sure," smirked their father.

"I will ride my horse," she answered, smiling sweetly at Killian, "for I much prefer riding to being in a cart."

The three young men nearly fell on top each other to help Alainn, but it was the young soldier who stepped forward and gently, but capably, lifted her upon the horse. His hand lingered longer than necessary on her leg as she positioned herself upon the chestnut mare. Alainn looked into his eyes in the moonlight and thought perhaps she should have recognized him.

The young man was tall, still possessing the thin body of a boy not yet fully matured, though he seemed stronger than his slight form suggested. His hair was light-colored; his eyes a smoky grey-blue. She reasoned that one day he would be a grand man.

Their eyes met, and she felt the attraction. This took her off guard for, in all the time she'd loved Killian, she'd never felt a hint of attraction toward another man. Why would this boy, surely younger than herself and a stranger, appeal to her? She shook her head to dispel the confusion.

"Will you be quite well, Alainn?" Killian asked in a displeased tone, looking back and forth between the two.

"I will, Milord." At hearing the title, the musician driving the wagon bowed his head in respect. His dark-haired adult daughter gazed brazenly at Killian as Riley and Mac sped off toward the castle. Killian's horse reared up and ambled to where Alainn sat on her mare. The steed nuzzled the mare, and she whinnied in response.

"They like each other, father," said the girl. "Perhaps they'll be needin' to stay together."

"'Tis unlikely daughter. If the steed belongs to the chieftain's nephew and the mare to a servant girl, they'd never be permitted a time together lest they mate, for surely that would be less than desirable to the chieftain."

Alainn stiffened and pulled her mare away from the affectionate nuzzling. The horse snorted loudly in protest.

"I know it well, girl," she whispered. "Life is entirely unfair."

* * *

Alainn led the way, the soldier riding beside her on his pitch black horse.

"Are all of the bonnacht so young then?" she asked the lad.

"There are soldiers of many ages. When duty calls age is oft not a consideration."

"And have you been made to fight many battles with the English?"

"Not many. Mostly, they stay confined to the Pale in Dublin, but more seem to arrive in our country each day. I feel it will be an age before Ireland is free of conflict."

"Do you suppose Ireland will ever truly be free of conflict?"

The young man shrugged.

"And what brings you to Castle O'Brien, away from your fellow bonnachts?"

"I was a minstrel and musician before I became a soldier." He patted the case that hung from his saddle. It obviously held a fiddle.

"And is it common for a soldier to be allowed time away from his duties to perform for a chieftain?"

"Is it common for a healer to be allowed time away from her duties to spend time with nobles?"

She glanced at him suspiciously.

"You have the gift of second sight?"

"Aye, since I was a wee boy?"

"Are you druid?"

"I am uncertain, for I did not know my parents. I was left in a basket upon the steps of a churchyard."

"Who raised you, then?

But, he did not answer, for they were at the guard tower leading to the drawbridge.

Chapter eleven

Once Alainn had seen her mare to the stable, she headed straight to her bedchamber. The number of people arriving for the week of celebrations was stunning. The village was overrun with entertainers and vendors. The courtyard was filled with actors, jesters, and musicians for the entertainment of guests. The halls of the castle were teeming with people, mostly lords chatting amongst themselves with drink in hand.

Hiding her face with the hood of her cloak, Alainn hurried to the back stairwell. She passed many servants, mostly menservants assigned the task of keeping goblets filled, with the odd woman carrying a tray of food. Breena, who was not often employed as a serving girl, was presently removing an elderly lord's hand from her arse.

Breena and Alainn had never been close though they'd both lived in the castle most of their lives. In truth, the servant girl had often treated her unkindly. Breena threw her an odd look as she recognized her; Alainn continued on her way.

So enormous was the crowd of visitors, she could scarcely comprehend how they would all be fed and housed for an entire week. As she passed the great hall, she heard many loud, drink-affected male voices. Hugh O'Brien's hearty laugh boomed out above the rest, making her skin crawl. With her powers so uncontrollable at present, she thought it best to pass the room quickly.

Alainn had just rounded the last bend before her chamber, when brawny arms pulled her into a darkened alcove. She stifled a scream and beat at the arms until Killian's face was illuminated in the soft light of the sconce.

"Killian," she chided. He kissed her passionately, and though she responded without hesitation, it was she who ended the embrace.

"'Tis unwise, Killian. Should your uncle discover us, I fear there would be dire consequences."

"Then come to my bedchamber."

"Killian, there are dozens of people scattered about the castle, 'tis not a possibility. Does your uncle know you have arrived?"

"Aye, he has requested I go to him, but I needed to know you were safe. I had reservations about you traveling with that family of musicians. I wanted to show the young lads my knuckles for their lusty looks. And when that brazen young soldier placed his hand on your leg, I could hardly keep from unsheathing my sword. Why did you look at him as you did?"

"I thought for a moment I recognized him, but it must not be so for I cannot recall ever meeting him."

"Aye well, he'd best keep himself distanced from you. No one else attempted to put their hands on you, did they?"

"Oh, Killian, settle you down. No one touched me. The young soldier is nothing more than a bold young boy. He meant no disrespect. And I am not without ways to manage men. I might have had him struck with a lightning bolt, but I thought that a bit rash. And you can wager much he wouldn't have attempted any such behavior had he known you think of me as yours. They see me as a peasant, Killian. I am their equal."

"But you are mine, Alainn."

He kissed her possessively again, and, when a servant girl and lord came up the steps, he turned his back to conceal their identity. They heard the woman's laughter as her companion led her eagerly to a nearby bedchamber.

"I must get inside before someone sees us together, Killian."

She stood on tiptoe and brushed her lips quickly against his, then started down the corridor and stepped inside her small chamber. As she lighted the candle, Killian followed her into the room. His eyes skirted the chamber. In all the time that they had been friends, he had never looked inside the room she had shared with Morag since childhood. He was appalled at how tiny it was.

There was a narrow cot at one side and upon it lay the saffron-colored cloak Morag had always worn. By the bed, a small hole in the wall let in the vaguest of light. It could barely be referred to as a window. The fireplace was surely incapable of producing much heat, for its size was meager. Two half-burned peat logs were now lying there waiting to be lit. And in the other corner, there was a tiny bed of straw, beside which stood a wooden table. Upon the table stood a pitcher and basin, one candle, and a small stack of books. Two worn and shabby dresses hung from a peg above the bed. Alainn saw the pity in his eyes and, with cheeks aflame, turned away from him. He gathered her in his arms and whispered in her ear.

"I had no notion, Alainn, that this was how you have been made to live all these years."

She turned and placed her fingers to his lips. "Don't pity me, Killian. I have never gone hungry and I have always had a roof over my head. The work I do is not back-breaking. There are others far worse off than I. Though, I am ashamed to admit, after spending time in the lavish inn at Galway and sleeping within your grand bed in your castle, I do feel some displeasure at returning to this place."

"I will speak to my uncle this night about finding a more suitable chamber for you until we are wed."

"You will do nothing of the sort, Killian! I am much accustomed to this life. I will soon settle into it once more. And do you actually believe your uncle will be accommodating to me in any way when he learns you plan to defy his wishes and scorn Mary MacDonald?"

She bent to light the turf fire and he knelt beside her. His eyes held a torment within them. She longed to remove the deep creases in his brow.

"I should have listened to you, Alainn. We should not have come back here," he said in a ragged voice. "We should have run off together." He stood and began to pace. She went to him and placed her hands on his cheeks.

"Do not be vexed, Killian. You must go to your bedchamber and get you some sleep. The night grows exceedingly late and you are expected to be in perfect form on the morrow when the games begin."

"I care not for these hellish games! All I can think of is you. Christ! My bed is as large as this entire chamber, and this window will not allow a breeze on a warm summer's night." He gestured in complete disapproval of her meager surroundings.

"Your bed is not entirely this big, though it's been a good many years since I've actually seen your bed." But his foul mood would not be dispelled with her humor.

She affectionately placed her hand upon his cheek.

"No good will come of your temper, Killian, nor of trying to change what has always been."

They both jumped as the small wooden door crashed open, and Hugh O'Brien stood in the doorway. He was flanked by two guards.

"Ah nephew, you have returned unharmed," he sneered. "I am most grateful, though it seems it was unnecessary for me to send out half my army and both my sons to retrieve you. And here I find you in the arms of a peasant girl when you have been ordered to come to my chamber. You might have taken such urges to a brothel."

"Uncle," Killian warned.

"So is it by sheer coincidence that my healer has arrived back from her mysterious departure on the same night my dearest nephew has returned from his business in Galway? One might be driven to believe the two of you had been together, though I am sure this is not the case. For the loyal, intelligent man I know as my nephew would surely not jeopardize his forthcoming marriage to be with a commoner, who by her present actions, appears to be nothing but a whore."

"Watch your tongue, Uncle. You speak of the woman I love and plan to marry."

The older man threw back his head and laughed raucously.

"I think not nephew. You are promised to the Scot and so it shall be. Whatever infatuation you have with this girl will pass when you allow yourself to spend time with the Scottish lass. She is quite beautiful, though I admit your wee harlot is not without lovely attributes of her own. But the Scot is a lady. She will be an adequate and suitable wife. Sure you'll come to care for her when you are removed from the distraction of this enchantress. And should you find the MacDonald lass less than satisfactory, I'm certain you will have any number of mistresses to still your needs. Women have always gladly lifted their skirts and parted their knees for you."

Killian's hand went to the hilt of his sword. The guards sprang to his side and roughly grabbed his arms.

"There is no need to restrain my nephew."

"Should his weapon be collected, Milord?"

"No, he may keep his sword. My nephew is a not a stupid or impulsive man. He knows what penalty would befall him should he attempt any harm of the O'Brien."

"You cannot force me to marry a woman I do not love!"

"The truth of the matter, Killian, is that I can. The alliance with her clan is necessary, and this love you speak of is no more substantial than tales of fairies. You are young and do not yet understand that love is fickle and fleeting. You will marry the Scot. That will be the end of it! Believe me, I was no more eager to marry Lady Siobhan than you are to wed the Scot. She was a Druid priestess for Christ's sake, and our family staunch Catholics, devout Christians. It was heresy to be sure to unite with a pagan clan, but it was necessary for the betterment of the O'Briens. You will accept your fate, Killian. You have little choice in the matter if you want to gain your father's title, his castle, and his land."

"I will relinquish my title, and to hell with the land and the castle. 'Tis a pile of rock put together centuries ago by men whose names I do not know. And my father would understand; he would see me as happily wed as he was with my mother."

"No Killian, you cannot!" cried Alainn.

"Ah, so the healer speaks. She has kept silent her bitter tongue for longer than I believed possible. But, you might listen to her. She is not worth the consideration of giving up all that will be yours."

"Truth be told, Uncle, she is all that I care about and I would give up more than you know to share my life with her."

"I sympathize with your plight, lad, for I well know the affect she has on a man. I still feel an aching in my loins for the temptress after being with her myself."

Killian lunged for him.

"How dare you! I did not think you would sink so low as to fabricate such matters!"

"She did not inform you of our time together in the great hall?" the O'Brien asked, a crafty gleam in his eye. "We spent a most memorable time there."

Killian glanced at Alainn. Her eyes were filled with despair.

"Aye, I heard how you beat her for taking your horse."

"I warrant much she did not reveal the details in their entirety."

"What are you saying, Uncle?"

"Why do you suppose she was not hanged, or lashed at the very least?"

Killian looked from his uncle to Alainn, and his face turned to a sickly pallor.

"You raped her?"

"Did I rape you, girl?"

"No!" she whispered vehemently.

"Why you vile, lecherous liar!" Killian spat, his hand on the hilt of his sword. "Why would you make such filthy statements? You only wish to tear us apart. You had to know when I left it was Alainn I intended to be with."

"Did you mention who you planned to marry? You only said it was a commoner. It could have been most anyone, Killian. You have an affinity for bedding peasant girls, the miller's daughter, the cobbler's, the tailor's. Shall I go on?"

"I cannot believe you did not know."

"Is that why you enlisted my captain's son to protect the girl? And instead, she ran off with him and the Cook's son. Took them both to an inn in Galway. Spent the entire night with them, I am told. Can you not see what a wanton woman she is? How little she cares for you and your reputation? Really, Killian, she is a trite, sullied little whore. How many others do you think she has been with?"

Killian tackled his uncle onto to the hard stone floor, grabbed his throat, and squeezed as the older man kicked and thrashed. The guards fell upon them, trying to pull Killian from his kin, and, with considerable effort, succeeding.

"Should we take him to the dungeon, Milord?"

The O'Brien held his hand to his throat.

"No, I think that will not be necessary," he rasped. "He cannot be flayed for being passionate. 'Tis an O'Brien trait. He will see reason soon enough."

"You'd best take me to the dungeon if you don't want your chieftain dead!" Killian shouted, struggling to escape the guards.

"Killian, you must refrain from this!" Alainn pleaded.

"I will not allow him to cheapen you with his vicious lies and insinuations!"

"Tell him girl," his uncle sneered. "Tell him you were with me, that I know you as he knows you."

"No one knows me as Killian does."

"I assure you, I know what it is to have your woman, Killian. I know what desires of the flesh she inflicts. I realize what you will be sacrificing to end what the two of you share, for I can barely fight the seductress and would like nothing more than to throw her down upon that very bed and have her even now. For her skin is as smooth as any I have touched, and her breasts as delightful. I think my cock will never feel such entire satisfaction."

"You will die by my hand, Uncle, mark my words!" Killian cried. "If you utter one more word, I swear I will see you dead by my sword!" The two guards strained to keep the man from hurling himself at his uncle.

"Ask my priest if you will not take my word for it, for he happened upon us and witnessed some of our time together. Do you actually believe she would not offer herself to me to save herself a lashing? And are you so vain to think you would be the only man she would ever service. I am the O'Brien! When she heard you were off fetching your promised bride, when she learned of all the women before her, she was not unwilling. In truth, I have never seen such a spirited young vixen when it came to it."

"She would not be with you, I know her! You have no proof, and I would take her word above yours any day!"

"So its proof you need?" he asked, his voice sly. "The wee soft tuft she possesses is nearly the same shade as her lovely locks." He ran his tongue over his upper lip. "And as soft as eider down."

Killian threw the two men off him as though they were twigs, grabbed his sword, and placed it to his uncle's throat.

"Killian, you will be hanged!" Alainn screamed. The tiny peat fire roared into flames that caught hold of the bedding and the cape upon it. She shrieked in terror as her skirts caught fire. Killian dropped his sword and ran to her, pulled off his overcoat, and extinguished the flames with the garment.

"I do hope the fire did no damage to those lovely silken legs. It would be a pity to have another scar on that otherwise flawless body."

Both Killian and Alainn stared at the man as he spoke.

"Another scar to match the one above her right nipple."

Killian's head jerked back as if he'd been struck. He looked at Alainn and his eyes were filled with accusations of betrayal.

"Take him to his bedchamber and lock the door. He will be needed in the bouts tomorrow so a night in the dungeon would not be beneficial to the outcome. Take the girl, and see to it she has a cell to herself. There is no need to cause a riot over which prisoner will have her first. She has been promised to Liam O'Hara, and though the farmer has been warned she's no virgin, I think he would not take kindly to having his new bride raped by the lot of them and unable to partake in the wedding night activities sure to happen mid-week."

Killian slipped a dagger from a concealed pocket of his tunic and hurled it at his uncle. The man, who was swifter on his feet than he appeared, jumped out of its path, but it sliced his shoulder. Deep red blood poured from the gash. Alainn watched the hilt of the guard's sword slam down upon Killian's head, and in her terror, her powers took a course she could not control. The guard's swords flew from their hands, met in mid-air, and drove into their chests. She pulled her own dagger from her pocket, and her eyes blazing with rage, she hurried toward the chieftain. He unsheathed his sword, knelt, and held it against Killian's throat as he lay unconscious upon the floor.

"Go on then," hissed the chieftain's, his eyes daring her to continue. She stepped back and dropped her weapon. "Call off whatever unnatural powers you possess, woman. My priest believes you are a daughter of the devil and thinks you should burn for your evil deeds. I may be inclined to agree with him after this night's events. If you had simply done as you were instructed and kept your distance from my nephew, all this evening's unpleasantness would not have been necessary."

"I tried to leave, I meant to stay away. I had no knowledge I would meet up with Killian in Galway. Please tell me you will see no harm come to Killian, and you must allow me to go free."

"What do you have to bargain with?"

"I will no longer encourage Killian."

"By the look he just gave you, he'll not be wanting any further dealings with you. He will clearly never trust you again."

"Nor you, Hugh O'Brien, but I do have a powerful asset with which to bargain. I have means to end the curse."

"How could you possibly bring an end to it?"

"I am the daughter of the Glade Witch."

The man's jaw dropped open.

"But what inducement would you have to end this curse when my nephew is promised to the Scot? Why would you aid the O'Briens?"

Alainn held her head up, and, though her eyes were filled with tears, she spoke with sincerity. "Even if he is never to be mine, I love him entirely and want him to know happiness, to produce many fine children. And I want that for your sons as well. Don't think I do any of this for you, Hugh O'Brien, for if it were only you made to suffer by my mother's curse, I would gladly watch you live out your days in utter misery. I ask that, you will see no harm to Killian and let me go free." She added as if in afterthought, "And I shall want the brown mare Killian recently gave me and the oldest of your dogs."

The man took a few moments to consider her words as if looking for a deception.

"You shall have what you ask for," he said finally. "But you are my servant and my word will still be abided. Your services as a healer will be required, and you will continue to work with my physician, assisting him wherever necessary. Since my sons and nephew are not yet wed, there is surely no need to hasten; the prospects of a child are surely still many months away."

Alainn blushed.

"Ah!" he said, smirking with evil intent. "So that's the whole of it then! Does my nephew know of your condition, is that why he is so set upon marrying you?"

"He does not know, and I ask you keep it concealed. It will be best if he marries the woman you have chosen for him. Should I fail to end the curse, I do not wish to see him suffer."

Killian stirred, and she knelt to examine the gash on his head. Taking her dagger, she slit her palm and allowed blood to drip onto his wound. The chieftain looked on, clearly disturbed, then surprised as the wound healed as if it had never been there.

By this time they could hear the footsteps of more guards approaching. Alainn tried to avert her eyes from the two wounded men on the floor. One of them began to come to. The chieftain stood over him and, with no hesitation, drove his sword through his heart. He roughly pulled the weapon from his chest and slit the throat of the other.

"Why?" she asked simply.

"I can hardly permit you to go free when they have witnessed your powers. Though my army is loyal, tongues are sure to wag, and rumors will run amuck. If my priest catches wind of this, when he already believes your abilities are born of evil, he will not soon be silenced on his quest to see you burn. So," he shrugged, "their lives needed ending."

She threw him a look of complete despair as he threw back his head and laughed.

"You think me shrewd and unfeeling, Maiden McCreary, but I do what I must to ensure the safety of my kin and the strength of my clan."

Killian had begun to gain consciousness. Alainn grabbed her cloak and her weapon, and threw the O'Brien a look of loathing. The guards clustered at the door parted, as if moved by an invisible hand, and let her pass. The chieftain shivered as she glanced back at him, the hairs on his neck standing on end.

Chapter twelve

Killian awoke in his own bed with a throbbing headache. He tried to remember what had happened and then wanted badly to forget. When he tried to stand, he was overcome with dizziness. His sword was no longer in its sheath, and his knife was missing. When he could finally stand without falling over, he headed for the door in an unsteady gait. To his surprise, the door was unlocked. Stumbling down the hall to his uncle's bedchamber, he pounded on the door, calling his name angrily when no one answered.

"Killian, 'tis so good to see you!" It was his aunt, Lady Siobhan, peering out of her own chambers. "I was overly worried when you were so late in returning. I feared you might have fallen into some trouble, for I heard the English had been spotted in the area."

"Aunt Siobhan." He bowed respectfully, felt himself growing dizzy again, and fell back against the wall. His aunt rushed to his side to steady him.

"Killian, you are hurt! Whatever has happened to you? There is blood all down the back of your garment. Come inside with me, I will see to your wounds!"

"'Tis nothing! I have come in search of my uncle. Do you know of his whereabouts?"

She was dressed in a nightdress with a thick shawl around her shoulders. Her yellow hair, always piled neatly on her head during daylight hours, hung loose. She pushed the lengthy strands from her eyes and shook her head.

"I do not believe he has come to his chambers yet. He was in the great hall earlier, and I heard mention of some discord and someone being taken to the dungeon, but I am not certain what happened. Your uncle does not share such matters with me. But, Killian, you must come inside my chambers and tell me what troubles you."

"I mean you no disrespect, Aunt Siobhan, for you are well important to me, but I have no time for discussion this night. I have a miserable ache in my head, to be sure, but I believe there is no fresh wound."

He placed his hand to his head and felt a raised welt but no open gash. His aunt instructed him to bend so that she might examine it, and he obliged her.

"Killian, it is healed! Surely, this is not a most recent wound. Were you wounded in Galway or on your journey?"

"It appears I am not so very clear on the details of my injury."

He could only vaguely remember a sharp pain in his head before he met darkness. He pulled on his tunic to straighten it, for his clothes were still slightly askew, and the amulet around his neck dangled free for a moment. His aunt gasped.

"Where did you get this, Killian?"

"It was given to me," he said gruffly, offering no further explanation.

"May I see it?"

Remembering Alainn's warning, he gently shook his head. "I am apparently not to remove it."

"It has been charmed for you?" Her eyes were filled with excitement and confusion.

"Aye."

"Wait here for one moment!" she instructed.

"Aunt Siobhan, I have matters to attend to," he complained.

"One moment, Killian, that is all I ask." She ran back into her chamber.

Leaning against the wall to steady himself, he waited with growing impatience. When she came back, her face was pale.

"What is it Aunt Siobhan? You look most unsettled."

"Aye, Killian, I am unsettled, to be sure."

She touched the amulet that still hung from his neck, carefully studying how it had been charred. The front still bore the druid symbol of the trinity knot, the triquetra, but her face fell when she saw the back.

"There is a piece missing. Do you know where the other side of the amulet is?"

"I've never seen any other portion, bar this."

She pulled her own amulet from her neck and passed it to him. He noticed the symbol was entirely the same and noted that it had also been scorched by heat at one time. When he turned it over he saw a crest.

"What crest is this?"

"'Tis my family crest, from our druid ancestry. The bearer of the amulet you wear is of our druid sect, but without the crest I am unable to distinguish what line it lays claim to. She must have cared for you dearly, for a druid is only ever to give away their birth amulet to the one who claims their heart or to a child they have birthed. I had the blacksmith forge two amulets for my sons when they were infants, but my husband would never allow them to wear the mark of the druids. I thought perhaps they had been stolen, but they remain securely hidden. Please, you must reveal who the owner is. This is of great importance."

Killian was about to speak, when he heard his uncle's voice. He stiffened. The man came round the winding corridor, accompanied by someone Killian had not seen before. His uncle's chest was bare, and a large bandage was wound around his neck and shoulder.

"Hugh!" cried Lady Siobhan. "What has happened to you? How were you wounded?"

"You might ask your nephew that very question, wife."

"Killian, you did this? The two of you have quarreled violently? What could have caused such a serious rift between blood kin?" Both men stared defiantly at one another. The third man who was considerably shorter and smaller of girth, spoke for the first time.

" Milord, you must not exert yourself, I have sewn up the wound, but it may reopen if you are not cautious."

"I am quite well enough. 'Tis not the first time I've suffered a blade and, in truth, not the first time I have suffered a blade by my kin. But, 'tis usually on a playing field or in a soldiering bout. You must tend to my nephew, for he too was wounded this night."

"I don't need to be tended to. I only need a word alone with you, Uncle."

"My physician is most knowledgeable. He will make certain you are in fit form to begin the bouts in the morning. The O'Brien's are counting on you to score points for our clan."

"And why would I want to take part in anything that would benefit you, Uncle?"

"The challenges and jousting matches are excellent ways to stem anger and frustration, Killian. Direct your anger at your opponents and you will have a clear advantage."

"I desire to speak with you alone, Uncle. We have many subjects to speak on."

"The night is late, Killian. We both must rest, for this week of events and celebrations promises to be a time of great happenings. You must greet your cousins in the morning, as well. And your intended, Maiden MacDonald, will be most eager to make your acquaintance again to be sure."

"If you do not speak with me in private, Uncle, I will air subjects best left between only the two of us!"

"Hugh, if Killian wants to speak with you, grant him his request."

"You stay out of this, wife!"

"He is like a son to us, Hugh. You cannot be suggesting he harmed you?"

Killian threw a caustic look at his uncle, but spoke to his aunt.

"I am proud to be referred to as your son, Aunt Siobhan, but I am not this man's son. He is a stranger to me. In truth, he is dead to me. I will stay this week, to be here for my cousins, but when it is through, I will be gone from your castle, Uncle, and I'll not care to ever see you again."

"You'll change your mind, Killian"

"I would not count on that."

"Killian, you must tell me what has caused this unpleasantness between the two of you!"

"'Tis nothing I can discuss with you, Aunt. Forgive me if I have upset you, it was not my intention."

His aunt looked from him to her husband and back again, great despair on her face. The physician stood to the side most uncomfortably. Killian turned and stalked down the lengthy corridor.

"Killian where are you off to? You should rest, for that wound on your head might still cause you grave concern."

"'Tis not my head wound that has caused this night's unpleasantness!"

"But where is it you intend to go?"

"I am off to the dungeon and to find the ale-wife. But, not necessarily in that order."

Chapter Thirteen

Killian's head throbbed painfully, and this time not from a knock on the head. He and Riley had spent the better part of the last two days and nights drinking to a staggering drunk. When they'd slept off the drink, they began again. After Killian learned Alainn had not been taken to the dungeon but was safe and staying with Cook and his family, he had found the ale wife and procured as much liquor as he could carry.

He'd run into Riley, looking as grim as he, and they found a place to drown their sorrows. Though Killian had not spoken of what had him so upset, Riley knew well enough it concerned Alainn. Riley was most displeased with the woman his father had chosen for him.

And so, they drank.

It was fortunate for them the skies had opened up and rained steadily for two days. It had poured so hard the tournament was postponed until the rain stopped and the ground dried. The rain continued to tap on the roof. Killian wondered if the storm was Alainn's doing. When he thought of her, he reached for another jug of whiskey and heartily drank the pungent liquid.

He knew he should go to her, speak with her about all that had happened, about what his uncle had said, but he did not want to be near her at the moment. She had lied to him.

"I trusted her completely," he grumbled and put the jug to his lips again, enjoying the burning sensation as the ale slid down his throat. It left his throat as raw and irritated as his heart. He rubbed his jaw; it was covered with stubble. He wet his lips. His breath was sour, and his hair and clothes were unkempt.

Riley moaned from his position on the floor. "Christ, my head thumps as though there were thunder inside it."

"Aye, you're not lookin' altogether well, either, cousin." Killian squinted at the man beside him as he lit the small lantern.

"Nor are you, Killian. Your Mary will not recognize you, I think, when you finally decide to go see her. Whenever that might be!" he barked.

"Your mother was not pleased when we refused to attend the banquet last evening."

"No, she looked more than displeased. In truth, I think she wanted to throttle the two of us. At least Rory seems agreeable about his intended. And yours is at least a pleasant girl. I have never met a woman as entirely abrasive as that wench I am to wed. She has a voice that would make one's ears protest. I'm sure she frightens animals and small children with the whining. Iona has not one kind or pleasant word to say about anyone or anything, and she will scarcely leave her mother's side.

"I dearly hope she'll run off with another and save me the unpleasantness of wedding her. I've a grand notion, Killian. What say we trade women? You'll not be happy, regardless of whom you wed, unless it is Alainn. So you wed the carrot-top, and I'll take the Scot. Your Mary is quite lovely. A happy sort. Sure she must wonder why you are avoiding her."

"Aye, wed her if you like, for I've no intention of it."

"You cannot disobey my father, Killian. He will have his way in the end, so you might as well just go along with it. He's a shrewd and cunning man who'll do most anything to achieve what he wants."

"I've no desire to speak of your father. And you speak as though this is as minor as him assigning us to a bout. This is to be for a lifetime, Riley. We are to be wed to these women for the rest of our lives. I cannot fathom the finality of it. I cannot be saddled with a woman I barely know! In truth, I may choose to join the McKenna clan."

"Killian, you must be drunk, he'd have your head if you joined our enemies."

"Perhaps, but it might be worth it to make him see how it feels to be betrayed by someone you trust."

"Curiosity has got the best of me, Killian. What in hell happened between you and Alainn? "

"I'll not discuss it with you or anyone else, Riley," he warned.

"Then drink another few jugs of brew and tell me if you feel any better for it. Maybe I'll just sit here and join you. Though, if the sun begins to shine, I suspect we'll be in less than fine shape to begin the challenges."

"Aye well, 'tis not a likelihood. It is sure to remain dismal for a time."

"So you've developed Alainn's talent for foreseeing the future, have you?"

The door to the windowless tower chamber opened and light from the hall flooded the room. The men cried out in pain and covered their eyes.

"Christ, but there is a horrid stink in here." When they saw it was only Rory, Riley flopped back down on the stone floor. Killian held the jug up in a welcoming gesture, taking another swig himself.

"You smell like you've bathed in that whiskey instead of drinking it."

"Would you care to join us, Rory?" his twin asked.

"I can barely stand to be near you, the reek is so unpleasant. You might want to wash and shave, for if you don't attend the banquet this evening, mother will be fit to be tied. She thinks you are being entirely rude to the women you are promised to, and their kin are displeased as well. Your absence was difficult for our parents to explain. The only saving grace is this gloomy weather. With no challenges to watch, half the guests are in a drunken state themselves. But, when the ale wife runs out of brew, which is sure to be soon if the two of you keep up the way you have been, it will be more difficult to explain. You're not lads anymore, hiding out to escape a whipping. 'Tis time you face your responsibilities like men. For our mother's sake, if nothin' else."

"Always attempting to make peace, brother. And how is your intended? Have you taken her to your bed yet?"

Killian snorted.

"Riley, you're completely irredeemable," he said, scowling. "Just because I do not despise the girl as you do her sister, does not mean I have bedded her. That will surely wait till after the wedding. And if you'd happened to have attended the banquet last night, you would have learned our father has announced that all of our weddings will take place at the conclusion of the celebrations."

"What!" Both men sat up at this proclamation, moaning loudly as their heads protested.

"He should get used to the idea that I do not intend to wed the Scot this week or any other!" Killian shouted, sinking back down to lean weakly against the wall.

"Killian, you're being unusually difficult. If you don't intend to wed her, then I think you might at least tell the girl and her family. In all fairness, that would be the gentlemanly thing to do. If you're not wedding her simply to defy my father, I think it's not the best strategy. But, if you're not wedding Mary because you truly love Alainn, then you'd best get off your arse and get yourself sober, for she's scheduled to wed the farmer, Liam O'Hara, in three days time."

Rory shook his head in disgust and headed back out the door. There was silence for a time as each man contemplated his own fate.

"So what is it you plan to do then, Killian?"

"I haven't the slightest notion."

"Well, I'm heading out to see if I can't find Alainn, for she has a surefire remedy to deal with the effects of too much drink. Are you coming with me, cousin?"

"Not just yet. I've still a lot of thinkin' to do."

"Well don't think on it too long, Killian, for you'll never forgive yourself, if you allow her to slip away. Sure, she's all you've ever wanted since you were just a lad. Can you truly bear to see her wedded to another?"

"What I want and what I can bear are apparently of little consequence at the moment, Riley."

"Aye, I know well what you mean, cousin."

The door closed and Killian welcomed the darkness once more to match his gloomy thoughts.

***

Washed and shaven, Killian stared into the looking glass in his bedchamber. His eyes looked as if some wee fairy with sharp heels had done a dance upon them. And they felt no better. Gravelly and irritated, like his heart and soul. He sat down upon the bed, still unsure what to do. He knew he must find Alainn and speak to her, but every time he tried to rehearse what he might say, he became enraged. Could he allow her to be wed to another? Did he have a choice? He didn't know Liam O'Hara well, but he seemed an honorable man. He'd make a good husband. She would have a home, and though not a castle, it was a good deal better than what she had now. But, could he live with the knowledge that the woman he loved belonged to another?

Then there was Mary MacDonald. She was not an objectionable woman. If not for his deep feelings for Alainn, he might believe she was a suitable match for himself. If not for what he'd learned about Alainn and his uncle, he would not be tormenting his mind with this one-sided conversation. He would be with her now, willing to throw away all that he had once believed so important. It now seemed trivial, inconsequential.

There was a soft knock upon the door to his bedchamber. A feminine knock. His heart began beating wildly. Perhaps it was Alainn. He leapt to the door and flung it open. Mary MacDonald stood quite still, looking rather nervous.

"Killian, I thought I should come to see how you were faring. Your uncle informed me you were in an altercation some days ago. It is to be hoped you are well enough to attend the feast this night."

He looked at her shiny gold dress, her dark hair piled upon her head, a few loose curls hanging prettily down her back. Her hands were clasped tightly together, and she nervously twisted them when he did not respond. He found himself thinking of his own mother. She would have chastised him severely for his unbecoming behavior toward this girl.

"Aye, I am quite nearly recovered," he said meekly. "I shall be at the banquet this night."

"Should I wait for you, then? Might we walk to the banquet together?"

"Aye, if you would find that to your liking, it would be agreeable to me."

As they walked together, she placed her arm through his and smiled up at him. They had gone only a short distance, when they came face to face with Alainn, who was carrying a tray containing many small vials. Upon seeing Killian and Mary, she glanced at the direction from whence they'd come. Her eyes, already deeply saddened, seemed to grow even more disheartened with the knowledge they had surely come from Killian's bedchamber.

" Milord. Milady," she curtsied softly, making certain the vials stayed put on the tray. She intended to simply walk on after the brief exchange, without making eye contact with Killian, but the woman called after her.

"Alainn! I am so verra pleased to see you have returned. Rory and Riley seemed uncertain. But, I believed you would come back, for how could the castle be left without its healer?"

"This castle employs a physician now, Milady. A healer is perhaps no longer necessary. But, I must take these elixirs to Lady Siobhan. She has asked to be excused from the feast this night, and I must attend to her."

She curtsied once more and started off, but the feminine voice called again.

"Might I come see you on the morrow? I would be most interested in your remedies and your herb garden, if this dreary weather ever lifts. I find myself growing homesick for Scotland, for 'tis not so prone to such weather, though Riley tells me this is not common to have such a long spell of objectionable weather. I have heard much about your herb garden. Riley tells me it rivals any healer's garden. Would you be willing to show me when the sun shines again?"

"If you it is to your liking, Milady. Sure, 'tis your choice." She started down the hall.

"Alainn?"

"Aye, Milady?"

"Please call me Mary. I insist."

"Aye, if it is as you wish." This time, she fairly ran down the hall.

Killian had avoided looking at Alainn, and it made her heart ache. She found herself torn between despising Mary and feeling drawn to her, for she wasn't unlikable. However, the thought of what the two of them had surely been doing to pass the rain-filled afternoon left her in tears again. She tried to compose herself before knocking upon Lady Siobhan's door, but the lady opened the door while she was still dabbing her eyes.

"Alainn, dear, Alainn! I had heard of your return. I have missed you so much, my dear girl!" She opened her arms in a warm embrace. Her affection proved to be too much, and Alainn burst into tears, weeping openly before the chieftain's wife. "There, there, child," she crooned. "Come inside with me, and we'll have a womanly heart to heart. Tell me all that has you so distressed."

They entered the room and shut the door. The kind woman stood with her arms around her while she wept.

"Forgive me, Milady. I should not be so prone to emotion. 'Tis most improper to carry on so in front of a lady. I have brought you the remedies you require. I will leave you to your rest."

"You will do no such thing, Alainn. You will tell me what has you so tearful!"

"You needn't be burdened with my plight, Milady. 'Tis nothing, or at the very least, there is nothing to be done about it. I should get back to my potions before that man takes over entirely."

"That man? The physician my husband has procured. Is he the reason for your despair? Has he been unkind to you?"

"No, truth be told, he has treated me fairly, perhaps more fairly than I to him. 'Twill take a time to adjust to sharing the space with him, but he is not opposed to healers as many physicians are."

"So what then, my sweet wee girl? What has you so saddened? I think I've never seen those blue eyes so filled with pain and hopelessness. Through the years you have been a bright ray of sunlight in my life, your eyes always so full of joy and gladness. What has taken the light from those sapphires?"

"'Tis nothing I can discuss, Milady, and nothing that any amount of discussion can mend."

The gracious woman patted the spot beside her on the settee.

"Come sit with me, and we won't speak of what has you so maudlin. We'll just talk of other things, for you look as though you need the company of a woman. I have felt just that way so many times in my life. I have longed for a daughter since I was old enough to think of such things. It was not to be, and though I love my mother dearly and we have always been close at heart, she lives far from here. Even now that she is here in the castle, she is not entirely present as she once was. 'Tis a sad thing to have her look at me as though she is uncertain who I truly am."

With that, tears started to pour down her own cheeks, and Alainn took her hand. They wept together.

"You are so like my own departed sister, Alainn. I know I have told you so many times, I am certain you must feel I am a foolish woman to speak of it as often as I do. But, when first I saw you, I thought my eyes played a cruel trick, you were so like her. Your coloring. Your smile. Your hair." She reached out to smooth the soft hair tied back in a plait. "Your eyes are your own, though. And you were always somewhat more spirited than my wee sister, Shylie. But, your expressions and the way you wrinkle your nose when something displeases you, 'tis as if she still lives when I spend time with you.

"I know how that must sound to you. My husband always discouraged me from talking about it, for I think it disturbed him. He likely thought I was losing my mind. After the loss of all my babies, I thought so more than a time or two, myself. 'Tis fortunate I had my lads to carry me through. Rory, I am close with. He speaks to me, tells me his heart. But Riley is his father's son. He is an O'Brien through and through, and belongs to his father, I think." She stared off, deep in thought. Alainn touched her hand.

"Not so entirely as he would have everyone believe for Riley loves you dearly, as well. 'Tis only he feels he must impress his father."

"Aye, I know it. You know so much of my sons and my nephew. You were always a friend to them, though my husband did not always approve. I would look out upon the moors and watch you with my sons and my nephew, and it would make my heart glad. To look at you and Rory, to me it was as though I had crossed a bridge through time, as though I could look at my younger brother and sister. It has brought me great comfort many times, for they are both lost to me now."

"Aye, I heard of the discourse between your father and brother."

"You have heard of my family? Who has told you of them? Was it my sons?"

"Forgive me, Milady. I have misspoken. 'Twas not my place to repeat what should have been kept within. I am not usually without tact. You must accept my apologies."

She stood to go, sat the vials upon the bedside table, and collected the tray. Lady Siobhan stepped in front of her path.

"I am not displeased to hear you speak of my family, Alainn. In truth, I think it would be a comfort to speak of my brother. My husband does not care to hear of problems for which he has no solution. And I cannot speak to my mother, it grieves her so, and she has lost so many children. I cannot even speak my brother's name to father. He will never forgive himself, for he feels he has driven him away. But, few know how much I contributed to him leaving as well. I should have been there for him; he went through a most difficult time.

"I was so engrossed in my own life. My sons were only young children, and I was trying to adjust to living with a man whose opinions differed so much from my own. I was selfish, and now I am filled with chagrin to know I will surely never be able to tell my brother how much he meant to me. The last night I spoke with him, his heart was so grieved; I should have told him how very dear he was to me."

"I'm sure he knew, for you are a kind and loving woman, a doting mother, and you still grieve so openly for your sister. He would have known, nay he did know. I feel it within my heart."

"Oh Alainn! You are a treasure! You always gladden my heart. 'Tis what Rory used to say about you. He said you made his heart glad, and you most certainly gladdened Killian's heart. Whatever you said to him all those years ago made him come back to us. And what a fine man he has become. You were once close to him. Have you spoken to him lately? Do you know what has happened between him and my husband, for neither will confide in me? But, I fear there is a divide so great it will not be capable of mending. I believe Killian intends to leave our clan over it."

The girl's skin turned a sickly hue.

"But, he will surely leave and go back to his home! He must become chieftain and live in his father's castle! 'Tis such a grand, majestic castle, and he has always been so proud of the fact he will one day return to follow in his father's footsteps. 'Tis how it must be!"

"It is a magnificent place, and I had always hoped he would return, but I think whatever has transpired between the two of them has colored Killian's way of thinking."

"He cannot throw it all away! He must not!"

"You care for him very much." She looked intently at the young woman. "Are you in love with him?"

Alainn turned away, but Lady Siobhan took her hand. The tears began once more, this time accompanied by heaving sobs. Alainn was barely able to speak, her despair was so deep, but she finally managed to tell her companion what lay within her heart.

"I know how foolish this must seem to you. I know it is an impossible love, that nothing can come of it, but I love him just the same."

"Oh my dear girl-child, love is never foolish, and the heart cannot be ruled by the mind. Perhaps we wouldn't be made to feel the pain if our minds were stronger, but they never are. Does he know? Have you told him?"

"Aye, he knows. But, whatever we shared is now over. It was ill-fated from the beginning and is now ended with no hope of a reprieve."

"And he feels for you the same way? I have suspected since you were children that one day your hearts would belong to one another."

"But, he will wed the MacDonald girl, and I am to wed the farmer O'Hara. It is as it should be. And he will return to his castle, and the best I can hope for is that one day when he thinks of me he will hold no contempt in his heart."

"You must fight for him, if you truly love him. You must fight for him!"

Alainn continued looking somber.

"Fight for him. To what end? To marry a commoner? The cost is too great, and the chieftain would never allow it, and how am I to compete with her? She is a lady, with all her grace and breeding, a high station and a title. I pale in comparison to what she is."

Lady Siobhan's face set with determination.

"You have his heart. 'Tis a tremendous advantage. And you have me on your side. Together, we will show Killian who he should wed."

Alainn appeared less than convinced. "But, he would lose his title, his land, all that is important to him."

"Ballocks."

Alainn laughed through her tears.

"Pardon me!" Lady Siobhan said, a twinkle in her eye. "I doubt Killian's mother's kin would denounce him because he chose to marry a commoner. They are reasonable people; they admired his father. I am certain they will be anxious to have him, no matter what wife he brings. And, once they meet you I am certain they would have no reservations about you. You are beautiful, educated, full of grace and compassion, and—" she took Alainn's hands in her own "—he loves you. When a man truly loves a woman, he is better for it. A better man and a better ruler."

Alainn dared allow her heart a trickle of hope. "But what of a dowry? I have nothing to offer as inducement for a clan to accept me as Killian's wife."

"My father is the wealthiest man in Ireland and chieftain of the strongest most influential clan. He has but two grandchildren, and both appear loyal to their father and intent on staying here at Castle O'Brien. My father adores Killian. He would offer what coin is necessary if he wants you as his wife."

"But, why would your father want to do such a kindness for me?"

"Because I would ask it of him, and I am most certainly his only living child."

"I could never ask such a favor, such immeasurable generosity."

"I would like nothing more, so we must speak with Killian," she insisted, seeming well-satisfied with the arrangement. "Tonight would be as good a time as any."

The younger girl sank back down into a chair, once more wearing a dejected expression.

"Killian is not willing to speak with me. I have lost his trust and kept many secrets from him. I am not entirely confident that he even desires to be near me any longer, much less want to marry me. He is at the feast with his betrothed. I believe they have grown close; most likely they spent this day in his bed. And, I am to be wed myself in only a few days."

The lady appeared to be deep in thought after hearing this information.

"Since you are to be married in only a few days time, then that is the first situation we must contend with. Leave that to me. You must find a way to communicate with my nephew, and between the two of us, we will make certain he knows what woman is the better match." She hesitated a moment before asking, "Are you lovers?"

"Pardon me, Milady?"

"The question is simple enough, Alainn. You are a healer and therefore know a great deal about anatomy. I know you have an understanding of the term, since you have attended births and know more than many a maiden. You are aware that a child enters the womb the same course it exits. You surely know what passes between a man and a woman. So, I will ask once more. Are you lovers? Have you and Killian been intimate? Has he bedded you?"

"I…we…I think…" Alainn blushed until she thought her head might erupt in flames. The older woman chuckled.

"I must conclude the answer is aye. And I think that is another stroke in your favor." The girl looked puzzled, so the older woman explained, "Once a man has had you in that manner, they become most possessive of you. Even if they don't have strong feelings for you, which I do not believe to be the case with Killian, they have a most difficult time accepting that another man will take what they believe is theirs."

"But he may have been with Mary in the same manner!"

"Nonsense. Killian has spent the better part of his return so filled with drink I doubt he would have been capable of performing."

"Aye, though I have mostly tried to avoid those appealing green eyes, they did seem quite blood-red. And I thought I detected the scent of ale. But, I've another conundrum. He already believes I have been with another man."

"And have you?"

"No, but I led him to believe so."

"'Tis a strange way to act toward the man you claim to love!"

"But 'twas a deception spurred by good intentions, for I thought it would ensure he'd marry the Scottish woman and procure his position and title."

"Your love for him is great, but now we must work together to make certain the two of you find happiness."

"The chieftain will oppose this without question." The girl trembled when she spoke of the man.

"I do not fear my husband."

"But, I do."

"Then you shall leave those dealings with me. Before long, I will have him seeing things my way."

Chapter Fourteen

The woman appeared most excited about the scheme. Alainn wanted to become caught up in the excitement of it, but she could not forget the hurt in Killian's eyes when he'd realized she'd been deceiving him. She felt herself sinking into the doldrums once more. The woman patted the girl's cheek in a loving, affectionate manner.

"Don't despair, Alainn, the O'Brien men don't know what a match they have before them. It will be far more entertaining than any of the bouts they have scheduled. Now, if this blasted rain would ever quit, we could make certain the men folk are kept occupied while we set our plan into motion."

Alainn looked toward the window and willed the clouds to disperse, forcing the sun to peek through the veil that had concealed it for nearly three days. She hadn't used her powers since the night of the guards' wounds; it was enthralling to exert them again. The sun was shining, though it was near to sunset. A knowing smile crossed Lady Siobhan's lips.

"'Tis your amulet Killian wears around his neck."

"Aye, 'tis mine. 'Twas my mother's."

"The farrier's wife?" the woman quizzed, an odd expression on her face. "Though I did not know her, everyone talked of how unusual it was for her to carry a child at such an advanced age. I never thought of her as druid. She seemed entirely Christian to me, though I suppose she might have kept it closeted, for many are fearful or ashamed to admit they adhere to the old religion. I never sensed a connection with her, though, and your father is not a druid, is he?"

Alainn grew uneasy with this line of questioning, for, as much as she loved and respected the woman, she could hardly relate that her own mother's curse had caused her many infants to perish. The woman would surely feel only loathing toward her, and however prone she was to want to aid her in her quest to earn Killian's love, she would clearly change her mind if she knew the actual truth. And, she still didn't know who had fathered her.

"Do you know that giving away your amulet leaves you unprotected against danger?"

"I have heard as much. But, I had a vision that frightened me so; I needed to ensure Killian was kept safe. I would ask you to find a way to have your sons wear their amulets; the ones you had made for them."

"How did you know of the amulets?"

"I know you are druid, and I have learned a druid parent has one crafted for their children before they have seen one moon on this earth."

"Aye, and if you suggest my sons must wear theirs, I am to assume you have seen them in grave danger as well?"

"Aye, I have seen it. But, I have yet to learn when the peril will present itself."

"You are an apt seer. I have only a small measure of premonition ability. My sister was more gifted in such areas. Though she must not have been alerted to her own danger. She could not have foreseen her death or surely she would have done what she could to prevent it."

Alainn looked toward the door before the loud rap could be heard. They both turned. It was Rory.

"Mother, you must come. Alainn as well. Grandmother has taken a spell and fallen into a deep sleep. Grandfather is sorely worried. Please come now."

Lady Siobhan's already pale face became ashen at the news. She took Alainn's hand, and they hastened off down the corridor.

***

The elderly woman lay unconscious upon a table in the great hall. Many lords and ladies were gathered round the ailing woman. An elderly man, who Alainn realized must be Lady Siobhan's father, held his wife's hand. Rory did not need to push through the crowd, for it opened as he and the two women made their way to the table. The physician stood by the old woman, his head on her chest. When he saw Alainn, he frowned.

"Milady, you have brought your healer. Do you feel her more skilled in healing your mother?"

"Alainn has proved her abilities to me time and time again, Thomas O'Donaugh. Though I do not question your abilities, I trust Alainn."

Hugh O'Brien stood with legs wide and arms crossed, a disapproving expression on his face. She was undermining his physician, and she'd come to the hall in the presence of all of their guests wearing her nightclothes. But, the determined expression on her worried face told him he should not challenge her on this. Alainn was surprised to see the physician step back from the matronly lady and gesture her forward. O'Brien's priest, who was standing next to him, made a sound of contempt and moved off into the crowd.

The old woman was very tiny of stature with snow white hair laying in soft curls about her face. Rory and Riley wore identical expressions of concern on their faces, and Alainn was aware that Killian stood close-by, his hand on the elderly man's shoulder. She pressed her head to the woman's chest as Thomas O'Donagh had done. Her expression turned bleak.

"Her heart is gravely weakened," she said. "I may be able to administer foxglove, which will cause her heart to beat more evenly for a time. I will attempt to heal her, but I fear it will only be a temporary solution, for regrettably there is no cure. I am most certain."

"Perhaps if we conduct some bloodletting, it will serve the purpose?" the physician suggested.

"It will serve the purpose of weakening her so that she will possibly never regain consciousness. With the foxglove, she will surely be allowed to speak with her family again, to spend what time she has left with them, and perhaps to live to see her grandsons wed."

"Get the herbal remedy then, Alainn. Please, hurry, for we must speak with her again! There have been too many deaths without chance of farewell in our family." Lady Siobhan looked to her father for confirmation, but he only stared at Alainn with such an odd expression, he seemed completely unaware that his daughter had spoken.

"Siobhan, are you certain you won't let this man attempt his craft, for he has much experience!" She ignored her husband entirely.

"Father, are you in agreement with me, that we allow my healer to proceed with her remedies?"

"Aye, do whatever the girl says. We must listen to what she tells us."

"Aye, you must allow Alainn to do what she will for our grandmother." It was Rory who spoke, and Alainn thought that was possibly the first time he had ever dared openly disagree with his father.

"I shall go retrieve the potion. I know where it is kept in your chamber, if you will allow me to touch your remedies," offered Thomas O'Donagh.

"Aye, it would be much appreciated." Alainn felt slightly ashamed at how she had treated the physician. She had childishly drawn a line down the center of the chamber they were to share and told him he was not to enter her half of the room or to touch any of her supplies. She'd said if he felt inclined to use any of her herbs in his efforts to heal anyone, he would need to ask her permission to go near them. She'd also referred to his many instruments, as liken to weapons you would find in a torture chamber. The man had not shown a temper when she'd been so rude to him, he'd simply gone about his business and shown her no disrespect. One day, she would apologize to him for her unbecoming behavior.

Alainn placed her hands to the old woman's chest and attempted to will the heart to beat strongly and evenly. It responded but with only minimal improvement. Foxglove would be needed. She hoped it would see the woman through the next week. She closed her eyes to concentrate completely on healing the woman's heart, when the woman beneath her hands gasped loudly.

"My darlin' wee Shylie, you've come home at last! Or have I gone on to the beyond then and been reunited with my youngest babe? I have missed you so!" She grasped Alainn's hand.

"Mother!" Lady Siobhan cried out in joy at seeing her mother's eyes open.

"Ah Siobhan, my beautiful girl. I was blessed with such dear lovely daughters and such fine handsome sons." Lady Siobhan's eyes filled with tears of joy, for since her mother had arrived at Castle O'Brien, she had not recognized her as her own daughter.

"Mother, I am much relieved you are well," she whimpered softly as she touched her mother's cheek.

"Niall, is it not the most wonderful sight to behold, our two beautiful girls together again. And Teige is here as well. Are all my children back, then? Come stand by me, dearest Teige, my youngest son. What a fair and handsome man you have become!" The woman beckoned to Rory. "Your father has grieved most terribly for the sore words he spoke to you. You must embrace, and Niall, you need tell our son how you have missed him." Her husband obliged her as well and hugged the younger man with a deep affection as though he truly was his son, back from wherever he had been all these years. "And where are Finn, Conan, and Collum?" She spoke the names of her dead sons. Then the old woman had an entirely lucid moment. She closed her eyes, and a tear slid down her wrinkled cheek. "Aye, I remember now, they are gone, killed in battle. They died as warriors, but 'tis little consolation to a mother who is made to lay her children in the ground." She looked into the sad eyes of her daughter. "And my lovely Siobhan, you have given so many babes back to the earth as well. There's no greater pain for a mother to bear than to live on while her children are taken from her, one by one." She noticed Killian.

"Killian O'Brien, my grandsons' cousin. You were my grandson and I, your grandmother, for all the years when we were too far from our actual kin to keep close touch. You used to steal the sweet cakes when you thought I wasn't lookin', but I always purposely left them there for you. And you would tell me your dreams, how you would be a great chieftain one day and marry a girl with lovely yellow hair. Have you found her then?" Killian smiled and nodded so only the woman could see. She reached for her husband's hand and then only had eyes for him.

"My dearest love." He embraced his wife, though she remained holding tight to the young girl's hand. "We have bore the pain together, you and I, Niall. I have been happy to be your wife for all these years, my only love."

"And I have been honored to be your husband, Katherine. I would not change a day I have spent with you, through the laughter and the tears. For nearly five decades we have shared all, and to me you are as beautiful as the day we first met. You looked as Shylie does now, your hair as lustrous and your skin as clear and youthful."

She smiled up at him as he bent over to place a tender kiss on her lips, and she patted his cheek affectionately. She glanced at Rory and took his hand. "My son, you are so dear to me. Now that you have returned, you must seek out the woman you loved so desperately. For if you loved her as you claimed, her feelings for you will surely remain unchanged. How could a woman not love you? You are so kind and sensitive. Your father believed you to be dead, but I could never allow myself to think you would be gone from us forever!"

She then seemed to notice Riley and called him over, as well. She obviously believed him to be his father, for she spoke to him as such. "O'Brien, you be good to my daughter; she'll be a good wife to you. Treat her kindly and fairly, and allow her to practice her beliefs, for they are sorely important to her and part of who she is. Though they may not be your beliefs, if you take them from her, she will never allow you into her heart entirely." She patted his hand as well, then looked up to Alainn. "I'm ready to join you now, Shylie, for sure you've come to take me with you, my lovely girl. We will go to meet your brothers!"

"Aye, Wee Mama, they're waitin' for us," soothed Alainn. The woman's husband looked at her sharply.

The old woman smiled tenderly at her husband, her daughter, Rory and Riley. Then, her eyes went back to Alainn. She squeezed her hand as though to never let go, and her eyes slowly closed.

The physician arrived with a vial in his hand but, noticing the somber expressions, lowered his head. The priest stepped forward, but her daughter and husband, both gave a resounding "No!" The woman's hand was still wrapped around Alainn's. She was so profoundly affected by all she had seen that she could not move. It was the woman's husband who finally took the girl's hand and lifted his wife's away.

"I give you thanks, from myself and my family," he said kindly, handing Alainn a handkerchief to wipe the tears spilling down her cheeks.

"But, I could not save her. I could not even give her the days I claimed she might still have."

The man, whose voice was both gentle and strong, held tight to her hand as his wife had done.

"You gave her far more than life. You brought Shylie back to her if only long enough to believe they would go to the next life together. And you allowed her to remember her grandsons, to know me again. She has not recognized me in months. Do you know what a treasure it was to have her look at me with love in her eyes and recognition of all we have been through together? If she'd lived another decade in the fog she'd come to live in, it would not have been the same as these mere moments you allowed us. I thank you." Tears were now filling his eyes as well. "If there is ever anything we might do for you to return this great deed, you must tell us. You have only to say the word."

He gave his son-in-law a stern look, as if to order him to heed his words. Then he smoothed his wife's hair and gazed at her with love, seeming to see her as he had the first day they'd met.

"If I am taken now," he murmured, "it would suit me well, for I look forward to the day we will be reunited once again."

Alainn nodded to him through her tears, embraced his daughter, and offered her hand to the twins with deep condolence. With that, she pushed through the crowd. Hugh O'Brien attempted to take her arm, but she pulled away from him furiously and fled the room. She heard Killian's voice calling after her, but she kept on running.

Once through the castle door, she expected to see ominous rain clouds to match her shattered heart, but the sky was dark and stars shone brightly. A star streaked across the sky, not downward like a falling star, but upward. Her heart gladdened, for it was a belief that, when a druid left this earth, the path could be seen all the way to the next life. She believed it now with no uncertainty.

Killian caught up to her as she crossed the courtyard, but when he tried to take her in his arms, she pulled from him in objection as surely as she had moved from Hugh O'Brien. He did not attempt to touch her again, but his eyes held a deep sadness.

"That was a great kindness you did for Lady Katherine. I thank you for it, for the O'Rorke's are both dear to me."

"Allowing the woman to believe I was her dead daughter could hardly be considered a kindness. Anyone would have done the same under the circumstances. And you needn't look so surprised, I am not the malevolent woman you believe me to me."

"Alainn, I do not—"

"You are such a kind soul, Alainn!" The words, spoken in a feminine Scottish accent, interrupted them. They turned to see Mary approaching. She took Killian's arm with a familiarity Alainn did not care to witness. "What you did for that woman and her family was angelic. I am proud to know you, and I hope one day to be considered among your friends." She reached out and hugged her no less tightly than if she were Cook's wife, Margaret. Alainn closed her eyes and tried to keep her thoughts kind.

"I thank you for your caring words, Milady. I must be off, for I am staying at Cook's cottage and should like to catch him before he leaves for home."

"You do not stay within the castle? I was under the assumption you lived here. Riley told me so, but perhaps I misunderstood."

"With the many people here now, I find it far too crowded."

She curtsied before the couple and, with a formal address to them both, set off for the kitchen through way of the back entrance.

"Killian, did Riley not tell me that the cook and his wife have a large number of children and a small cottage?"

"Aye, they've thirteen children."

"Hmm," was all the Scottish girl said as they walked back into the castle.

Chapter Fifteen

Alainn lay in the bed she shared with Molly and her sisters, Fiona and wee Eileen. She listened as Cook and three of his sons quietly left the home while the rest of the family slept. It was not yet daybreak and the house dark, but she had slept little through the night. At present, Eileen had her arms wrapped tightly around Alainn's neck, and she found her warmth and closeness comforting. She'd heard Margaret up through the night with her youngest child, who'd been fussy and discontent. Alainn surmised that new teeth would soon appear.

She felt movement within, and her hand caressed her stomach in growing adoration of the child that grew there. She must soon arise for her need to find a privy was growing more urgent. It was sometimes as bothersome as the nauseous morning stomach. The cottage was tiny with so few divisions, she did not feel comfortable using the chamber pot beneath the bed. She disentangled the wee child's arms from her neck, fumbled for her warm shawl, and made her way through the maze of beds.

The air outside was cool; the freshness of the early morning, inviting. She found a tree behind which to conceal herself and was thankful for how much more comfortable she felt. When she lifted the latch to open the door, she saw a small candle burning in the kitchen and a kettle upon the hearth. Margaret sat beside the large table, holding her youngest child to her breast. Alainn washed her hands in the basin and pulled up a chair.

"I hope I did not wake you, Margaret."

"Nay, 'twas the babe. She had another restless night."

"I shall bring some more ground juniper, for it often fights the pain of new teeth approaching."

"Aye, 'twas most helpful last time."

The two women sat in silence for a time, the only sounds were the kettle beginning to heat and the infant suckling at Margaret's breast.

"Do you not have something you care to say to me, Alainn?"

She looked at the older woman uncertain what she meant, so she broached a subject she had been avoiding.

"Aye, I've yet to apologize to you for keeping Cookson so long when he was off to Galway. I have told Cook how sorry I am regarding that matter, but it was very wrong of me to cause you worry, as I'm sure you did fret when Cookson's return was delayed."

"Oh, it is a mother's burden to worry, but I bear no ill feelings toward you for that. Joseph is a grown man and two of his younger brothers are already wed, so I think I should not question him regarding his being away from our home for a time. In truth, though I hoped against it, I thought perhaps he sought out the company of a harlot, for I know that there must be many in the city. However, that was not the topic I'd thought you'd maybe be wantin' to discuss with me."

The baby cried at the moment and squirmed in her mother's arms. Alainn noticed the dark circles beneath the woman's tired eyes. She held out her arms and Margaret passed the baby to her with some relief, pulling her chemise over her exposed breast. In all the time Alainn had known her, she had been with child or nursing another. As she rose to take the kettle from the hearth, Margaret clutched the small of her back.

The baby grabbed an adequate handful of Alainn's hair and tugged at it quite steadily As she giggled and talked sweetly to the child. Margaret prepared a pot of herbs and hot apple cider. The child noticed her mother and began to whine. Margaret sat back down, took the baby from Alainn, and put her to her breast once more.

"You are tired, Margaret, and your back is ailing you."

"Aye, my body feels older than its five and thirty years. Sure 'tis the many babies I've carried that have taken a toll. Though I'd not wish any of them away, for I love them all, but I would be most pleased if this wee girl is the last babe I bear."

"Have you tried the herbal remedies that sometimes prevent a pregnancy?"

"Aye, off and on through the years, Morag would pass me some, knowing I would birth a child with less than eighteen months between the one next to it. I am certainly most fertile."

"But there are nearly three years between your last two daughters?"

"Aye, well my husband and I attempted a time apart from each other. But, 'tis an unnatural thing to share a bed with a man you love and desire, and not to be together in an intimate fashion. It was I who ended the time of celibacy for, though he was displeased with it, he would never have forced himself upon me as some men do. And so, we have our wee Sheena now. 'Tis both a blessing and a curse to desire a man in a physical manner."

Alainn smiled slightly but did not comment.

"You are quiet this morning, Alainn. In truth, you have been quiet since you came back from Galway. Did events happen there that have you troubled?" The girl only shook her head and poured the drink. "So is it the event of last evening, Lady Siobhan's mother's passing, that leaves you so melancholy this morning?"

"Aye, 'twas a sad thing to watch the woman slip away. Though I did not know her, I felt a deep connection to her. And her husband appeared to love her very much. It was obvious how great was her love for him as well. What a wondrous thing to behold, a love that has spanned five decades. To be allowed that much time with the man you love must be the greatest of bestowments. But to have it taken away after such a lengthy time would surely cause the deepest heartache known to a soul."

Margaret watched as the young woman's eyes brimmed with tears that overflowed down her cheeks. Alainn angrily wiped the tears away and stood to busy herself, wiping the table and setting out bowls for the children.

"Alainn, would you fetch the jug of milk from just outside our door? Seamus always pulls it from the well for me and leaves it ready beside the stoop so I don't have to leave the cottage. You might pour yourself some as well."

"I'm not so overly fond of cow's milk, although 'tis better than that of a goat."

"Aye well, whether you've a fondness for it or not, you should drink it. 'Twill be beneficial to the child you carry and aid in producing the milk you'll need to nurse it."

Alainn stilled, a disconcerted look on her face.

"It is not yet outwardly evident, is it?" she asked in a tight voice.

"No, your body is as trim as always. Perhaps your bosom has grown, but surely only a woman who knows what causes that condition would notice, or maybe a man who knows you intimately. But, sure you'll not be able to keep it hidden for very long."

"Cook told you?"

"No, I guessed it, and then he confirmed it. Joseph told me how ill you were on your journey to Galway, how you were unable to keep food settled in your stomach. With how quickly you left, I thought you'd gone to keep your condition concealed."

"That was not the reason entirely, but perhaps a part of it. And 'tis doubtful I shall ever need milk to nourish the child, for he'll surely never live more than hours."

"So 'tis an O'Brien child you carry within you!" the woman fumed. "Which one of them has been at you? Was it Sean, the chieftain's youngest brother?"

"Sean? Why would you think it was Sean? He's never been anything but gentlemanly toward me. I quite like the man."

"Sure, he's not known to be as wanton as some of his brothers, but I caught him starin' at my Molly the other day and wanted to rip off his ballocks!"

Alainn giggled. "Well Molly's a lovely girl, and Sean does have an affinity for redheads. His late wife had red hair as does their son. But I've never known Sean to be rude or disrespectful to any of the servants or commoners. He was surely just observing how lovely Molly is. She's of an age when men are beginning to look at her, and though I know how protective you and Cook are, 'tis unrealistic to think she can be protected entirely."

"Aye well, she will be protected as long as her family is around. I know well how a woman must fight to keep herself virtuous for her husband, for men are a depraved lot when it comes to matters of the flesh. And you,

Alainn McCreary have surely been made to fight off an army of men with the great beauty you possess.

"Ever since you were a child you were lovely. And now that you're a woman, so radiant and blossomed, I suppose men cannot be faulted for wanting you. When I see those eyes of yours, 'tis nearly impossible to turn from you, as though you hold my gaze. Aye but you have old eyes, Alainn."

"Old?"

"They seem to hold a knowledge far beyond your years. And when they are sad, as they are now, it is painful to look within them. So tell me, Alainn, is it the fact you carry a child that has you so entirely maudlin, or is it the father? Has he forced himself upon you, is the child a product of a rape?"

"No, I gave myself to him, completely, entirely, with no reservations and no regrets."

"It's Killian, then." Alainn glanced at her as if to question how she could know, but the woman answered before she could speak. "The love shines in your eyes when you are around him. It always has. I have worried over that from the time you were a child. I knew it would bring heartache, as did my husband and Old Morag. Does Killian know of the child?"

"No, 'tis of no benefit for anyone to tell him for he is to wed by week's end, and me, day after tomorrow. Killian is the only man I have ever been with, and he'll be the only one I shall ever desire to be with in such a manner."

"Liam is a good man, Alainn," she said, taking her hand and patting it. "I believe he will accept the child, and perhaps you might make him believe it is his. Babes are oft born before their expected time."

"Sure it will not even be a consideration unless the curse is lifted."

The woman looked at her with sympathetic eyes for she clearly believed that was not probable.

"How far along are you, child?"

"I missed my second monthly past a week ago, and the sickness in the morning has begun to ebb, so I doubt I could convince the man the child is his." She glanced down at their entwined hands and whispered, "Molly will think so little of me. She is much insistent she will never be with anyone until she is wed."

"She is young, Alainn, and has not given her heart to a man. 'Tis easy to declare statements of intent when the circumstances have not yet been presented. She does not know how a woman burns for a man when she has fallen in love. But, you needn't worry about Molly, she'll not judge you, for you are gravely important to her. She loves you well."

"And so, do you judge me, Margaret, for giving myself to a man without benefit of matrimony?"

"I could hardly judge you when I did so myself." Alainn's eyes widened in surprise.

"You and Cook were together before you were wed?"

"Aye, I wanted to ensure the first time was with someone I loved and not with a lord who simply wanted me for a night or two to ease his desires. Hugh O'Brien's father was a lascivious man in his later years. I was always unable to understand how a man who had been honorable and noble all his life could change so drastically. After his wife died, he did not care how he behaved toward women. I had a deep respect for the man, and then almost overnight he became an unreasonable, insatiable tyrant."

"Like his son. I suppose the apple truly doesn't fall far from the tree, for I always believed Hugh O'Brien to be a good man. I sang his praises, and now I am being made to pay for trusting him."

"So, he's raped you?"

"No, but he attempted it, and it was the closest I ever hope to come to being violated. I would have killed him, I think, if he were not Killian's uncle and the O'Brien."

"You have not mentioned any of this to Killian?"

"No, he believes I've been with his uncle but not that it was forced. I think he would kill him if he learned the truth, and no matter that he is his nephew, Killian would pay for taking the life of a chieftain, regardless of how warranted his actions might be."

"So you allow him to think you have been unfaithful to protect him."

"Aye, to save his life. To keep him safe, I would do much more."

Alainn sipped the warm drink. As some of the children had begun to awaken, Margaret passed the sleeping child to Alainn and added oats to a large pot of water. Alainn placed soft kisses on the child's fine hair and inhaled the sweet scent. Love for her own unborn child filled her heart, and, for the briefest of moments, she felt content. When a knock came to the door, she jerked upright, for she knew whose knuckles rapped at the thick wood.

"'Tis Killian. You must tell him I am not here. I cannot speak with him!"

"I will not speak falsehoods for you, Alainn. I will attempt to dissuade him, but we both know he is not a man to be discouraged easily." Moments later, she came back from the door, shaking her head. "He will speak to you now or wait outside the door. He looks sorely grieved and wears the armor of battle, so he is clearly slotted for a match this morning. The sun has risen, and sure his uncle will not take kindly to him missing a bout. You might as well face him now, Alainn. I am certain there are words that must be spoken between you."

* * *

Alainn reluctantly stepped out onto the stoop still carrying the sleeping child in her arms. She did not meet his eyes but closed the door behind her, pulling the blanket over the sleeping baby. She looked down the path and toward the stone fence.

"Are you expecting someone, Alainn?"

"No, but I thought perhaps your intended might be somewhere close by."

"No, I've come alone. There are subjects that must be spoken between us, matters meant for our ears alone."

When neither spoke, Alainn sighed and looked toward the distant hills. The sun was just rising and a lovely mist covered the horizon. How odd that it could be such a pleasant morning when her stomach felt knotted and her mind full of torment. When still he did not speak, she dared glance at him. He wore his leine, his heavy tunic, with a light armor covering his chest and arms. She didn't want to think of the fine brawny chest that lie beneath the armor or the powerful arms that had so often held her.

"Broadsword or pith axe?"

"Sword," he said shortly.

They fell to silence once again. She looked down at the sleeping child to keep her eyes from looking at him. The clanging of dishes from inside the cottage brought her head up.

"I must go assist Margaret with the morning meal. And I will be needed to go to the healing chamber, soon enough. I should take leave now."

"And so you mean to never discuss our situation?"

"What situation do you refer to? The fact that we are both to be wed this week?"

"You know very well, that's not what I speak of! I need to know of your time with my uncle. I know you've been with him, but you told me he did not rape you. Am I to conclude you simply allowed him to have you? I have seen you create thunder and lightning. I have seen you call upon the ocean's fury. Sure you might have kept him from bedding you, unless you actually wanted it."

"You know little of my powers, Killian O'Brien!" she spat. "They are unpredictable and ever-changing. We clearly have nothing further to discuss, for it is evident you have already formed an opinion on the matter."

"Tell me it isn't so, Alainn. Tell me you weren't my uncle's whore!"

Her eyes grew stormy, and she turned to open the door.

"I'm not done speakin'!" he shouted, taking a step toward her.

"Do not dare move from where you stand!" Her tone was both taunting and furious. "Aye, we are surely not through yet, Milord, but I'm taking the child within so you do not frighten her." The door opened and Margaret popped her head out. She glowered at Killian as she scooped the child from Alainn's arms and closed the door.

Alainn turned, drew back her arm, and slapped Killian's face with all her might. His head snapped back from the force of it, and she grabbed her stinging hand. His cheek held an angry red mark. His lip was bleeding.

"I have only ever been one man's whore, Killian O'Brien, and I rue the day I ever went to his bed!"

She pivoted on the stoop to leave, but he caught her arm. With gritted teeth in a grimace, he passed her a package tied with cloth ribbon.

"This is for you. I bought it in Galway. It is a gown I chose for you." She refused to take it from him.

"I want nothing from you, Killian O'Brien, save solitude and distance."

"You must take it. It was intended for you."

"I'm sure you'll find someone else who would be suited to it." She tried to keep her eyes from the welted handprint on his cheek, the trickle of blood on his chin.

"'Tis the gown I hoped you might wear at our wedding. Perhaps you'd like to wear it when you wed the farmer." Bitterness had seeped into in his voice, and his green eyes held ire. Her heart twisted painfully.

"It would be shameful to accept a costly garment and wear it for such a short time, so eager will he be to consummate the marriage."

She turned without looking at him, stepped into the cottage, and slammed the door in his face.

Chapter sixteen

He stood there for a time, trying to calm his confusion and jealousy. He looked toward the sun and knew he must get to the tournament before he had to forfeit a bout and begin the games with a loss to the O'Briens. He thought of rapping on the door once more, but it was unlikely they could say anything that they wouldn't later regret. When he started down the stone walkway, a most displeased voice called after him.

"Killian O'Brien, you get yourself back here this instant, for I've a word or two to tell you myself!"

Margaret Kilkenny stood with face flushed and arms crossed over her full bosom. She had a rankled look upon her motherly face, one Killian had seen before when she'd scolded her own sons. He turned fully around to face her wrath.

She saw the dark red mark on his face, his obviously wounded pride, and a forlorn heartsick expression.

"Aye, what is it you'd like to say, then?" he asked in a defeated tone.

"You can tell me this is none of my concern if you like, but I'm going to give you my opinion anyway. And if you don't like it you can take it up with the chieftain. And if he cares to dismiss my husband for my address to you, then so be it, for he'd back me in this, I know it well."

"This'll not go to my uncle," he mumbled.

"I only met your mother but a time or two, but she seemed a good decent woman. Your aunt who took over in her stead, is a lovely, gracious and well-mannered woman, and I know the two of them would be most disheartened to hear you speak to a woman in the way I've just heard you talk to wee Alainn. That was a horrid, disrespectful word you called her, and one she does not deserve."

"Aye, it was wrong of me, but she can rile a man in a way that would make the saintliest of men want to strangle her!"

"Aye, she's spirited and oft speaks her mind to a fault, but you cannot dishonor her. And while I don't know all of what has happened between the two of you, I know the two of you have been together as a husband and wife, without the vows and nuptials."

"She told you that?"

"Aye, just this morning, and she told me she gave herself to you freely. Do you not realize how esteemed you should feel? A woman has her virtue to give to but one man, and she offered it to you. You should feel honored. You should treat her as a treasure. She honored you with the pleasure of making her a woman, and now you throw it back in her face?"

"She's betrayed me and deceived me. I don't know if I can see past that."

Margaret put her hand on his shoulder. "I don't see Alainn as being deceitful. You must tell me what she's done to make you believe that."

"She's been with my uncle!" The words cut him as he spoke them.

"Are you certain of this? Has she told you so herself."

"Nay, but he has, and she won't deny it, so 'tis the same thing!"

"Why then would she tell me she'd only ever been with one man?"

"Perhaps she was ashamed to admit it to you."

"She admitted to me she lay with you willfully. If she values my opinion, why would she have me believe she's a wanton woman, yet not disclose the fact she'd been raped? If she allows you to believe she gave herself to your uncle what are the consequences?"

"I will never trust her again. All that we shared would be ruined."

"And what would your recourse be toward your uncle."

"I would hate him for the rest of my life!"

"And if you learned he tried to rape her, then what?"

"I would kill the bastard as sure as I breathe!" Killian seethed.

"Aye, and be hanged for killing the earl."

"To swing at the end of a rope would be worth it to avenge the woman I love!" he shouted.

"Maybe not to her," she said quietly.

He looked as if he'd been slapped anew. The woman watched as understanding dawned on his young, handsome face.

"She thought to protect me. She knew I'd avenge her wrongdoing."

"Aye, I believe that is the truth of it. But, should you act upon this now, make your uncle pay for his injustices, she will have risked losing your respect and your love, for nothing. Don't cause Alainn any more pain. She's a delicate girl, and though she puts on a bold front, you have wounded her."

"She's stronger than you think."

"If you speak of the powers she has, then I'll explain somethin' to you. I have only ever known two other women with such abilities. One died in childbed with a broken heart, so clearly her powers were of little use to her. The other lives in a cave banished forever and shunned by everyone she ever knew. So think awhile on this, Killian O'Brien, if you think those powers can protect her. They'll surely not mend her heart if you leave it tattered."

The seriousness on Killian's face was evident, and he swallowed hard before asking, "You don't approve of our being together? You believe I should allow her to marry the farmer and go near her no more?"

"I like you fine, and I believe you to be a good man. And at the moment she believes she will never be happy without you. Who can say what the future will bring for either of you? I will say that you and your kin have done her no favors through the years."

Stunned at this, he touched her shoulder.

"You think we have been unkind to Alainn?"

"Aye, well it's not to say you haven't done what you thought was right by her. And she has been forever grateful for the schooling and education she's been given. And I know she'd not trade a moment she spent with you and your cousins. But, it's left her between two worlds. She does not fit in your world for she is still a servant and not allowed within your circle. She's remained a commoner no matter how many lessons she had or books she's read. The other servants and peasants have resented her terribly. She was never included entirely with them either. They believe she thinks herself above them. She's no female friends, save Molly. She has been like a daughter to us, but we cannot protect her as we do our own daughters, for we've truly no say when it comes to her life."

"I had no notion she had been shown cruelty by others because she had spent time with the O'Briens."

"Aye well, one never truly knows another's lot in life, no matter how well we think we know them, or how dearly we hold them within our hearts."

Killian heard the bagpipes beginning and looked toward the castle.

"I must be off now, but I thank you for this conversation, and for setting me right about a good many things."

"Aye well, I may not be schooled or important, but I've an abundance of knowledge and a good deal of experience at motherin' and handing out advice."

"But you've not told me what you think would be best for Alainn."

"Sure, I don't know the answer to that. The two of you will have to find that out yourselves. I do know you'll be needin' to mend her pride as well as her heart if you ever intend to be more than a memory to her."

He looked toward the door, but the pipes called loudly and the cheers had begun. He nodded respectfully to Margaret and headed off at a steady trot.

"Keep your wits about you, Killian O'Brien, for you'll be no good to anyone if your head lies apart from the rest of your body!"

He smiled to himself for the first time in days.

Chapter seventeen

The morning dragged on for Alainn, though she had passed the time with readying bandages and sorting through her remedies. The physician had spoken a few words to her but then left her to her temper. There had only been a couple of men from neighboring clans brought in from the challenges, and their wounds had been bloody but quite minor.

She could hear the roar of the crowds in the playing fields. The cheers were always the rowdiest when an O'Brien was on the court, and when they'd won a bout, there was no need to be watching to learn the outcome. Two generations of O'Brien's were competing in one or more event. Though Hugh and all of his brothers were scheduled to take part, it was Riley and Killian who brought the greatest pride to Clan O'Brien. They were undefeated champions in all of Munster, Connaught, and Leinster, as well.

She was standing on a wooden crate straining her neck to look out the tiny window at the current match, when the wee babe within her moved.

Is it your da who's battling for the honor of his clan? she silently asked the child, smiling. She wondered if he would resemble his father.

"How far along are you, then?" She nearly fell off the crate at the physician's words.

"What? How? Is it evident?"

"No, you cannot tell by the look of you, to be certain. But I've noticed the scent of herbs on you. Now, the only reason people ingest that combination of herbs is if they are squeamish, which is surely not the case for you, since you have not flinched nor seemed the slightest bit disturbed by the amount of blood you see, or they have a stomach ailment. You eat later in the day, never in the morning, and you're moody and disagreeable. Yet, every so often you smile and place your hand to your belly. I have seen it before."

"Most physicians are not so knowledgeable or accepting of herbal remedies."

"They've been used for centuries. I can hardly discredit hundreds of years of proof." He smiled. "My mother was a healer, and my father a physician. Sometimes the two complement each another."

"Is it you then who's been leaving bits of thyme throughout this chamber?"

"No, I've not gone near your herbs, and though I do not discredit the use of herbs, I only use them on occasion. Why do you ask me this?"

"I have found scattered sprigs of thyme on my table, in my mixing vessels, and even occasionally on my pillow. The old healer, Morag, who has recently gone to the beyond, found great favor in thyme. Of course, it cannot be denied to be a heal-all and beneficial in any number of remedies, but Morag adored the scent of it. She carried it with her always."

"But you've not answered my query, when is your time?"

"The babe will be born early in the month of December."

The words were barely out of her mouth when Riley entered the healing chamber assisting a limping Killian. There was a large, dark red stain on the front of his thigh. Rory followed closely behind, scolding his cousin.

"Killian, you are being reckless! Your mind is not on your opponent!"

His brother added, "Aye, Killian, you're lucky the wound was not over a wee bit or you'd be of little use to your wife. With your wedding only days away, I think she'd not be so keen on being wed to a gelding."

Riley looked up and, upon seeing Alainn, his face colored. "Forgive me, Alainn."

"'Tis of no concern to me," she sniped.

When Riley headed Killian toward her, she shook her head. "Take him over to the physician straightaway! His side of the room is clearly marked. You may find me in the kitchen should anyone else need my attention." Before leaving, she handed the physician two vials. "After the wound has been cleaned with this solution, this ointment should be applied before it is sewn together. If you don't care to take the time to sew it up, I'm sure one of your many saws would work fine to amputate, or perhaps you might employ his betrothed, I'm certain her needlework would be fine and as perfect as she is!"

Not one of the men spoke until she'd left the room.

"I wonder who's put her in such a fury this morning," Riley remarked, looking accusingly at Killian.

"She's in a rare temper, even for Alainn," Rory agreed.

"What is that ointment?" Killian asked suspiciously to the man cleaning his wound.

"'Tis a heal-all, and she knows her herbal medicines as well as anyone I've ever known. But she's got half a dozen others that would serve the purpose just as well as this one without—"

He'd stopped mid-sentence and hesitated, with his hand suspended over the wound.

"Without what?" Killian asked impatiently.

"Without the pain," he finished, pouring the medicine into the wound as Killian sucked in his breath and swore. "This one burns like fire," he added needlessly.

"Why the wee bitch!" Killian snapped through gritted teeth, and at that moment, the physician was quite certain he knew who had fathered the healer's child.

When she returned nearly an hour later, Alainn was startled to find Killian still lying flat upon the table, the physician continuing to work on his wound. Rory sat to one side.

"Is it serious, then?" she asked in a voice that unwittingly revealed her concern.

"No, 'tis deep enough but not apt to become purulent, I believe."

"And you cleaned it with the water I gave you earlier?"

"Aye, woman, I have closed a wound or two before. I once served as physician to men in battle."

"Ah, so you haven't always spent your days looking through bodily fluids and excrement."

The man glanced at her for a moment but then went on with his suturing.

"Much can be learned from the examination of bile, blood, and excrement. Many cures will be found by such studies."

"Christ is that the smell that fills this room?" Rory coughed and jokingly put his hands to his throat as though he were choking. Alainn giggled at the sight, and Rory grabbed her and playfully swung her.

"Stop that, Rory O'Brien, my head grows dizzy, I beg you, stop it this instant!" she squealed. "What was that about?" she asked dizzily when he finally relented and the room stopped spinning.

"I like to hear you laugh, and it's been a time since I've heard it."

"Where is Riley?"

"He's gone to spend time with Iona, his intended. They're not hitting it off well, and father thinks if they spend more time together they might begin to see eye to eye."

"I'm sorry to hear it. But I see you and your betrothed are getting along most splendidly."

"Aye, I like Brigid. We are able to talk freely with one another. And though she doesn't have quite the same sense of humor as you and I, she is not without humor."

"Aye well, you and I share something uncommon, no one can question that. I shall miss the times we have spent together." With that, she threw her arms around his neck, and they embraced openly with a familiarity that left the physician wondering if he had been incorrect about the father of the child, after all.

Killian lay still as the man continued with the closing of his gash. He was happy that Rory had made her laugh. It had been a very long time since he too had heard the sound so dear to his ears.

When Alainn peered over the physician's shoulder to gauge how apt he was at repairing a slice by a sword, she saw that the wound truly was quite close to his most sensitive area. Though his tunic covered his masculine parts, his trews were removed for the procedure, and she found herself thinking about that part of him.

"Is it to your liking?" the physician asked, and she felt her cheeks color slightly. "The wound, is it as able a job as you might have done?"

"Aye, your stitches are sturdy and precise."

"Would you care to accompany me to the banquet this night?" he asked as he laid a clean cloth to the wound.

"It is not permitted for a commoner to attend the feast of nobles."

"But your chieftain has told me to be in attendance and insisted I bring someone of my choice. I would welcome your company."

"Because you have found no one else so entirely welcoming and charming as myself?" she jested, knowing how poorly she had treated the man since he had arrived. "'Tis sorry I am that I can't attend as a guest, but the earl has ordered all who are able to assist with the feast this night. Nearly all the lords and ladies have arrived, and the hall is sure to be filled to the limits with nobility. I suppose every extra hand is needed, though I am uncertain how much help I will be when I have never carried a tray of food anywhere but within the kitchen."

"You're sure to do fine, Alainn. You're graceful and most capable in anything you do," Rory offered.

"How are your mother and your grandfather, Rory?"

"They are doing as well as can be expected. They are planning a druid burial ritual, which has my mother and father at odds. My mother wants Riley and me to attend, though my father is much opposed to the notion."

"Aye, I suppose he believes you'll be sacrificing virgins or dancing about naked worshipping trees."

Killian opened his eyes as the physician finished his chore, saying, "You'll need to move slowly and cautious for a while."

"I have another bout before the feast this evening."

"You can't seriously be thinking of fighting in another challenge!" Alainn scolded. "You've lost a good deal of blood, and you are surely weakened. 'Tis a jolt to one's constitution to have a wound such as that inflicted on a body!"

"Nonetheless, I am scheduled to partake."

"That will be three challenges this day! That is not safe, and you know it well, Killian O'Brien!"

Her eyes flashed as she pulled the dagger from her apron and handed it to him. He did not take it or understand her meaning.

"And what is it you are indicating?"

"If you are trying to see to it you go to your grave instead of the altar, you might just as well end it now, for it will save us the trouble of cleaning up after you twice!" She pointed to the blood that lay upon the table and floor.

"I'll take that under consideration," he said dryly. He attempted to put weight upon his leg and sucked in air deeply as pain seared through his thigh. Alainn went to her cupboard and pulled out a bottle of clear liquid. She filled a cup and handed it to him.

"Drink it," she ordered.

"And what is it, some type of poison?"

"There are none fast enough or painful enough to my way of thinkin'!" she saucily answered. "'Tis water from the spring in the glade. Drink it."

"When did you become so entirely bossy?"

"Nearly ten and eight years ago, I'd wager." Riley jested as he came in through the door. She tossed a rag at him. He caught it as he ducked, then aimed it back at her. He blocked her next shot. Killian cast him a sour glance. Riley ignored it entirely, picked up Alainn, and threw her over his shoulder. It was then that Mary MacDonald came to the door. She looked at Killian and his blood-stained trews, then Riley, who still had Alainn over his shoulder. She looked most displeased with both sights.

"Are you quite well, Killian?" Mary asked, going to his side. "Is it terribly painful?"

"No, 'tis only a scratch."

"A scratch that nearly left him emasculated," Alainn scoffed.

Mary's cheeks turned bright red. "You were able to heal him, then? You've mended what has been damaged?"

No, 'twas the physician who so capably has seen to the wound, so he should be well enough for your wedding. You might use your connection to him to urge him to withdraw from this day's event."

"You don't truly intend to partake in an event when you are so recently wounded?" the Scottish girl asked, unhidden horror and disbelief in her voice.

"I have fought more difficult matches with far worse wounds."

"Go then, Killian O'Brien," Alainn snapped. "But, when the pith axe slices off your head, make certain someone brings it to the physician to be examined, for I think he's sure to find it entirely empty!" Upon seeing how pale Mary's face had grown, she felt chagrined. "Are you still interested in going to the herb garden?" She looked at the young woman and attempted a smile.

"Aye, it would be much to my liking!"

As the girls headed toward the doorway, only the Scot called out a farewell to the men left behind.

Chapter eighteen

As the two women sat in the garden, Alainn couldn't help noticing how Mary did not seem like the noble women she'd known before. She sat upon the soil as Alainn did, though she'd been offered her a blanket to sit upon. She didn't mind getting her hands dirty and followed Alainn's lead as she weeded out unwanted plants, and pruned and trimmed others.

As the young woman reached to pluck one of the plants, however, Alainn swiftly knocked her hand away, crying harshly, "Don't touch it!"

"I'm dreadfully sorry, Alainn!" Mary said, turning red in the face. "I'm so clumsy. I'm ruining your beautiful garden, aren't I?"

Alainn held a hand to her chest for her heart was thumping wildly. "I could care a whit whether you pull a plant, but 'tis evening nightshade! It's a most powerful and deadly plant. At best 'tis known to cause hallucinations and madness; at worst, a slow and hideously painful death. I am not accustomed to having others in the garden, so I did not take the necessary precautions. I am disbelieving of how careless I was. My mind is muddled this day."

"But, Alainn, I saw you touch it. And you are well and unaffected."

Pushing hair away from her face, she explained, "'Tis only that I have handled tiny wee bits of it since I was a child and have become immune to the poison. It has no affect on me. Although," she smiled, "many might say it would explain much, for I have been accused of madness more than a time or two throughout my life."

"So everyone who touches it in small quantities will build up a resistance to the poison?"

"No, that is not always the case, sometimes, if a person takes a tiny amount orally, it can drive them quite mad as well, and change their personalities entirely."

"Then why would anyone knowingly risk it?"

"Some believe it will allow them eternal life, that somehow it will poison the aging parts of their body and allow the youthful to be retained. Quite a lot of malarkey, I'd say."

"But why would you grow such a horrible plant, if it is so dangerous?"

"The wall around the garden is high, and most know a healer's garden holds many dangers." She shrugged. "'Tis a heal-all and can be most effective in healing wounds if the healer knows what they are doing. Few people are immune to it, though, and nearly everyone reacts badly to it. Killian has built up some immunity to it himself, for his many battle scars have been managed with the plant."

"You seem to know Killian well, Alainn, and the chieftain's sons. Do you know…is Killian always so distant? He has not been unkind to me, but I feel he has much on his mind and is not so very easy to become acquainted with. He is unquestionably handsome. His eyes are so intense, so vividly green. Would that I knew how to become closer to him. In truth, I am uncertain if he will be a good match for me. Riley speaks to me often, but he seems displeased with Iona. I have never opposed arranged marriages. I have never dreamed of marrying for love, as many girls do. Of course, I hope that one day my husband and I will find love, but I am not so certain that Killian and I will ever come to that."

The girl sighed and brushed bits of soil from her skirts.

"Do you ride horses?" Alainn asked impulsively.

"Aye, we have horses at home. I much enjoy riding."

"Then let's go find some horses and be off for a lengthy ride."

"Unattended? Without telling anyone of our intentions?"

"Aye well, the farrier, my father, will know where we are off to. Unless, you need to seek out permission."

Mary looked unsure for a moment, then her face set determinedly. "No, it shouldn't be a concern." She jumped to her feet and clapped her hands. "Then, we shall have a glorious afternoon riding the hills!"

Strangely enough, Alainn believed they would.

***

The entire time the farrier was saddling the black mare, chatting pleasantly with Mary, Alainn's mind dwelt upon the evening nightshade.

"Do you want a saddle this day, girl?" the farrier asked, interrupting her thoughts.

"No, only the bridle; that will be sufficient. The earl has informed you of our arrangement, then? I will not be accused of stealing his horses this day?"

"He's spoken to me."

Mary MacDonald did not ride sidesaddle, as was often the custom with ladies, but she was surprised that Alainn lacked a saddle entirely.

"'Tis not uncommon for the Irish not to use saddles," Alainn explained. "But for me, the reasoning is I like to feel the horse beneath me. I can sense when the animal tenses. I am more aware of how the horse will handle. So, Scottish girls are allowed to ride straddlin' the horse? 'Tis not considered improper?"

"I have many older brothers so 'tis the way I learned. I have always ridden this way. I dinna ken why people think it improper for a woman to ride this way."

"'Tis men who don't like it. I am told they believe it might cause a woman's maidenhead to rupture, leaving her husband on their wedding night uncertain if she is virtuous. 'Tis a common excuse women give their husbands if they have been with another man. Or so I'm told."

Mary's face turned deep red.

"Would it be less painful, do you suppose, than the marriage-bed ordeal?"

"Ordeal? You think of your upcoming wedding night as an ordeal?"

"Aye, 'tis how my mother spoke of it. She says the first time is excruciating and every time after is repulsive, something to be tolerated because it is a husband's right. She says it is most offensive and that I should lie still like a proper lady, to not make a movement or a sound. That I should wait until my husband finishes with the unpleasantness and never allow him to think that I like it, for he will either think I am improper or that I want him to violate me more often. One of my handmaidens, Liza, did not share the same opinion as my mother. But she was not such a proper woman, for she shared the beds of many men. She seemed quite eager to do so."

Alainn wondered how she got herself into these situations. She was discussing physical pleasure with the woman who was to be Killian's wife.

"I suppose it depends entirely on the experience, whether a woman will ever find pleasure in the coupling," she said. "I also believe it is much dependant on how the woman feels toward the man, and how the man treats the woman. I do not think it wrong to reveal your pleasure, if you feel it. I believe that is what was intended for a man and a woman."

"Have you been with a man, Alainn?" Mary asked. Alainn tensed and her horse snorted softly. "Forgive me if I am seem forward, but I suppose knowing you are to be wed tomorrow, I am wondering if you are as nervous about your wedding night as I am."

"I try not to think about it, for I barely know the man. I have seen him only a handful of times. And though I am not certain you and I know one another well enough to discuss this subject, I will tell you your mother is much mistaken. Physical love can be as beautiful and precious as anything a woman can ever know."

"So, it isn't painful then?"

"Perhaps it would be best if you talk to someone else regarding this subject."

"Who would I speak to? Brigid is virginal and shy, and Iona is bitter. My aunt would surely have a fit of the vapors, and I have no sister. Did your mother speak to you of such matters, Alainn?"

She was about to say that her mother had died when she was just an infant, when there was movement in the thicket. She slowed her horse and came to a stop as Mara stepped out from behind a tree. Seeing Mary, she did not remove her hood.

"You risk being seen so close to the castle?" Alainn asked in a quiet voice.

"What do I have to lose, Alainn, other than my life, which has not turned out quite the way I imagined when I was a girl your age. It has been a goodly time since I last saw you."

"I have been away for a time," Alainn answered tersely.

"You are displeased about something?"

Alainn dismounted and walked up close to the witch. Mary looked curious, but stayed upon her horse at a safe distance.

"I would be hard-pressed to find something I am pleased about at the moment," Alainn whispered to her mother.

"Have you been to the dungeon? Have you located the crest?"

"I attempted it once, but sensed a dark presence within. I intend to go once again once the tournament and celebrations are complete. The dungeon would be a most undesirable place this week for it is surely filled with riff-raff."

Alainn turned and said in a loud voice, "Mary, this is Mara, an acquaintance of mine. Mara, this is Mary MacDonald, Killian O'Brien's betrothed."

The older woman nodded respectfully to the noble woman.

"*So this is what has you so disturbed?*" she asked Alainn with her mind. "*The father of your child intends to marry another. And is that the reason why you wait till week's end to go to the dungeon? You want to see him wed before you learn your true identity? You may be most rueful if you allow that to happen.*"

"*It might be simpler if you would just tell me who my father is instead of being so elusive about it.*"

"*I could tell you, but there would be no proof, and then the curse will never be ended. It is up to you, Alainn. But do not wait too long, for your powers grow, and they may bring about more unrest. Perhaps knowing who your father is will be of no consequence. If you allow your man to be taken away, you will never experience true happiness. I will attest to that most assuredly.*"

The horses were moving restlessly, and Alainn looked up toward the sky. The day was growing late, and she must get Mary back to the castle.

"Have you seen Morag's spirit? Has she come to you?"

"*No, not since the day of her wake. I have not even sensed her around me.*"

"*Perhaps she has gone on then. I thought maybe she would stay awhile to assist you. There is a large black man with unusual patterns painted on his face and arms. He is often found just outside the castle gates, though I met him in the thicket outside the village one evening. He recognized that I was a witch. He knows much of magic. You must speak to him about dissolving the curse. He may know how to assist us. But beware, his powers are great. Make certain he can be trusted before you discuss our dilemma.*"

Alainn nodded to Mara, and set off at a gallop back to the castle, Mary keeping pace behind her.

Chapter nineteen

"But, Siobhan, why did you not tell me she was so like, Shylie?"

"I tried, Father. Years ago, I told you of a girl who reminded me very much of my sister, that the first time I saw her, I wept for days."

"But, you did not say she was nearly her double. You should have pressed me on the subject. I would have come to see her for myself if I'd known how greatly she resembled your sister."

"My husband made me believe it was wild imaginings on my part, and no one else at Castle O'Brien had ever met Shylie."

"Your husband does not give you the respect you deserve, daughter. If not for my grandsons, I would tell you to leave the man and return to your home."

"You would have me leave my husband?" She considered it for a moment but shook her head. "Father, I could never desert my sons. No, my home is here now."

The elderly man patted her arm consolingly.

"But, tell me of this girl, Siobhan. What do you know of her? Could she be our kin?"

"I have wondered that very thing for years, Father. I have tried to reason how it could be possible, for, in all the years she has been in my life, I have seen resemblances to Rory as well and Teague; sometimes I think I see myself as a young girl. But, I cannot come up with a reasonable explanation for the likenesses."

"I know this will be a painful subject, my daughter, but could she be your child? By some cruel treachery could one of your lost children have lived and been raised by others?"

"There is no possibility of that, Father. I only bore one daughter and she lived but a matter of hours. I saw her laid in the ground. I met Alainn shortly thereafter, but she was already past three years of age."

"Then what of her parents? Might they be kin to us?"

"I think not, the families of the old farrier and his wife have been servants to my husband's family for nearly a century. They have no druid connection that I know of."

The old man's brow grew increasingly furrowed.

"Does she possess any abilities, mental or physical? Does she speak the language? Does she have the voice? Do you think she knows of our ways?"

"Father, so many questions! I will tell you what I know. She is a healer and a seer, and I suspect she has control of the weather."

"By the gods, Siobhan, perhaps she is the one of legend!"

"I am uncertain, Father. I don't know what other abilities she might have. If she doesn't know of our connection to those abilities she might keep them guarded so as not to draw suspicion to her powers. I have never spoken the language to her, and though I have listened to her sing a time or two in her garden, 'twas done softly, so it was difficult to tell. And though Rory has a fine singing voice, Riley is tone deaf. Perhaps, as time passes, the druid ways are being lost."

The elderly man grew sad and nodded. "Aye, as the druid blood grows more dilute, the ways are being lost. And with men such as your husband and many others so opposed to passing the teachings onto their children, one day we will be no more, I fear."

"But there are qualities passed on through the blood, memories that are inborn."

"Aye, how else might we explain the girl knowing the name your sister always called your mother? She said, 'Wee Mama.' She must be ours somehow! Your eldest brothers were never near this part of the country so they could not have fathered a child, but what of Teige? He was here for those months many years ago."

"Aye, he was here." The woman grew saddened at thoughts of her younger brother.

Her father spoke on, "I know he loved a woman, that he spoke of wanting to marry her, but he told me she died. He wanted me to bring my army and start a feud with your husband's father. That is what our quarrel was about all those years ago. What do you know of this woman, Siobhan?"

His daughter had risen and was watching the jousting in the field below. Rory was galloping toward his opponent. She turned her back and could not watch. The games always unnerved her. Her eyes met her father's. His stern expression induced her to declare the truth.

"She did not die, Father. Teige was told that falsehood, I found out later. My husband's father forced them to be kept apart then told Teige she was dead. He left without farewell to me, I think, perceiving me as the enemy as well, for I was helpless to assist him."

The man became agitated; his face filled with hope. "Could he have fathered a child then? Was there a child, a daughter? You must tell me."

"Aye, a child was born, but not a girl-child, Father, a son. And I could never be certain it was Teige's child, for Hugh's father told us the woman had been with many men."

"Where is the son? You must take me to him so I can decide for myself."

"He has died, Father. He was never able-bodied or sound of mind. I tried to view him from a distance but could never see a likeness to Teige or any of our kin. He died some weeks ago. Although I came to despise his mother because of her hellish curse, I felt grieved that she and her son were made to live in such dismal conditions. On the possibility that he could be Teige's boy, I often had a servant leave food and provisions for them. But, I feel within me he was not Teige's child.

"I thought perhaps twins were born, that the farrier and his wife took the healthy child, but why would the woman send off a healthy twin and keep the boy who had so many difficulties? None of it made sense to me, and I know the farrier's wife was with child. She was of an unusually advanced age to carry a child, so everyone in the county knew of her condition. I can make no sense of any of it, for Alainn was surely born to the farrier and his wife, yet I feel such a connection to her, even beyond the physical resemblance to our family. I feel drawn to her."

The elderly man sat down upon the settee in his daughter's chambers. "Have you used your seeing ability to think on it, daughter?"

"Aye, I have, but I am not so well skilled in that area, Father. Each of your children was given a druid gift. I have the voice and the musical abilities. Shylie had the gift of second sight. My older brothers, unusual physical strength. But 'twas Teige who had some of each. And you are gifted in many areas, Father. Perhaps you might try to see what you sense from her.

"And there is more, Father. She possesses an amulet, one of ours. I am certain. But the crest has been removed. Until it is found, we cannot be entirely certain of her identity. Did you sense anything when you were near her?"

"Aye well, I was much occupied with my own concerns for your mother, but indeed, I did feel a strong bond to her. If she has the amulet, it must surely be Teige's. The only others were buried with your siblings and our kin. We must learn more about her. You must arrange for her to be with us for a time. I must see the amulet. Perhaps on the morrow. Would you be opposed to her attending your mother's burial ritual?"

The woman considered it and smiled sadly. "No, Father, I would be greatly pleased to have her with us, and because she was the last to touch mother, she should be there to bid her a final farewell. I will speak with her at once. But it is Killian who has the amulet at the moment."

"Why would he have it?"

"She charmed it as well with a protection spell and gave it to him. But, if she is a daughter to the woman who I think is her mother, then I believe she may be more powerful than we know."

The grey-haired man stamped his foot with impatience.

"Daughter, tell me what you know, the whole of it!"

"I believe she may be the daughter to Mara, the woman Teige loved, the woman who cursed my husband's line."

"Was she druid?"

"No! But she is witch. Her mother was a tweenling, half fairy, half human. If Alainn is the product of druid and witch, of a line of fairies, her powers are sure to be great."

The man tapped his fingers against his chin and considered this for a long while.

"And she is without her amulet to protect her and calm her powers. We must deal with learning her identity at once."

Lady Siobhan's eyes widened and she gasped, "Oh dear, Father! I have been so consumed with losing Mother that I nearly forgot what day this is. Alainn is to be wed tomorrow, and I promised her I would assist her in this matter and see to it she is allowed to wed the man she truly loves."

"She will wed no one until we discover if she is connected to our kin!" the man's voice boomed. "Who is this man she is to be married to?"

"My husband has selected a local farmer, but Alainn does not care for him."

"And it is your husband's nephew she loves? It must be or she would never have given the amulet to him." The man smiled broadly. "I would be proud to have a kin of ours wed the lad. He has always been a strong young man with honor and conviction. We must search for the crest to ensure they may be married."

"Aye and he is promised to the Scottish girl, a match my husband has also arranged, though Killian is much opposed to the arrangement."

"Then I will see what might be done to alter the plans of Killian's betrothal. You speak with the young girl, and I will seek your husband. He will not care for any interference on my part, but I think I will be capable of making him see reason."

"Pray that you will, Father, and I will do what I can to make certain Alainn does not wed the farmer. We have little time. I must be off, Father. May your audience with my husband be fortuitous."

Chapter Twenty

Alainn stood outside Hugh O'Brien's bedchamber waiting most impatiently. The guard at the door insisted the chieftain was not willing to see anyone at that time, but she was not planning to be sent away so easily; they had matters to discuss. She stood with arms crossed, glaring at the guard who refused to tell the chieftain she was waiting. When she glanced down the long arched corridor and noticed Killian heading toward his own chambers, she quickly turned her back to him to hide her face, for he would surely be displeased.

The door flung open before her and Breena McTeer came out, straightening her crumpled clothing and carrying a chamber pot. She glowered, red-faced, at Alainn and hurried away. Before the guard could prevent it, Alainn pushed her way inside the door and strode toward the partially-clad chieftain.

"Get her out!" he hollered to the guard was already in the process of trying to grab her struggling body, when Killian barged inside.

"Uncle!" he cried.

"What the hell is this!" roared the chieftain. "If either of you is here to talk to me about the marriage on the morrow you'll not persuade me to cancel it. It will happen! There have been far too many people seeking me today regarding this topic. There seems to be as much interest in it as there was when the English King Henry took his bride!"

"Aye well, maybe if someone had convinced him not to wed her," Alainn goaded him, "she'd not be locked in the Tower of London awaiting execution." The chieftain signaled for the guard to go back to his station outside the door.

"I doubt the farmer will have you killed, Maiden McCreary."

Killian stood in the middle of the room, a cantankerous look on his face. Alainn ignored him completely.

"Where are the potions you consume?" she asked the O'Brien.

"What potions? What are you referring to?"

"You know very well what potions I speak of. The one Morag prepared for you and the one you procured from the alchemist in Galway."

When he did not seem inclined to respond, Alainn closed her eyes, envisioned the vials, and walked to the small basket hidden beneath a bedside table.

"You have no right going through my possessions! You could be thrown in the dungeon for forcing yourself in here and attempting to search through my personal belongings. Have you gone mad? Or are you thinking of poisoning me?" he added nastily.

"I would like nothing better than to see you dead," she spat, "but, no, that is not what I am hoping for this day. I am trying to prevent you from being poisoned."

"And are you her protector, Killian? Have you come keep me from stopping her actions?"

"No!" they both shouted.

"We are not here together," Alainn stated emphatically.

"Aye well. I see what you're doing, woman," he said as she inspected the bottles in his basket. "What are you up to, Killian?"

"Just making certain you keep your distance from Alainn. I'll not see her harmed."

Alainn glanced at Killian briefly, but then went back to what she was doing. As she pulled a vial from the basket, she shook her hand as though she'd been burned and cursed loudly.

"'Tis little wonder you have been acting altogether asinine in recent months. I cannot believe you are not entirely mad after taking this combination of herbal potions. You might have killed yourself. Have you been having any hallucinations?" She continued to shake her burning hand and blew on it as she queried. "I would estimate you have had very little sleep lately either?"

"Not a great deal," he mumbled, frowning.

"Well, you must stop taking both of these potions immediately," she said, holding them out for the chieftain to see, "or you shall soon be dead or irrefutably driven to madness. There is no potion available that will allow you to retain the characteristics of youth." She looked at him disdainfully. "Your alchemist in Galway has misled you. And if it were only you who would suffer, I would tell you to take the entire lot of them, but sure your family would be affected as well."

She placed the vials in the pocket of her frock when the O'Brien growled like a wounded animal and ran toward her. Killian grabbed the charging man as the guard stepped through the door, weapon drawn. Alainn screamed, retrieved the vials and shoved them in the chieftain's hands. He scurried to the other side of the chamber, holding tight to the two vials.

"These are my potions, mine, do you hear me!" he hollered wildly in a high-pitched voice. "You have no business touching them! I will consume them whenever I desire, in whatever combination or amounts I desire, young healer. And you cannot prevent it!"

Alainn stepped backward. Killian took her arm.

"Aye, Alainn, if he wants to end his life, by all means allow him to do so. This is not the man I once knew to be my uncle."

"You wish me dead!" the man snarled. "'Tis treasonous to freely admit such thoughts." The guard still stood with his weapon drawn, looking uneasily at his chieftain.

"If you are dead, you can do no harm to Alainn or anyone else," Killian said, his jaw tensing as he stood protectively in front of the young woman. "And since you refuse to accept her advice or listen to her wisdom, then you choose madness and the possibility of harming all those around you."

The chieftain's eyes appeared glassy. He placed the vials within his tunic and went to stare out the window as if forgetting they were in the chamber.

Killian gently guided Alainn toward the door.

"Maiden McCreary," the O'Brien said in a calmer voice, still looking out across his lands, "you've truly not come to see how you might get out of your intended wedding?"

"What I want is clearly irrelevant, so I will not defy you." She swept past Killian and out the door.

"You are wise to allow her to be wed, Killian," the O'Brien continued. "Though you appear to care much for her, in truth, allowing her to marry one of her own kind is a good choice."

"I don't care to take advice from you, Uncle. Not since I've heard you are near madness. Not since I learned you dishonored the only woman I have ever loved. You will pay for what you attempted to do to Alainn."

"Forget about that unpleasantness, Killian. It is long since passed. I warn you," he said, turning to face him, "do not interfere with the nuptials tomorrow. If you truly care for her you will not saddle her with the O'Brien curse. 'Tis a sad thing to see babes torn away from the woman you love." He turned back to the window. "Spend more time with the MacDonald woman and forget all things connected with the farrier's daughter."

Killian turned and hastily left the room.

Chapter twenty-one

Using her mortar and pestle, Alainn ground herbs and added them to the mixture in the cauldron. She had found yet another sprig of thyme upon her work table this day. Was Morag truly attempting to leave signs of her presence? But why then did she not simply come to her as she had done before? How Alainn longed to speak to the old woman who had been a mother to her most of her life. She would give much to tell Morag of her many woes. Attempts to summon the old healer's spirit had met with no results. Though she was certain she detected the strong scent of thyme that had accompanied her previous visitations, the spirit would not materialize.

Alainn's mind returned to her worries. She knew she could not marry the farmer, but was still uncertain how she could prevent the wedding. She had not talked to Lady Siobhan, but felt certain her thoughts would now only be filled with the loss of her mother. Perhaps she could go to the glade. No one would search for her there. But surely, it would only prolong the nuptials and enrage the chieftain if she jilted the man, especially now she knew how deranged the chieftain had become. He had always been a dangerous man, but to toss madness into the mix was an entirely different predicament.

She could feel the physician's eyes on her as he stood across the room watching her. She knew he was curious as to what potion she was mixing, but he would not ask her. Her respect for the man was growing; he had proved more adept in his capabilities than she would have believed. She turned as the door opened and Riley came in. He embraced her with an open affection he rarely displayed, and she hesitantly returned the embrace.

"I have spoken to my father regarding your wedding, Alainn. He will not be persuaded to cancel the arrangements. I am apologetic to you for I know it is not what you desire."

His concern moved her and she touched a dark curl that had fallen over his eye.

"I am thankful that you spoke to him of it, Riley. It was kind of you, and more than I would have expected."

"You know I would see you both happy."

"Perhaps happiness was never something we should have hoped for," she said in a forlorn tone.

Alainn could hear the physician's thoughts intruding on her mind. He was now undoubtedly confused. He had been certain it was the nephew whom the healer was involved with, but she appeared unusually close to both the earl's sons. *Could she be involved with all three? But, who had fathered her child? She did not seem to be the sordid type, but she was unwed and with child and displayed an uncommon affection for the noble class.*

Alainn cast a suspicious look toward the man as he stared at Riley.

Riley had moved away from Alainn when Pierce MacArthur threw open the door and rushed inside.

"Killian is to duel!"

"Whom is he dueling?" asked Riley with obvious concern.

"Not Liam O'Hara!" Alainn gasped.

"No, 'tis the steward's son, Henry McGilvary!"

"He is no match for Killian. He'd never choose to duel Henry knowing he is much superior in skill and weaponry." Alainn added more to herself than the others.

"Aye, he tried to decline, but the man pushed him and challenged him publicly. He finally managed to force Killian to agree to it by telling him what happened in the forest that day, Alainn!"

"He knows what they attempted?"

"Aye, and he's gravely angered."

Riley and Pierce quickly left the chamber, Alainn close behind, while the physician stayed behind, shaking his head. But as she hurried down the corridors toward the courtyard where a noisy crowd had gathered, a vision so filled her mind that Alainn was left frozen in place.

Henry and Killian were already involved in swordplay, but it was clearly one-sided. The onlookers watched, deeply intrigued as Killian toyed with the man. Henry swung his sword in a wide arc. Killian stepped deftly aside under the blade, dropped the tip of his sword and smashed the hilt into Henry's jaw. The young man's head flew back as he staggered. He shook his head to clear it and threw out his sword in front of him in a weak defense. Killian tapped the sword aside and swiped at his exposed forearm, drawing a deep line of blood. Henry leapt back as Killian smiled. The man was clearly out-skilled, and he well knew it.

Killian advanced, his sword cutting the air in small arcs getting close enough for Henry to feel wind against his cheek as it passed, backing up, further and further, into a dry stone wall, until he was clearly trapped with nowhere to move. Then, Killian's sword lifted high overhead and cleaved through the air, striking the other man's blade with a resounding metal clang. The force of the hit wrenched the sword from Henry's grasp and it was flung from his hand, clattering onto the cobblestones.

"You are fortunate that was not your head," Killian said shortly, wiping his bloodied blade on the edge of his tunic. He desired to end this man's life for his part in attacking Alainn. But in his gut, he felt certain the man was only following his brother's unscrupulous lead as had so often proved to be true. With Henry's lack of skill and experience, killing him would hardly be more reasonable than killing an unarmed man. But, he was faced with the need to defend Alainn. It was an unenviable dilemma.

"Did you attempt something untoward against the healer, Alainn McCreary?"

The man looked up at Killian, and his voice shook as he replied, "Well…aye …well… no… not actually… I was there, 'tis true, but I was simply to keep the captain's son from aiding her. Aye, that was to be my part in it."

"And if you had managed to keep him from assisting, Alainn. Then what?"

The man was hesitant to answer, but Killian drew nearer and placed the point of his sword against the man's soft throat.

"Well, my brother was to…to have his way with her." He was so afraid he could barely spit it out.

"And you would have allowed a young woman to be violated by your deplorable brother? You would have simply watched while he terrorized her?" Killian's soft voice was more menacing than any shouting would have been.

"Aye, well he is not a man to cross, Milord." Henry's eyes filled with dread as he spoke of his younger brother. He glanced around nervously. "And in truth, Milord, I would have little choice, for though my brother would have done so most willingly without inducement. It was by order of the chieftain that we were to see harm brought to the healer in as vicious a manner we could see fit."

Killian stepped back, stunned at this revelation.

"Killian!" Alain cried, pushing through the crowd. She looked toward the south wall where she spied the other McGilvary brother, Richard, just as in her vision. He was positioned atop the wall with his arrow pointed toward Killian.

"The south wall, Killian!" she screamed, trying to make herself heard over the din of the crowded courtyard. He turned and saw the arrow as it was released. He threw himself out of the way, as the courtyard erupted in chaos, and jumped toward the stone wall. In so doing, he lost his footing and toppled against the wall.

"Behind you!" cried Riley, and Killian turned to see Henry, his retrieved sword in hand, charging towards him with sword held high above his head, wailing as if charging into battle.

"You foolish bastard," hissed Killian. He righted himself and stood there as Henry closed the distance. He held his sword low at his side, bent his knees, turned his blade, and slashed it up forcefully at an angle that met with his opponent's neck, beheading him in one fell swoop.

A second arrow, which would have hit its mark without question, strangely came to a halt, as if it colliding with an invisible barrier only inches from Killian, and simply dropped to the ground. Alainn looked toward the despicable younger brother and a billowing gale suddenly gathered around him, forcefully hurling him to the ground below.

Killian turned to Alainn and questioned her with his eyes.

"'Twas not me." She pulled back the collar of his tunic as if to determine whether he may need healing and noticed the amulet around his neck was glowing. "'Twas the charmed amulet that prevented the arrow from striking you," she offered in a quivering voice. He took her arm for her steps were unsteady.

The group of onlookers had grown into a huge, rowdy crowd that gossiped and gestured as the guards walked toward the body. Alainn clung to Killian, relief clearly evident in her blue eyes, though he noticed how she continued to tremble. Riley joined them after he had gone to see the condition of the younger McGilvary.

"He's alive, but injured. The guards have carried him to the physician, but should he live, he'll be taken to the dungeon as soon as he is able."

The chieftain was hurrying toward them across the square, his face filled with consternation.

"You are well, Killian? No harm has befallen you?"

"I am unharmed."

The earl glanced at the gruesome sight upon the ground. The guards had come to remove Henry's body and the crowd was abuzz with the happenings.

"What prompted the duel?" he demanded.

"He openly challenged me to a duel. 'Tis law a public challenge must be accepted."

"Aye, you had no choice in accepting the challenge. But, clearly you had an underlying motivation to finish the task so brutally."

"I was defending Alainn's honor and seeing to it he paid for the dishonorable deed he attempted with her. And if the brother lives, he too will meet with the same fate, as will anyone who has wronged her!" He glared at his uncle as he spoke, still holding tight to Alainn's hand. She pulled away angrily.

"I do not require you to defend me, my honor, or my life, Killian O'Brien! You are not my keeper, and you could end up dead yourself. I'm certain your intended will be less than pleased to know you dueled publicly only days before your wedding to defend the honor of a peasant. I do not ask for this nor do I appreciate it!"

"I doubt your farmer will duel in your name!"

The fury in his emerald eyes was unmistakable. She returned the glare with equal displeasure.

"Then, perhaps he is the sensible man!"

"Even without your blessing, I intend to defend the wrongdoings toward you, for until the morrow you are still a maiden without a man to protect you. There is another debt yet to settle." He glanced at his uncle, his eyes blazing. "Therefore, Uncle, I challenge you to a duel!"

"Don't be ludicrous, Killian," his uncle scoffed. "I am a quarter century your senior and, though I may have been a match to you at one time, 'tis no longer the truth and you well know it."

"Then you choose the details, the weapon, the location, the time, the whole of it!"

"Killian, stop this! This is not necessary or reasonable!" Alainn demanded.

He ignored her entirely and, when Riley and Rory, who had just arrived in the courtyard, also attempted to dissuade him, he only charged on with determination.

"I am challenging you publicly, Uncle!" he said in a voice loud enough for the entire crowd to hear.

The older man's face grew serious, and he spoke once more. "Do not force this, Killian. Do not allow us to come to blows over a peasant girl who by this time tomorrow will be wed to another."

"Choose the weapon," he seethed, "or I will state that part of it as well."

"Have it your way then, nephew!" the older man shouted. "We shall duel, but in fairness to a man of advancing age, you will battle two others of my choice before you do battle with me." Killian nodded without flinching. "I choose the weapons, and the bouts will be consecutive, on the last day of the challenges, the day before you are to wed!"

"I will meet your terms, Uncle."

"Killian," pleaded Alainn, "they are too greatly slanted in his favor."

There was a hush over the crowd, and Alainn felt her anger and fear begin to soar. She threw a disgusted look at both men and pushed through the onlookers again. Thunder rumbled in the distance, and she tried to calm her power and her trepidation.

When Alainn entered her chamber, the physician was standing before the unconscious McGilvary and attending to his head wound. Alainn hoped she would see his aura waning, indicating he would soon die, but it remained unchanged, as black and murky as it always had been. When the physician crossed the chamber to seek more supplies, the injured man's eyelids snapped open, and he looked directly at her.

"Young witch! I told you we would meet someday soon!" he whispered in a low, ominous voice that frightened her to the core. "You cannot run from me, nor hide, for always I will locate dark souls willing to assist me. And one day I shall have your powers and take them for my own."

She jumped back as his lips curled in a wicked smile.

"Did you hear that?" Alainn asked the physician who was now beside his patient. Richard's eyes were once more closed.

"You did not hear this man speak?"

He regarded Alainn as though she had lost her mind. He pulled back the man's dark hair to reveal a deep wound and a large swelling on his head.

"He is surely unconscious and, with an injury such as this to his head, it is quite possible he may never be capable of speech again. In truth, he may never regain consciousness."

"One can only hope," Alainn whispered.

He noticed how she trembled.

"How fares the chieftain's nephew?" He had barely uttered the words when the man in question bound into the chamber wearing a most displeased look. He ignored the physician, cast a caustic glare at his patient, and grasped Alainn's shoulders, shaking her.

"Get your hands off of me, Killian O'Brien," she demanded, "or I swear, I will kill you before your uncle has a turn at it." He ignored her entirely.

"The McGilvarys tried to rape you, and you didn't think to mention it to me!"

"It is not up to you to defend me. I have told you that surely a hundred times, Killian O'Brien. You will end up dead to honor a woman who after tomorrow can never be anything more to you. The cost is too great! You must go to your uncle and tell him you have reconsidered. Tell him you were temporarily suffering from a bout of madness. I think he will accept that for, even in his troubled state, I believe he does not want to battle you, Killian."

"I suppose I should be grateful to McGilvary. If he hadn't challenged me publicly, I would not have discovered my uncle ordered them to harm you or thought to publicly challenge my uncle. I should have known he could not simply turn from a challenge and suffer dishonor."

"If you wanted a pissing contest with your uncle you didn't need to involve weapons, Killian. They are unbeatable odds. Three bouts back to back. He will surely choose heavy weapons to tire you!"

"Surely."

"And if you lie dead at the end of it all, do you suppose Mary will be pleased?"

"This has naught to do with Mary! Alainn, you show me great disrespect in questioning me on this. It was because of me that my uncle tried to harm you. You may not approve of my methods, but I need you to understand. You must allow me to honor you, for it is because of me that he nearly violated you!"

"Do you think I will be honored to know I caused the death of the only man I shall ever love?" He held tight to her arms though she tried to pull from his grasp.

"Tell me you respect this decision, Alainn, for it is of great significance to me that you understand."

"I will not disrespect you, and I understand how important honor is to you, but, Killian, the amulet will not prevent your death should it come to that!" She burst into tears and fled the room.

The physician stood by the table, as still as his patient. Killian growled in pain and left the room, but he did not follow Alainn, for he could offer her no comfort or consolation.

Chapter twenty-two

Standing in the kitchen next to Cook, donned in clothing provided by the chieftain, Alainn pulled displeasingly at the low neckline that left half of her breasts exposed. Cook glanced at her with a sympathetic expression.

"Sorry I am to hear of the challenge and that you must wear that absurdly revealing garment."

Alainn only shook her head, trying to keep out thoughts of Killian and the challenge he had forced.

"There's not to be done about either. All the serving women, the young women at any rate, are to wear these garments. I suppose the chieftain is providing his guests with added entertainment."

"Aye, I heard that you sent Molly home when you saw the serving gowns. I very much appreciate that, Alainn. She is timid around men, and I think she would not be able to defend herself for we've always sheltered her so entirely. And sure my mind would only be in the hall with her instead of in the kitchen where it should be. I am not pleased that you will be there either."

"I am not so innocent as Molly, or as sweet, so I think I shall be capable of defending myself against any lewd advances."

When Breena McTeer came in to the kitchen to discuss a matter with Cook, Alainn caught the sneer she threw at her, yet again. Alainn inhaled deeply. She was in for a long night.

*　*　*

As the serving girls stood outside the hall, waiting for the kitchen servants to bring the food to them, Alainn glanced over at Breena and some of the other young women and heard her name being whispered. In truth, it was often Breena who lead the attack on her, they had never been close. She had never been certain why she was the target of such bitterness.

Because her mind was already filled with many quandaries and the lot of them seemed more drastic than an uncharitable serving girl, she ignored the group. But when Breena roughly pulled the tie from Alainn's hair as she walked by her, she decided she had had enough.

"Breena McTeer! I need a word with you straightaway."

The girl ignored Alainn and spoke to the others. "Surely the gifted healer does not speak to me, I am neither male nor of nobility, therefore I am hardly worthy of her time or company." The other girls smirked and tittered at the remark, but Alainn would not be swayed.

"So, 'tis because I have spent time with the young lords that you harbor such dislike toward me?"

"'Tis because you believe you are above the rest of us servants, Alainn McCreary. You think yourself the great healer and our tasks are surely beneath you. How belittled you must feel to serve food with the rest of us peasants."

Alainn straightened at the insults and felt her claws coming out.

"Aye well, sure the grass is green on the far off hill, Breena. You think my tasks as a healer are all grand and important?"

"I imagine they are better than hauling piss-laden chamber pots for the earl and his kin."

"Do not be so certain, Breena McTeer. Do you think healing only involves a mortar and pestle, that it is only the mixing of potions, the handling of elixirs? Well, you'd best think again," she snapped furiously, "for I have lanced festering carbuncles on aged men's arses. I have been covered in blood, soaked in urine and excrement, and drenched in emesis. I have attempted to patch up limbs that have been hacked through to the bone. I have held stillborn babies in my arms and helplessly watched women die in childbed. I have been forced to tell parents that their children will not live and wives that their husbands cannot be saved. So if you loathe me because you think my position is grander than yours, perhaps you might come try my tasks for a time!

"Now, you've had a deep dislike for me for as long as I can remember, and I have listened to your unkind remarks and your snide comments for as long as I will. If you loathe me because I have schooling and you do not, I will not apologize to you for that. It's sorry I am that everyone, male or female, peasant or noble cannot be schooled, for I have never been as grateful for anything as my learning, but what is it you would have had me do? Decline the offer to be schooled because I was the only female offered the privilege? And I know you disapprove of the fact I have spent a time with the earl's kin, but though you may find it difficult to comprehend, I think of them as my friends, for they have been better friends to me by far than any of you ever have!"

The girl's eyes had grown wider as Alainn spoke and, when the women all curtsied, she turned to see the reason why. Rory, Riley, Killian and their respective betrotheds stood staring, clearly having heard every word she'd just said. She felt her cheeks flame, but she did not speak. It was Mary MacDonald who smiled warmly at Alainn and Killian and spoke.

"I believe Alainn is waitin' for your answer, Breena."

The pretty young servant girl squirmed and appeared terribly uncomfortable, but she looked at Alainn and spoke.

"I had no notion your tasks were oft so unpleasant," she said softly, "and aye, I was jealous of you, not only about the schooling and your beauty, but because everything you do, you do well, better than any of us. Sure, it's envious we all are of you, Alainn. And I offer you my apologies for sure we have not treated you fairly."

A few of the others nodded and said their own words of apology.

"Perhaps I have acted unfriendly toward you as well," said Alainn, "though it was never my intention. Sure, sometimes being excluded from your circle made me prickly."

The kitchen servants appeared, carrying trays laden with food, and there was no more time for discussion. Alainn noticed how Killian's eyes followed her, and she felt a nervousness within her, knowing she would be attempting tasks she had never done before hundreds of nobles. Killian winked and smiled, then headed into the great hall with Mary on his arm.

***

The evening had gone much better than Alainn had thought it might. She'd not dropped a tray nor poured drink on anyone. She'd been forced to push away a few hands from her backside, but none that would not be dissuaded from the forwardness. She had only needed to venture near the chieftain and his kin a time of two. And each time, Lady Siobhan was exceedingly friendly to her. She'd even introduced her to some of the nobles and their wives, singing her praises, telling them what a gifted healer she was, listing the many potions she'd created to aid in beauty and cleanliness. Several of the ladies wanted to speak to her regarding this, and she found Breena looking at her jealously. But when she rolled her eyes at the girl, she received a smile.

Lady Siobhan's father showed an unusual interest in her throughout the evening, and she was startled to hear him request she attend his wife's burial ceremony the next day. She knew he was very appreciative of her attempt to save his wife, but she thought he was carrying the gratitude somewhat far. Though she said she was most honored but was to be wed the next day, he acted very unusual and told her he wanted a word with her later in the evening regarding that subject.

The only person who treated her with disdain and snobbishness was Rory and Riley's future mother-in-law. When she made a rude comment regarding Alainn, Lady Siobhan leaned over and whispered to Alainn, "'Tis a pity there's no potion or remedy for pomp and arrogance, for I think it would be in great demand this night." Alainn had smiled warmly at her and seen the chieftain's disapproval at the exchange.

Mary MacDonald talked to her several times in a manner typical of a friend, not a servant. Even Rory's intended, Brigid, had been unusually pleasant to Alainn. And though Iona, the older sister, had not been outwardly friendly, neither was she rude or snooty.

Alainn found herself feeling a deeper respect for the servants who had the task of serving food every day, for her feet ached. She was pleased, however, to hear and see some of the entertainment, for she adored the musicians and the vocalists. The jester and the actors were also clearly skilled at their crafts.

As the evening wore on, she noted that she had not seen Killian in some time. Mary remained sitting with her kin, and Rory and Brigid had danced a few times, but both Riley and Killian seemed to have disappeared. When she made a trip to the kitchen to fetch another tray of sweets, she found Riley in a most passionate embrace with one of the young servants. He had indeed had too much to drink. She remembered seeing Killian with a goblet in his hand most of the evening as well.

When she returned, Lady Siobhan caught her arm and asked if she might come to her chambers for a short discussion with her father. Many of the guests had already retired for the evening, and Alainn thought no one would miss her if she departed for the night.

As she walked down the quiet castle corridor, she heard voices around the bend in the archway and was startled to find Killian in a group of three young women. They were surely beguiled by the fact the hero had slain the villain this day. Two were servant girls. Killian had his arm around the dark-haired one, the daughter of the musician with whom Alainn had ridden to the castle, the night of her return. Another leaned against him unabashedly. Yet another had her hand on his chest and was at present touching Alainn's own amulet. His eyes appeared glazed, and she thought he looked entirely dangerous in his brooding state.

She threw him a nasty glance and continued walking past without comment.

"Was that a disapproving look, Alainn?" he slurred. "Why do you hold your tongue? You're not usually prone to keeping your opinions to yourself."

"What you do and with whom you do it is hardly my concern, Milord. But, perhaps you might think of your intended. Surely she would be displeased to find you cavorting about with other women when your wedding is only days away."

"But what I do is of no concern to you," he baited.

"And why would it be? I'm to be married myself on the morrow. I could care less if you diddle every woman from Kinsale to Larne and back again, or if your manhood rots and falls off from a sordid disease. 'Tis most fortunate I did not become infected with a contagion when I lay with you, Milord!"

It was not the tone or the comment that had the women fleeing his side and scurrying off down the corridor, but the furious eyes that stared at them as though she might strike them dead with their intensity. She sneered at him and kept walking. He came up quickly and pulled her to him roughly. She fought him but was no match for his strength, even in his inebriated condition. His hot breath trailed down her neck, and she wasn't certain she truly wanted him to stop, though she pushed at him as he spoke.

"You must create a potion for me, one that will take away the hunger I feel for you. Your face is etched on my eyes and is all I see when I close them at night. Your scent fills my nostrils, your voice my ears. I think it is not only my heart and my mind that is so bewitched by you, but my very soul. My blood hums with the need to have you, Alainn. Though you oppose me and disrespect me, keep things hidden from me that I have a right to know, still, every part of me burns for you. How am I to simply allow you to be wed to another?"

"Killian, unhand me, this instant!" she ordered.

"I see your body responds to me, even if you prefer to delude yourself into believing you no longer desire me."

"I do not desire you!" she snapped.

"So 'tis only the cool dampness of the castle corridors that has caused this condition?" he taunted as he caressed the hardened peaks of her breasts.

"Killian, let me go, you must let me go!" her voice lacked conviction, but she noticed he had loosened his grip on her. His eyes were filled with unhidden torment, two day's growth covered his jaw, and his hair was disheveled. He had a dangerous sensuality about him that Alainn could barely pull herself away from. He noticed, and she thought he derived a small amount of pleasure in knowing she yearned for him as well.

She stepped free of his hands and fled toward Lady Siobhan's chamber without looking back.

* * *

True to Lady Siobhan's word, the discussion with her father was short and soon she found herself back in the hall. Her mood was considerably lighter than when she'd entered the room.

As she made her way back down the corridor, she came upon Killian still standing outside the door of his bedchamber. She inhaled a deep breath and started to pass him. But as she approached him, she turned and looked into his tortured eyes, sensing a pull stronger than anything she'd ever experienced before. Surely the moon's pull on the tides could have been no more magnetic. Their eyes locked and she was in his arms, kissing him passionately, feeling him harden as their bodies met. The kiss was so ardent she was overcome with dizziness.

His hand went to the low bodice of her dress, the thumb slipping beneath the garment to caress her nipples. She moaned as she felt them peak. He held her up against the wall, capably lifting her skirts. He was barely able to stop himself from taking her there in the corridor, as he fumbled to open the door to his bedchamber. They were scarcely within when garments were removed in a haste they'd never known.

This meeting of their bodies was never tender and loving, but passionate and torrid and primal. He squeezed her buttocks with a possessiveness that would surely leave marks where his fingers had been, and she raked his back with her nails leaving a stinging trail. She bit his lip, which only spurred him on, and he roughly entered her. His thrusts were rapid and intense, and she arched her hips in equal fervor until they cried out in jubilance and relief. Moments later they lay on the bed, exhausted and panting and spent. They did not lie entwined in a lover's embrace, for love had little to do with what had just transpired between them.

When Alainn finally quit trembling, she pulled herself from the bed and attempted to locate her garments in the darkness. Having little success, she instinctively waved her hand toward the hearth and flames roared up in response. Killian lay on his side, resting on his elbow, gazing at her as she dressed, unable to find any words that could possibly relate what he was feeling. It was Alainn who spoke.

"I thank you for that, Killian O'Brien."

"You're thanking me for bedding you?"

"Aye well, sure you have more experience in being with a woman when it is only for basic physical gratification. What do you say in parting if not thank you? How do you speak to your other whores?"

"Ah, so you're still sore about what I said to you then?"

"On the contrary. But if I am to be wed tomorrow, I have little time to live up to the name you've given me."

He stood, a blanket draped around his waist, and took her arm.

"You know I did not mean that, it was said in bitterness and anger. I much regret my cruel words and how roughly I treated you just now. 'Tis hardly the way a man treats the woman he loves."

"You are not without battle scars yourself, Killian." She gently touched the deep scratches she'd left on his back, and when she pulled back the sheet covering him, he was truly uncertain what she had in mind. Her hand went to the deep scabbed wound on his muscular thigh. As she grazed it, he felt the warmth he'd experienced other times she'd healed him. He attempted to take her in his arms and hold her, but she would not allow it.

"No, 'tis better when there is no affection. Perhaps the meeting of our bodies will calm us for a time, Killian, for 'tis not only you left burning when we are parted. But, we both know we cannot share a bed again. Ten years ago this very night, I stood in this room. A child of seven I was, I came with the intent of healing you and giving you purpose to live on. 'Tis perhaps fitting this is where it ends between us, for it has been a decade our lives have been entwined. Whatever debt you felt you owed me for healing you has long since been paid. And if you should die to save my honor, I feel I am unworthy, Killian. I will not ask you to withdraw your challenge for I have told you, I will not, but, if you should die, I swear I shall never forgive you. I will see to it your soul knows no peace. Mark my words. You well know what I am capable of in this life; sure the next will be no different."

She pulled her hands through her long tresses and retied the knot. He did not respond, but felt his heart ache as she closed the door behind her.

Chapter twenty-three

Alainn had not intended to go near the great hall, especially not to speak with Mary MacDonald, considering where she had just come from, but the young girl spotted Alainn and called out to her. She was friendly and considerate, and Alainn found herself feeling consumed with guilt, but clearly there was little to be done about it. When Killian appeared only a moment or two later, she tried to avoid looking at him, though the memory of his touch still lingered on her skin.

She finally made her excuses to Mary, ignored Killian, and went into the great hall just in time to see Iona, Riley's intended, stick her foot out as Breena passed by with a huge tray of filled goblets. Throwing her arms out toward the girl, Alainn concentrated all her efforts on stopping time.

When she opened her eyes, she was amazed to see that everyone stood still as stone. Not one person moved; not one muscle twitched. Killian walked into the room, eyes wide in astonishment, as if he were in a world he did not recognize.

"What have you done, Alainn?" he asked more in amazement than accusation.

She smiled as he drew nearer to her.

"I wondered if the amulet would keep you from all my magic or only from the type that might harm you. I see you are unaffected by any of it."

"What have you done?"

"I believe I have stopped time."

"But why? For what purpose?"

Alainn pointed to Breena and Iona. It was clear what would happen next.

"When she falls, the contents will surely spill on the nobles around her, and 'twill enrage the chieftain."

Killian nodded his agreement. "She's horridly spiteful, that one. But why do you attempt to save Breena humiliation when it sounds as though she has caused you much grief through the years?"

"I would like to think I am not an evil woman, though the fact I just spent time in your bed and then had a lengthy conversation with your betrothed only moments later might indicate otherwise."

"You are not evil, Lainna, not ever have you acted evil. Not for all your power and your supernatural abilities, and, in truth, I doubt many could state that claim if they possessed the capabilities you do."

Alainn felt her concentration slipping as she walked toward the two women. With her witchcraft, she carefully moved Breena out of the way of the girl's foot, turned the red-haired girl, and placed her in the direct line of Killian's Uncle Sean who was in the midst of laughing with two young red-haired men who looked very much alike. With that done, she ever so gently pushed the girl, and she began to fall.

"Now what are you up to, Alainn?"

"Setting a plan in motion." She smiled at him and walked back toward the door. When she snapped her fingers, the room was instantly full of noise and movement. She turned in time to see Sean catch Iona and watch her beam up at him with a startled but appreciative look. Killian grinned to himself and turned toward the door, but Alainn was already gone.

Riley staggered over to him.

"Where have you been?" Killian asked.

"Out beddin' a servant girl, trying to forget the fact that I am to marry that miserable woman who at present seems quite taken by our uncle. And where have you been, cousin? Were you out spillin' your seed and trying to forget Alainn?"

Killian did not respond, so Riley goaded him further.

"You're truly going to allow her to marry the farmer? Why then would you challenge my father when 'tis Alainn's honor you fight for? Seems all a bit muddled to me. But, Christ did you see her in that dress tonight, cousin? 'Tis little wonder you are so bedazzled by her. I never thought Alainn to be so well-endowed in the bosom area!"

"What by God's nails were you doing lookin' at her in that manner?" Killian growled.

The other man shrugged. "Well, if you're going to allow her to wed the farmer, you can wager he'll have done more than look at those fine young breasts by this time tomorrow. And you can't order me not to look at her if you're going to allow her to be married to another. Come to it, I might do more than look, since you're clearly out of the runnin' and this is her last night to be ravaged."

"Are you purposely trying to annoy me, Riley?" he asked darkly. "Is this some ploy to force my hand and stop the wedding, or are you so entirely drunk that you think I'll take pity on you and not break your nose before your own wedding day?"

"Even half drunk, I estimate I'd fare better than the steward's son."

"He only got what he deserved and so will any who attempt to hurt Alainn!"

"I've no intention of hurting her, cousin, but still I tell you she's never looked lovelier or more bewitching than she did in that revealing dress. She was almost voluptuous." He licked his lips. "Now you would have had much closer contact with her in that regard, but I swear to you she has blossomed most appealingly and surely only recently."

"Go take a walk to sober up, Riley, before your own head lies at your feet."

The other man narrowed his blood-shot eyes, and smiled a lopsided grin as he left the great hall. Rory approached Killian with their betrotheds on each of his arms.

"We're heading out for a walk to the grove. There's talk of a gathering, and we thought we'd go see what we will. Are you up for the outing, Killian? I've already ensured Brigid's parents that we'll take good care of the girls."

"Aye, then I suppose we're off for a time," he said almost absentmindedly, as Mary hooked her arm through his, his mind still back on his conversation with Riley.

Chapter twenty-four

As she sauntered along the narrow path on her way back from the glade, giddy and refreshed from a swim in the spring, Alainn almost bumped right into Killian and Mary. She giggled when she saw the look on Killian's face.

"Are the two of you off to the round tower?" she asked, purposely taunting him.

"To the round tower! That sounds most exciting, might we go, Killian?" Mary pleaded.

He scowled at Alainn and discouraged the girl on his arm.

"'Tis a long walk and the grass is certainly damp with this night's dew. Sure your lovely skirts would be ruined."

She seemed disappointed then noticed Alainn's wet hair.

"Have you been for a swim, Alainn? That sounds heavenly, where is it you swim?"

"I've been to the spring in a nearby glade," she said vaguely, "but it is also a considerable walk, and my skirts are not as fine as yours, Milady."

"I've told you, Alainn, you must call me, Mary! And do you always walk alone in the darkness? Is that a wise consideration, does that not frighten you?"

"I like the dark if there is some moonlight, as there is tonight, and I was not alone."

Killian's eyes flashed with jealousy.

"I was with Wolf," she snapped.

Mary's eyes filled with horror, and she looked around with panic, shrieking with fright when Rory and Brigid came up the path.

"What's wrong with you, Mary? Your face is ashen?"

The girl still scanned the area with her eyes, and when she heard a rustling in the grass behind Alainn, she screamed and clutched Killian as though she were being pursued by demons.

"What is it Mary?" Killian asked his voice laced with genuine concern. Just then, a wolfhound came bounding up behind Alainn, and Mary became nearly hysterical.

"She's terrified of wolves," Brigid offered.

Alainn snapped her fingers and the dog lay down at her feet in submission. She put a hand on the other girl's arm.

"I apologize for causing you such a fright. He is just a dog, Milady, an Irish Wolfhound. Though I refer to him as Wolf, he is gentle and obedient. How long ago was it your brother was attacked by the wolves?"

The girl's large brown eyes were filled with tears, her bottom lip quivering. "I was just a wee lass," she managed to whisper. "He was protecting me when they attacked. He was not much older than I, and I saw him killed before my eyes, could do nothing but watch. I have been terrified of all dogs ever since."

"I don't blame you for that, no one could," Alainn said soothingly as she took the girl's hand. Killian cradled her protectively, and Alainn smiled at him approvingly as he gently calmed her.

"How did you know of the attack, Alainn? Mary has never spoken of it to me or my sister," Brigid asked.

Alainn sighed deeply and admitted, "I am a seer, though oft I wish otherwise."

"Where are you off to then, Alainn?" Rory asked, hoping to change the dismal subject.

"There's a gathering. 'Tis to be a grand crowd with entertainers and musicians. Sure, it will be a lovely night."

"And where is your intended this night, Alainn? I had hoped we might meet him?" Mary asked, seeming calmer now, though her voice shook lightly.

"I couldn't say. I haven't seen him. But I must be off, for I told Molly I would meet her at the gathering. She'll be wondering where I am." She clicked her tongue, and the dog followed her as she headed down the darkened path. Alainn was truly surprised when Rory's betrothed, Brigid, followed her down the path.

"Might we come to the gathering? Would we be allowed to partake?"

"You are nobility; no one could stop you from attending if that is what you wish."

"But would we be welcomed?"

By this time, all three nobles had joined Brigid, and Alainn looked toward the bright light of the torches up ahead. She seemed to wrestle with the notion but finally answered the girl.

"Aye, you may come with me, if you fancy the notion, but there are rules of attending a gathering of common folk. You must leave your titles and positions at the gate. If you agree to be all of one class within the gathering, then aye, you are welcome. Rory, Riley, and Killian have attended a few similar events through the years, but not for an age, I would suggest."

When they got to the edge of the clearing, two village men greeted Alainn and called her by name. They glanced at her companions with suspicion.

"They are with me tonight," Alainn explained.

"The women as well?" they asked doubtfully.

"You are making me sound rather a harlot," Alainn jested, "if you suggest you've never seen me in the company of women!"

The two men laughed. "Are the ladies certain they want to be allowed within?"

"The stories and songs tend to be a bit rowdy and raucous at times," Alainn explained to the women. "You must be accepting of that or you may be offended."

"Not me!" Mary assured her.

"Nor I!" Brigid piped up as well.

"'Tis fine with me as well then," Alainn agreed. "But you're certain you'll take no offense to be referred to by your given names by common people?" Once more the girls shook their heads, and Alainn led them into the boisterous crowd.

There was much gaiety and frivolity, with people dancing and others singing. The smell of whiskey and ale hung in the air. Two young men were having a lively discussion about who would dance with the young girl standing between them, but Alainn deducted that neither looked as though they were in any condition to dance. Mary and Brigid giggled behind their hands.

They found a spot where they could watch the festivities, and soon Cookson and Molly approached them. Molly affectionately embraced Alainn, who introduced her to the young women. Killian watched as the quiet young girl was introduced to Mary MacDonald. Though an obviously well-mannered girl, she made no attempt to hide her displeasure and threw him an angry look.

"My mother will be wonderin' where I am," she murmured and excused herself from the group.

Cookson offered the men ale, and they accepted. Alainn located cider and brought some back for Mary and Brigid. It wasn't long before Alainn was whisked away by a young villager who Killian had seen a time or two. As they danced a lively jig to fiddle music, Killian tried to keep his gaze only mildly interested, when he wanted desperately to have her in his arms. She returned almost breathless from the lengthy dance but had no time to rest before being carried off to dance with another young man. Rory and Brigid soon joined the dancing circle, and when Mary looked at Killian quizzically, he took her hand and led her into line.

Several musicians and local fiddlers, harpists and pipers continued on with their music, playing a vast variety of Irish songs. There were fast-paced tunes that left everyone exhausted and laughing, and slow sad melodies that pulled at the heart-strings. The young soldier who had helped her upon her horse earlier that week played a tune on his fiddle to the delight of the crowd. Then MacKenzie MacArthur took a turn at playing a Scottish tune on his bagpipes. Mary squealed with excitement to learn that she was not the only Scot in the crowd. Molly came and retrieved Alainn, and with two other girls, one being Breena McTeer, they danced so aptly and in such perfect rhythm it looked as though they had practiced for months.

When Alainn returned to stand beside Killian, he whispered, "When did you learn to dance so well?"

With a mischievous glint in her eye, she whispered back, "When you and your cousins were off sowing your wild oats, I danced."

Molly came by at that moment and nudged Alainn.

"Are you up for a dare, Alainn?"

"I'm not sure, Molly. Breena and I have already locked horns once this night, I'm not certain I want to go head to head with her again."

"Come along, Alainn. Sure, it'll be fun!"

She pulled her to the end of a long line of women. Cookson described what was happening.

"The girls will all line up," Cookson explained. "The one at the end of the line chooses what steps the rest will follow, and if a step is missed, they must drop out. If the leader tires, she goes to the other end and allows the next in line to take over. 'Twill go on until there are only two left. 'Tis nearly always Alainn and Breena."

As the dancing began, slowly, one by one the girls dropped out until only Breena, Molly, and Alainn remained. Killian felt himself nearly out of breath just watching the girls exert themselves at their fast pace and for so lengthy a time.

Molly finally tired and, laughing, came to join her brother next to Pierce, who smiled and took her hand. Killian did not miss how the young girl grew flushed and thought it had nothing to do with the fact she'd been dancing for some time.

When Breena signaled to Alainn to take over the lead, she stepped up the pace, which Breena answered with a knowing look. Alainn continued on, untiring, until her glance found Killian's and their eyes burned into each other. She looked quickly away, but in that moment, missed a step, and conceded the contest to the happy disbelief of Breena. Smiling together, they went breathlessly in search of a drink.

Alainn was rosy-cheeked and breathing hard when she got to Cook. He passed her a drink of cool water.

"Still can't think of drinkin' ale, Alainn?"

She shook her head and drank the cool water, then loosened the lacing on her garment and poured the cool droplets down upon her bosom. She felt Killian's eyes on her and saw the desire within them.

As the night wore on, several locals took their turn at singing. There were songs of war and patriotic Irish songs, love songs and tales of heartbreak. And as promised, several racy tunes as well. When Riley joined the group some time later, he insisted Rory and Killian join him in a song. Though the other two assured him it was not a song to be sung in mixed company, they finally agreed and had the entire crowd roaring with laughter at the silliness and genuine affection between the three young men. Even Brigid and Mary were laughing uproariously upon hearing them.

When it was completed and Killian was standing between Alainn and Mary, Riley jested with him. "Pick one, cousin! Don't be greedy!"

Killian seemed to not understand his cousin's meaning.

"Pick one of the beauties who now flank you, and I'll take the other!" Killian looked into the dark eyes of the one he was promised to and then into the deep blue sapphires of the one who had so long ago captured his heart. When he seemed incapable of choosing, Alainn made the decision for him.

"Well Riley, since neither your intended nor mine are here, I suppose we must be forced to suffer each other's company." She curtsied to him, and he whisked her off her feet. There was truly something to be said about large tall men, for it was a grand thing to have a man sweep you off your feet in a literal way. They danced two fast-paced jigs, and, when the next song was a slow stately love ballad, Riley brought her in closer and linked their hands. He moved with an uncommon grace especially given how much he'd had to drink that night. When he stroked the inside of her wrist, she pushed his hand away, but in no time it was back. When he led her in front of him, casting out of the line, his free hand crept to rest on her backside.

"Are you purposely trying to anger me, Riley, or are you doing this for Killian's benefit?" she asked.

"Mostly for his benefit, I suppose, though I've always wanted to know what it would be like to fondle your wee arse."

"Aye well, you can wonder all you like, but you're not about to find out, Riley O'Brien," she laughed, looking into his smiling eyes.

"Oh fine, then ye wee wench," he murmured, kissing their entwined hands. "Keep me wonderin' for all eternity."

Killian paced at the side of the dance, watching them; Cookson cut in and saved her from the worst of his glare. When that tune ended, the young soldier asked her for a dance. She agreed, and he was most gentlemanly through its entirety.

"You've a rare talent with the fiddle. Where did you learn to play so well?"

"It seemed to come to me when I was a wee boy."

"I don't even know your name."

"'Tis Danhoul Calhoun. And you're Alainn McCreary. I've heard much of you. You're spoken of highly by both the villagers and nobles, it would seem."

When the dance ended, he politely bowed to her and smiled warmly. "I have heard you sing, and I was wonderin' if maybe you might sing a song with me?"

"I am not certain I care to sing this night," she said. Something niggled at Alainn, but she could not put her finger on it. She was certain he was unusually familiar. Though he was still a young man, perhaps younger than herself, there was something alluring about him. She felt a connection to him that she could not understand.

"Come on, lass, agree to sing a song with a lonely young man. I would be greatly honored if you would do me this favor."

She eventually gave in, and the crowd enthusiastically passed him his fiddle. Standing side by side, Danhoul began playing a lovely Celtic melody. They sang together as though they had done so many times before. Alainn had the oddest sensation that she truly had sung with him before, but she quickly dispelled the notion as she had never met him until mere days earlier. When they were finished the song, the crowd cheered, applauding the talents of the two young people and commenting on how wonderfully their voices blended.

After they'd finished and she began to walk away, Danhoul looked at her with such an intense gaze, his smoky blue eyes fixed so keenly on hers, it was as though they had known each other from another time. Or would. But Alainn had little time to dwell on it for Rory, who loved to sing and possessed a fine singing voice, asked Alainn to sing with him next.

When Alainn finally made it back to talk to Mary and Killian, Molly came to her with a request of her own.

"You must sing the Farewell Song."

Alainn looked at her young friend and shook her head, "Not this night, Molly. Not that song."

Mary was listening and added her opinion. "I'd love to hear you sing again, Alainn. You've a lovely voice, and it would be a pleasure to hear you sing solo."

"Aye, and you should hear her sing this song. She sounds like an angel come down from heaven. 'Tis the saddest song you'll ever hear, and my da says when Alainn sings it she can make many a grown man weep."

"There's no need to sing a song of sadness, Molly. There'll be enough time for sadness. Tonight I want only to be happy," Alainn whispered.

But, the girl would not be quieted. "Alainn you are my dearest friend, and I do not ask so very much of you. After this night you will be wed to the farmer, and I know not when or if we'll be allowed to spend time together. Please, you must show everyone what a lovely voice you possess."

"Aye, then choose another song, Molly, and I'll oblige you straightaway."

The young girl put her hands on her hips precisely, Killian noted, as her mother had only days earlier. "That is the song I request, Alainn, and 'tis the only one I will settle for."

Alainn turned her back to the others and pleaded quietly to her friend.

"Molly, 'tis a sad love song. You know I cannot sing that. Not with Killian here."

"Aye well, if you can't even bear to sing a song of farewell, how do you intend to be parted from him forever? Sing it now and I won't mention it again. If you can get through the song without fail, then I know you will be capable of wedding another."

"And if I can't?"

"Then I'll tell him of the child you carry."

Alainn's quickly steered the girl away from the others.

"I was not aware you knew."

Molly nodded. "Aye, I heard you and Mama talking the other morning. I can't believe you intend to marry Liam O'Hara when 'tis Killian you love, when you carry his child."

"Some things are not within our capabilities to change, Molly."

"Just sing the song then," she stubbornly repeated, and Alainn finally relented. As she went to join the musicians, Molly whispered a further condition, "You must look at Killian whilst you sing."

Alainn was doubtful of that, but she began. Her voice was clear and sweet and melancholic as she sang of two lovers being parted, the man never again to return to Eire or to his love. Her voice held through the first two verses and the poignant chorus, but when she began on the third, she allowed herself to gaze at Killian for but a fleeting second, but it was enough. Her voice cracked with emotion, and tears slid down her cheeks. By the end of it, she was nearly sobbing and not alone, for half the crowd was truly moved to tears. Alainn started off toward the gate, Molly following after her.

"I will tell him, Alainn. If you do not tell him now, then I swear to you, I will."

"No, you must not, Molly."

"How can you marry another when you love him so, when you carry his child! He has a right to know!"

Killian approached them at that precise moment, and Molly stubbornly went to him. "I must speak with you, Milord."

"Molly, 'tis not your place. I must speak with you further on this."

The girl seemed uncertain, but she went to Alainn's side. "You must trust me, Molly. I have no intention of marrying the farmer, but I must be sure Killian loves me enough to prevent the wedding. I cannot think the only reason is because of the child. And if he truly goes to battle with his uncle he cannot have a mind filled with thoughts of his child. Please trust me to know what is best."

The girl remained uncertain, but she left without further word to Killian.

"Alainn, are you well?"

"As well as can be expected for a woman whose heart is breaking," she managed. He took her in his arms and held her. His warmth enveloped her and stilled her tears, as well as her fears. She wrapped her arms around his neck and clung tightly as though she would never let go.

"How long have they been in love?" Mary asked Riley quietly.

He did not attempt to deceive her. "For as long as I can remember. From the first time they saw each other, I think, maybe a decade."

"Why are they not together then?"

"My father won't allow it. She is not of noble blood, and Killian is to be a chieftain. And he thinks you are the better match for him."

"Then your father is a fool," the girl stated simply and stalked off.

Chapter twenty-five

They'd spent the entire night together and sat watching the sun rise over the mist-covered hills. They'd barely spoken, only embraced once or twice, but held tight to each other's hand. Killian had touched her cheek to wipe away a tear as he left her at the garden gate near Cook's cottage. She knew how deeply he loved her, but she was not confident he meant to prevent her marriage.

Although the wedding was to take place late afternoon following the burial ceremony, the chieftain had changed the time of the ceremony to late morning, and this was a fact known by only a select few. Alainn was certain Killian wasn't one of them. She hoped he would not dally if he was inclined to prevent the nuptials.

She headed to the village abbey accompanied only by the captain. Lady Siobhan and her father, Chieftain O'Rorke, were nowhere to be seen. They entered the lovely chapel that Alainn had attended all her life; the farmer, Liam O'Hara, stood nervously at the front of the church with the village priest, a man Alainn both admired and respected, so opposite to the old priest the chieftain employed personally. He came to her and gave her a warm and caring smile, then spoke in a quiet voice.

"Though I am much opposed to deception, Lady Siobhan has explained the situation to me, and in my heart I do not feel this is wrong. Liam and Mellane, the miller's daughter have longed to be married for some time, but were waiting the appropriate mourning period till a year has passed since his wife's death. They had told me of their intent to marry many weeks ago. When the chieftain ordered him to marry you, they were both devastated by the arrangement, but fearing the chieftain would increase his rent or make life most difficult, he agreed for the sake of his child. Lady Siobhan has assured me Liam will experience no ill will, and I am trusting in her word and that of her father."

Alainn breathed a sigh of relief and looked up at the captain, realizing he had heard the entire explanation.

"You intend to allow us to go against the chieftain's wishes as well, Mac?"

The largely built Scot spoke to her in his gruff masculine voice, "Aye well, you and the father here have kept a secret of mine for over a decade. I think it is a noble thing to see two people who love each other be allowed to be together."

The priest nodded at Mac and went to the altar where the miller's daughter now stood linked arm in arm with her farmer. Alainn was genuinely pleased and the couple appeared entirely relieved that they would finally be united when it had seemed an impossible consideration. Alainn looked up at the large man beside her, and he escorted her to a bench near the back of the church.

She whispered to him, "How did you know I knew your secret?"

"From the time you were a child, you looked at me with that knowing expression and in truth anyone who has half a brain should surely see the resemblance between my son Pierce and Dermod, the boy Sean O'Brien has raised as his own."

"Aye, they're a good deal alike, though I don't think everyone sees it as you and I do. She was a wise woman to choose a man with hair as red as her own to father her child."

"Aye, she was cunning and beautiful and seductive, and I a widower for several years without the company of a woman. I do not think badly of her for it. She wanted a child in a fierce way, and I do not begrudge Sean the fact he raises my son. He is a good man, more so than his eldest brother as of late."

Alainn nodded her agreement, and the two sat quietly as the ceremony was performed and the couple joined in matrimony. Alainn thought what an odd twist of fate that the woman she had disliked so intensely for so long because she had once found her with Killian, was saving her from a marriage she would have been most unhappy in.

When the ceremony concluded, the couple was hurried out the door, but not before Alainn's cloak was given to Mellane. The women exchanged hugs, and the miller's daughter passed her cloak to Alainn. She accepted and watched as the priest wished them well. They headed off to the farmer's cottage to consummate the marriage before the chieftain learned of the deception and ordered the wedding annulled.

The captain seemed as though he wanted to speak to Alainn further.

"Tell me what's on your mind, Mac. You know I hold you in the highest regard and your opinion is important to me."

"Aye well, you're a lovely wee lass, yourself, Alainn McCreary. You remind me of a lass I knew back in my homeland, but that was near twenty years ago before I made the voyage to this land. And now it is unlikely I'll make the journey home, though I will admit, I miss it still."

"Then you must return, Mac. If, after two decades you continue to long for the country of your birth, then go back, for if I were parted from Ireland I think I would die of homesickness."

"But, I've Pierce to consider and Dermod as well. Though I can't claim him as my son, I still care for the lad, and I know Pierce would never care to leave. But, it is concern I feel for you, Alainn. The chieftain was once an honorable man, but I no longer feel so strongly inclined to believe it, and he has a deep dislike for ye, and a fierce determination to keep you and his nephew apart. He will be wrathful when he learns of this ruse, and I fear it will be you who is made to bear the brunt of his rage. Now, I know Lady Siobhan and her father will be able to keep him from you for a time, and I'll do what I can as well, but we can't see to your safety every moment.

"And Killian has perhaps already bitten off more than he can chew with that infernal challenge he's forced. Now, I know it was to defend your honor, and he's a proud, strong lad and he loves ye well, but if he gets himself killed in the process where will that leave you, lass?"

"Where indeed, Mac? Alone and heartsick and—"

"With child."

"And how did you come by that information?"

"I heard you telling the chieftain the night my two guards were killed in your chamber. I stood outside a moment longer than I might have so you would be allowed to escape, but I heard the entire exchange. It is fortunate he fears you and hopes you may possess a way to end the curse on the O'Briens, or he might have had you killed."

"Aye, it is a possibility. But If he would stop taking the potions he is consuming in such mass quantity, he could possibly be restored to the man he once was. Now, I feel that is unlikely."

"Aye, he's always been a might unscrupulous and not without many allies. So, you must watch yourself, lass. And if Killian goes ahead with the marriage his uncle has arranged for him, you'll be needing a husband."

"And are you offering to fill the position?" Alainn asked skeptically.

"Aye, well in a very awkward manner. But if Killian does not do right by you, then I will be honored if you'd accept my proposal."

"You are very kind, Mac, and in truth I have no notion of what Killian will do. He does not know of the child, nor will I tell him, until he has made up his mind what he wants. And if the curse cannot be undone, then there is little need for him to ever learn I carry his child."

"But, he should be told, lass. Surely he deserves to know."

They both stopped talking when the priest came toward them.

"I must be off to visit an elderly gentleman in the village. I wish you well, Alainn, and pray you will find the happiness you deserve."

She smiled at the priest but, as he left, called after him.

"Father, how long is it you have been here at the abbey? I remember you here all my life, but when did you arrive?"

"It would have been nearly ten and eight years ago, child? Why do you ask?"

"But what month?"

The man seemed perplexed by her question.

"It was early summer. Aye, for I was in Kinsale before that and did not arrive until mid-June, if I remember it correctly."

"And any wedding that would have been performed before then, who would have officiated?"

"The chieftain's priest once offered services to the commoners as well as the nobles. Sure, it would have been him. What wedding is it you are inquiring after? There may still be a record here in the cellar, for there are many found in the volumes below. You are welcome to search through them with me one day if you like."

"Sure, any documented record of the wedding would have been destroyed by the priest, or by the chieftain's father," she whispered. When she seemed unwilling to discuss it further, the priest bid them farewell, and the captain prepared to take his leave.

"Would you care for me to walk you somewhere, lass? I can take you back to Cook's cottage if that is where you intend to return."

"No, I must wait here, Mac. I need to know where I stand with Killian. If he comes, then who knows what will become of us; if he doesn't, then I know I must face the future without him."

"Aye well, for your sake, lass, I hope he does not disappoint you."

***

Killian wrestled with a most difficult decision the entire morning. He'd left her at dawn without word of promise or of love. And all morning he'd waffled back and forth between what was surely best for her and what he wanted for them. If he'd asked her he knew she'd gladly accept a life without children to be with him. And he would spend all eternity only with her, if it came to that, but could he truly do that to her?

Could he hope to keep her as his own, propose marriage to her when he may have no home or position to offer her, and perhaps the issue giving him the greatest grief was, could he actually marry her when the curse was still upon them? His thoughts went to the memory of Alainn on the beach in Galway city. Barefoot and happy surrounded by a crowd of children.

And the other morning, when he'd seen her holding Cook's daughter, she'd looked so radiantly maternal with the sleeping child in her arms. How could he take that away from her? She seemed to believe she might be able to assist Mara in ending the curse, but if it could never be lifted and would remain until the O'Brien line died out, could he purposely cause her such grief and sadness?

He had galloped across the meadow upon Storm's back and found himself headed toward the farmer's land. The very thought of Alainn being wed to another man, sharing another man's life and his bed, had filled him with a jealous rage. But as he came over the hill that looked over the farmer's land, he'd spotted the cottage. A sturdy stone cottage with a view of the distant rolling hills. A stone wall surrounding a garden, and when the door had opened, he'd watched as two dogs bounded out ahead of the man. Dogs inside the house.

And as he'd surveyed the entire scene, it came to him this was the exact picture within his mind he had formed of the place Alainn had described in her perfect day. He felt his stomach knot and his heart constrict.

With the farmer she would be cared for, he would give her a home and children and a life that, although not grand, would be comfortable and safe. But would she be happy? Could either of them ever be truly happy apart from one another? He'd pulled the reins and headed the horse back toward the castle. Loving her as he did, he thought perhaps letting her marry the farmer might be the best he could do by her.

* * *

As the chapel bell rang out twelve times, he knew he should prepare to attend his cousins' grandmother's burial ceremony. He'd already spoken to Rory and Riley, and though Riley was clearly displeased with attending a druid ceremony, he had agreed to go for his mother and grandfather's sake.

He went to his window and looked out on the games below grateful he was not slotted in any events this day, for he would have been at a great disadvantage. His mind was so entirely muddled, he could scarcely think straight. His thoughts went to Alainn singing that song the night before. Never had he heard a voice so beautiful or a song that shredded his heart so entirely. And she'd looked at him with such utter and complete sadness, such despair. He was drawn to her, and taking her in his arms and consoling her seemed as natural as breathing. It always had.

If he didn't make a move soon, she would no longer be his to hold, not lawfully, not completely. Her eyes came to him as surely as if she were there with him, and once more they seemed to plead to him. She wanted him to stop this wedding! She would never have agreed to it if his uncle had not forced it upon her. He would prevent it! He had to, for it was now or never.

He raced up the cobblestone street and past the villagers, now sure this was his destiny. She was his destiny. As he neared the abbey, he saw the priest heading down the steps. The man smiled in recognition of the chieftain's nephew.

"Killian O'Brien, you seem in a great hurry, my son! Where are you off to, then?"

He spoke breathlessly. "The farmer's wedding. Is it to be held soon?"

The priest's eyes filled with understanding. "The farmer and his bride were wed nearly two hours ago now. Your uncle changed the ceremony to earlier this morning."

The color drained instantly from Killian's face.

"No! That cannot be!" he cried.

"Aye well, I performed the marriage ceremony myself, Killian."

"Where are they now? Where have they gone?"

"To the farmer's cottage, I presume."

Killian sunk weakly onto the stone steps, his heart thundering in his chest. He dropped his head. His chest constricted and began heaving with emotion, tears pouring freely. He'd waited. He'd waited too long, and he'd lost her. He could not breathe. How would he live?

The last time he had shed tears was the day Alainn came to him as a child and convinced him life was worth living, that he should fight to survive. And he had never felt so desolate and alone again. Until now. Footsteps behind him warned that the priest had returned, but he did not care. He felt a hand on his shoulder and was certain the man had come to console him in his grievous state. But there was nothing he could say to ease his pain.

"Sure you took your sweet time, Killian O'Brien."

She dropped to the steps beside him, tears flowing down her own cheeks as well. She pulled his head to her bosom and held him tight. His arms encircled her and breathed in her sweet feminine scent, and his heart ached from the sweetness of it.

"Sorry I am that I deceived you so cruelly," she sobbed, "but I needed to know you would come for me." His arms tensed around her.

"There was no wedding? The priest lied?"

"No, there was a wedding." Killian looked up horrified. "Liam O'Hara married the miller's daughter, Killian. They've been in love for a time. The priest did not lie, not in actuality. And your uncle still believes I am married to the farmer. Lady Siobhan's father has been assigned the task of breaking the news to him."

Killian could not speak for a long while, but pulled her onto his lap and held her tightly. She wrapped her arms around his neck, and they were content just to be together. Killian thought he would never be as grateful to the Lord and to the O'Rorke as he was at this moment. When the church tower bell rang out one more time, Alainn nudged Killian.

"We must go to the burial ceremony. Lady Siobhan is expecting us both. I am uncertain why they wish to include me, but I will go. Please walk with me, Killian, for I think I shall never again release you from my arms."

"Aye well, I don't care to be parted from you any time soon, either, Lainna."

***

As they walked toward the clearing in the forest where they'd been instructed to meet, Alainn changed course and moved deeper into the forest.

"I believe it was to be held here," Killian suggested as she tugged on his hand.

"Aye, but the location has been changed. There is a larger oak grove deeper in the forest."

Killian allowed her to show the way. After they had walked for some time, they came into another opening, and sure enough the family was there waiting. All seemed to wear a look of relief as they came through the trees still holding hands. Riley was the first to greet them.

"So, you finally came to your senses then, Killian, and stopped the wedding?"

"Not entirely, but something along those lines."

Rory gave Alainn a heartfelt embrace and noticed how pale she appeared. "Are you ailing, Alainn? You look as though you are unwell."

"I am well enough, Rory. I suppose I am in need of sleep, for I had a rather late night."

Killian only then noticed the dark smudges beneath her eyes. He squeezed her hand, knowing they'd both had a difficult day.

Lady Siobhan and her father were standing beside the shrouded figure of their beloved. Killian went to his aunt and embraced her openly, whispering a thank you in her ear as she nodded and smiled with relief. She had not been entirely confident that Killian would go to Alainn. The elderly man nodded to them as well and cleared his throat, for it was time to begin the ceremony.

They were all given long white robes to don before the ritual could start. Riley appeared displeased but put on the robe with only minimal complaints. When his grandfather began speaking in a language he could not understand, he looked toward the trees as if planning a speedy escape.

"We will be calling the quarters," the old man declared.

Riley looked at his mother for an explanation, but she stood with her eyes closed.

Alainn whispered, "'Tis to create a boundary for protection and to raise energy." He looked at her as if she were mad. When his grandfather began chanting, Riley grew increasingly disturbed. Finally, he pulled off the robe, threw it on the ground, and began walking away, cursing under his breath.

"Riley, please don't leave!" Lady Siobhan called out, her face crumpling in distress. "This is important to me and to Father."

"'Tis horse shite, mother, and heresy!"

Alainn could not still her mouth. "Riley O'Brien! Perhaps your mother and her kin feel Christianity is horse shite! There are many questionable practices in that religion as well. To begin with, a man has supreme power in the Roman Catholic faith, some pray to the pope and not to God, and how can man be given the power to absolve sin? And besides, Druidism predates Christianity by thousands of years."

"How in hell do you know so much about Druidism, Alainn? 'Tis not as though the farrier or Morag raised you in the old ways."

"Riley," she pleaded in a softer voice, "your mother raised you and Rory in Christianity as your father has desired. She has attended mass for both the nobles and the peasants, and seldom missed it. Can you not abide her faith and that of her people for this one time in respect of your grandmother?"

"No, Alainn, I cannot abide this heresy! It goes against the Lord's commandments. Thou shalt have no other gods before me."

Alainn scowled. "You are somewhat selective in adhering to those commandments. I could list several that you break on a daily basis, one this very moment: honor thy father and thy mother!"

"You are overstepping your boundaries, commoner," he spat. "I have no intention of remaining here and listening to any more of this lunacy." He turned and walked toward the trees.

Furious, Alainn held out her hands and stopped him in his tracks.

"Who the hell are you, Alainn McCreary? *What the hell are you!*" he bellowed.

She stretched out her arms and looked to the west.

"I am fire!" And as she spoke the edge of the clearing to the west burst into a crackling wall of flame. "I am water!" To the south, a wave of black angry water rushed through the trees to crash as if against an invisible wall and stand suspended in space and time just beyond them. "I am earth!" In the east, an enormous mound of earth rose out of the shaking ground with a deafening rumble. "I am air!" Hundreds of screaming whirlwinds shrieked through the sky to merge together in the north. They tore through the trees and hovered at the clearing, completing the circle. Riley was going nowhere.

Lady Siobhan was the first to speak in a voice that trembled.

"Father, have you ever witnessed power such as this?"

The old man's eyes, still wide and in awe of the young girl's abilities, swallowed and croaked, "Never, Siobhan. In all my six and a half decades, in all the councils and druid gathering I have attended, never have I even heard of such greatness. Sure she must be the one spoken of in legend."

Riley, who could finally move again, was peering closely at the perimeter, realizing he had no hope of escape for the circle was not only unbelievable, it was clearly impenetrable. Rory shook his head but seemed to hold no fear. He smiled appreciatively at Alainn.

"I had no notion you had abilities beyond your healing and premonitions. Did you know of this, Killian?"

Killian held tight to Alainn whose arms were still stretched rigidly outward. He dared not turn to look around at his cousin but shook his head slightly as he spoke. "I've seen some of it, 'tis true, but never anything liken to this degree of ability."

Niall spoke before any other questions could be issued. "Before we go on with this, I would ask that my grandsons put on the amulets you carry for them, Siobhan. Please do not attempt to argue this, Riley. You may need protection. Killian has Alainn's amulet so he is protected. Your mother and I have our own."

"Why does Alainn have an amulet like this?" Riley asked as his mother passed him the chain. He did not need convincing to put it around his neck, nor did his twin.

His grandfather exchanged a knowing glance with his daughter. "We will explain more after we attend to the solemnity ritual," Siobhan said, "for Alainn will surely not be capable of holding the wall of protection for long." Alainn slowly lowered her arms, and the wall remained intact.

The man spoke in English and ancient Celt, of his beloved wife, of all they had shared. His daughter added a few tender words of her own. Then he glanced at Alainn.

"Would you sing the dirge, Alainn? Do you know the druid requiem?"

Alainn closed her eyes, called upon a distant memory, and a clear angelic voice flowed smoothly and beautifully from her. The song was solemn and mournful, and eerily enchanting, and no one could take their eyes from her. When she was through, Niall O'Rorke held an unlit torch high in the air and nodded to Alainn. As she stared at it, the object burst into flames. He touched it to the enshrouded figure of his wife, and the woman's body was set afire.

"That is surely not always part of a druid burial ritual," Alainn declared in a voice filled with horror.

"No, not with all sects," the elderly man agreed, "but so many grave robbers have desecrated the bodies of our loved ones, we have chosen to set fire to the bodies as an alternative. And since her ashes could not rest with her children who have gone before her, they shall be scattered to the wind so that they might find their way to them."

Alainn nodded her head in understanding, but she had begun to tremble. "When I die, do not allow anyone to do that to me, under no circumstance; I ask you put no flame to me!"

He nodded approvingly. "Aye, anyone with fairy blood running through their veins has a distinct fear of fire."

The old man spoke words in an ancient tongue and ended the ritual. Alainn said words of her own to close the circle, words that even the man and his daughter could only partially understand. Slowly the circle of the protective elements disappeared as though it had never been, leaving no trace left behind. Alainn immediately collapsed in a dead faint, Killian catching her in his arms before she hit the ground. His face a mask of fear and dread, he carefully lowered her to the grass. His aunt hurried to her side.

"What's happened to her father?"

"She is drained, physically, spiritually, and emotionally. Such a display of power will have weakened her greatly."

"But she is not harmed?" Killian asked, his voice stricken with deep concern as he gently stroked her hair and rubbed her arms.

"No, I believe she must rest and be kept protected, but I am confident she will soon waken," the old man assured him.

"Protected from what?"

The man looked hesitant, as if uncertain.

"Aye, you deserve to hear the truth. Any display of power such as Alainn showed, while it created protection for the ceremony, it would have most certainly alerted supernatural entities from many realms, perhaps from the Unseelie Court. There will be some who would attempt to take her powers, others who would tempt her toward the dark side, to an evil place."

"Christ!" Killian cursed loudly. "And how can she be protected from that?

"You can protect her, Killian," said his aunt, "for you have her heart. You are surely a guardian to her, and you possess her amulet."

"Then I must return it to her!" he shouted, grabbing the leather strand and lifting.

"No!" both druids answered emphatically. Killian released the leather as if burned, and Niall continued more calmly, "Keep it where it is. She has charmed it for you, and you'd both be at risk if you remove it."

"Grandfather, you must explain to us what you know," Rory said. "For you've left much unanswered." Riley sat away from the group, but his head tilted slightly toward them as if he could not control his curiosity.

"Aye, 'tis time we spoke aloud of our suspicions, Siobhan. All here have the right to know and a vested interest in the subject." He looked down at the girl whose eyes remained closed. Her long dark lashes, a contrast to her pale cheeks. With those striking, brilliant blue eyes hidden, her resemblance to his long dead daughter was even more startling.

As Killian continued tenderly stroking her hair, the man noticed the shape of her ears and gasped. Though they were much smaller and feminine, they were shaped very much like his son's. His voice was nearly choked with emotion as he said, "My daughter and I are convinced this girl is our kin."

Chapter twenty-six

"Our kin?" Riley scoffed. "How would that be possible?"

"Allow your grandfather to speak son, it will be explained in time."

"It is a great likelihood that she is the daughter of my son, your mother's brother, Teige."

"How would that be possible?" Riley demanded, hands clenched. "That would make her of noble blood, so why would she be raised as a peasant, passed off as the farrier's daughter?"

"And why has it only been discovered now?" asked Rory.

"And if it is truth, who then is her mother?" Killian's voice was filled with dread for he thought he knew the answer.

Niall and Siobhan looked at each other, uncertain how much to divulge, when a noise in the bushes drew all eyes to the thicket as a dark-haired woman in a shabby garment headed toward them. Lady Siobhan stiffened. Killian closed his eyes and inhaled deeply, for he realized he had been correct. Rory and Riley watched intently; neither had ever seen the woman.

The Glade Witch walked to Alainn and knelt beside her. She placed her hand to the girl's chest, and her blue eyes revealed her concern. Her long black hair swung over Alainn as she leaned over and put her ear to her daughter's chest, while furtively laying her hand to her abdomen. She was certain Killian did not see, but Lady Siobhan breathed in sharply and her eyes grew wide.

"What is it, Mara? Why do you look so worried? What do you sense?" Killian asked.

"Mara!" Riley barked. "This is the Glade Witch? The woman who has cursed our line and caused so much tragedy for our family?" Killian nodded. "Then why in hell are you allowing her to touch Alainn?"

Killian sighed as he continued to lovingly caress Alainn's hair. "Because she is her mother."

"Jesus, Mary, and Joseph!" Rory exclaimed, but he stepped closer to look at the woman, for he had been curious about her all his life. Riley was not so congenial. He withdrew his sword and began to walk toward her. Lady Siobhan and her father called out, but it was Killian who held out his hand and stopped him.

"Stay back, Riley," he said almost wearily. "She may be the only one capable of aiding Alainn. And I am certain she can tell us much that we must learn."

The woman continued to lay her hand near Alainn's chest. Her expression was grave as she looked at Killian.

"I cannot rouse her. She will not waken."

Killian grabbed her arm. "You must do something! What is wrong with her?"

"There must be a reason she is taking so long to come back. Her heart beats much too slowly. Talk to her, Killian, you are her most treasured possession and her strongest connection to this world. Tell her to come back to you, quickly, before she is unable!"

"You think she may die?" he asked in a panic. "Christ, Alainn! What the hell are you doing? Come back to me this instant! Do you hear me woman? I swear you'd best listen to me before I shake the life out of you!" With that, he began shaking her. Alainn gasped deeply, as though she'd been underwater and just come up for air. "Killian O'Brien," she snapped, angrily slapping at his arm as he continued to shake her. "Settle you down. I was trying to listen to Morag, and I've yet to hear what she was telling me. If you'd just given me another moment—"

She finally opened her eyes and saw that his arms were now shaking involuntarily. She rubbed his arms, sending through a calm warmth that stilled them. It was only then that she noticed Mara kneeling beside her. She glanced up sharply at the concerned and startled faces surrounding her.

"Sure, the cat is out of the bag, then?" she attempted to jest, but no one uttered a word. "I am an O'Rorke, then, am I, Mara? Teige O'Rorke is my father?" Alainn questioned.

The woman stared into her daughter's eyes as she softly spoke. "Aye, but its certain no one will believe that to be truth until you find the other portion of the amulet."

"I believe it without question," said Lady Siobhan. "I see many likenesses to my brother,"

"Aye, she is very much like him," Mara murmured.

When Alainn tried to stand, she was overcome with dizziness and fell back into Killian's arms. He cursed under his breath. "Alainn you are never ever to use your powers as you did this day. Not to that extent! Not ever, do you hear me, woman?"

"And you must not enter the spirit world, Alainn, for 'tis not always possible to return. Morag should have known that. Why did she call you there?" Mara asked.

"She did not call me, but I know there is something she must tell me. It regards the other portion of the amulet."

"Why does she not come to you then to speak to you?"

"I have not seen her since the day her body was laid in the ground. I don't know why she seems unwilling or incapable of coming to me."

Riley looked at them in complete disbelief of their unusual discussion, as if he would explode into a rage.

"You are the witch's daughter? How could you deceive us all in such a manner?"

"It was not a purposeful deception, Riley."

"How long have you known, Alainn?" asked Killian.

"I have only discovered my father's identity this very day. It finally came to me when I was standing here earlier. And I have known about my mother for not much longer."

"How long?" Killian asked flatly.

"A few weeks."

"And you didn't think you might share that information with me? 'Tis not as though there has been no opportunity to tell me!"

"Do not flay her for this, Killian O'Brien. Would you be so eager to share such information knowing what ramifications would surely follow?"

"She should have told me, Mara. You should have told me, Alainn," he chastised softly, his hands gently cupping her cheeks and framing her sad blue eyes.

Mara stood up and went to Lady Siobhan, who stiffened as if approached by a snake. The Glade Witch frowned. "I loved your brother more than a soul should ever love another. But, he was taken from me by your father-in-law, a truly loathsome man. He brutally violated me, and I uttered an impulsive, retaliatory curse born of desperation, and I have regretted it every day since. I've oft attempted to withdraw the curse but have not managed it. I do not expect you to forgive me, Siobhan, but I hope you might one day understand the reasoning."

"How a woman could cause such pain for another! You caused my babies to die! Five beautiful, precious babes! All innocent, all dead because of you and your damnable curse! How can you ever expect me to understand that?"

"I was young and heartsick and alone. The chieftain would not allow me to see or speak with Teige. He tore us apart. I know he would never have simply left me as the man claimed he did. We were deeply in love. We had just learned I carried our child!"

"So Alainn is my uncle's bastard child?" Riley accused.

"She is no bastard. We were wed, legally wed by the chieftain's priest, but when the chieftain learned of it, he had Teige sent off and the marriage annulled, but we'd been wed for over a month. The marriage was legal and binding. But, a chieftain has the power to do whatever he pleases to destroy people's lives at will."

"As do you, apparently. That's what you did with your vile, unforgivable curse!" the chieftain's wife exclaimed, her voice filled with rage; her eyes, with tears.

Alainn had heard enough. She pulled from Killian's arms and stalked over to the women. "Sorry I am to resort to this," she said in a testy voice, "but I feel it is the only way to resolve this," and she took her mother's hand in one hand, Lady Siobhan's in the other. "You think it impossible to know what the other feels? I assure you 'tis not entirely true, for 'tis something I am made to contend with every single day of my life."

With that, Alainn closed her eyes and focused, and in moments the two women tensed and cried out, each wearing a stunned expression that grew more intense. Riley ran to stop Alainn from touching his mother, but Killian and Rory grabbed him and wrestled him to the ground. The women were shaking, moaning, sobbing uncontrollably, tears spilling down their ashen-colored cheeks when Alainn finally released them. They grabbed each other in a desperate embrace and continued sobbing as they sunk to the ground together.

"What did she do? What just happened?" Rory demanded of his grandfather.

"Alainn must be an empath. She feels other's pain, a rare druid ability possessed by few, but she is somehow able to transfer this empathy to others. 'Tis an ability I've never heard of before."

Alainn walked away from the group and sat down, exhausted. She looked around at the various expressions, at the tension and unhappiness, the skepticism and betrayal and it was suddenly all too much for her to bear. She stood up and began to walk away.

"You'll not escape from me, Alainn," Killian said, clasping his hand around her wrist. "We have much to discuss."

"'Tis not the time, Killian, not when you harbor such embitterment toward me."

"Aye well, that will take some time to dissipate, I'd wager."

"Then, we'll not speak for some time."

"You should have told me, Alainn. It hurts me to know you trust me so little, that you felt you needed to conceal all this from me. That you had to bear this on your own."

"I tried to tell you—"

"You did not speak of any of this to me."

"In the letter I wrote to you, I attempted to explain it all to you."

"And you could not tell me face to face?"

She shook her head. "I hoped to never see the look in your eyes that I now see."

Alainn wanted desperately to be free of him at the moment. Could he not understand how tired she was with all of it?

"I have always treasured our friendship and valued highly our ability to talk to each other. Now you conceal much from me. You distance me from your life and try to push me away. I thought my greatest wish would be to spend forever with you, Alainn, but I am now uncertain if I can ever couple our fates."

Her blue eyes flashed with fury.

"I have never requested that you join fates with me!"

"If you have taken her virtue, Killian," said the O'Rorke who had slipped up behind them unnoticed, "then by druid law you are already joined. No ceremony or ritual is necessary, for the physical intimacy deems you are one for all time."

"With all due respect, Milord," said Alainn through gritted teeth, her cheeks flushing red, "I think my virtue is truly none of your concern. I feel in my bones you are my grandfather, but I hardly think whether I am virtuous or not is something to be considered when you have only just learned of my true identity. And even if I were to admit to having lost my virtue, why do you assume it is Killian who has deflowered me?"

Rory snorted. Killian looked affronted. The old man simply addressed her calmly.

"I doubt you would give your virtue or your amulet to just anyone. It is clear the two of you love each other, and if you have lost your virtue it is of great interest to me. The loss of innocence can cause a great many hidden powers to present themselves. Have you experienced new abilities recently or have you always had such abilities? "

"There have been some I did not possess until recently."

"After your virtue was taken?"

"It was not taken!" Alainn stormed, then she shrugged. "It was given as freely as my amulet."

"Then you are truly joined. Whether you believe it or not, it is so. But, I am certain your strong Christian upbringing will require an actual ceremony," he said, addressing Killian.

"Aye, there will be a ceremony."

"I will wed no one who only marries me out of feelings of guilt or obligation, and I will not have it decided for me as though I were a piece of livestock!" Alainn fumed.

The older man looked at her with dwindling patience. "Do not be unreasonable, child. You will need to be protected, and if Killian is the one who has claimed your virtue, then he must be the one to wed you."

"I will not be ordered to wed someone just because he bedded me, nor will I be forced to marry a man who just now voiced great displeasure in the very consideration of being with me for eternity!"

"Alainn, you must listen to reason. You are a female, and though your powers are strong and unusual, you need a man to watch over you, to guide you and protect you!"

"You cannot possibly know just how mule-headed your granddaughter is, Niall," complained Killian. "She is much opposed to being told what to do and is unreasonable to the point of exasperation a good deal of the time."

"Then as her husband, though you may not control her, you must ground her."

"It would be much appreciated if you did not refer to him as my husband, for he is not and surely never will be. And by the look on his face, it would appear it is truly not what he wants any time soon."

Alainn saw both her mother and Lady Siobhan coming toward them and felt herself being cornered. She glanced at Killian with a somewhat regretful expression, imagined herself in the fairy glade, closed her eyes, and disappeared, leaving everyone in complete disbelief.

Chapter twenty-seven

Alainn opened her eyes. Though she had wished herself inside the fairy glade, she was surprised to find she was not actually within the glade. She could see the thick briar bushes surrounding the fairy glade, and as she stared up at the portal, it begin to glow and hum, a sign that accompanied the portal's opening, but it remained closed.

Perhaps with her mind so filled with her many quandaries and without her amulet to ensure safe passage, she was not allowed access within the glade. And perhaps it was truly not a wise consideration to attempt it at such a precarious time. The beings in the perimeter realm of the Unseelie Court might latch onto her, since her heart and soul were presently filled with deep uncertainty and torment.

She jumped when she heard a deep mellow voice behind her.

"You would be wise to stay clear of this location, White Witch."

It was the large, dark-skinned man with many peculiar markings on his skin who she had met once before; he had called her a white witch. Mara claimed he knew much of magic and may be able to help end the curse. But she had warned her to be wary of the man until they knew whether he was trustworthy. "I am Alainn," she offered, "what is your name?"

"I am called Ramla, foreseer of the future. Heed my words, White Witch. Though the magical place deep within these brambles is filled with many a benevolent being, you must first pass through the outer edges where much evil lives. There are those who would be interested in learning your magic. I sense it."

"And what do you know of my magical abilities?"

The large man moved closer, and his aura grew steadily brighter. When he dared touch her hand, she too was surrounded by the ethereal light. She sighed deeply, feeling that he meant her no harm.

"I was alerted to your great display of magic this day. Anyone who possesses supernatural abilities, whether dark or benevolent, will surely know of the event for it was of an unusual magnitude not often witnessed."

She was about to question him further when there was a rustling in the nearby trees and out stepped Wolf. She cried his name, and he came bounding over to her. She was surprised to see the young soldier, Danhoul Calhoun, following him.

"Why is Wolf with you?" she asked.

"He came to me. Seemed insistent I follow. Are you unharmed, Alainn?"

"Aye, I am safe and well."

"I would not see harm befall her," the other man said defensively.

"Aye, 'twas not you I was implying would see her harmed."

The dog ran to her side. Even in his advancing age, he was a large, strong animal and so tall his back was in line with Alainn's waist. He nuzzled her hand, and she rubbed his snout.

As Danhoul approached, his skin began to glow as well. They stood together, and the circle of light encompassed them all, growing steadily more brilliant. Alainn felt her skin tingle and grow warmer. Her body became less taut. Her cares began to lighten.

"Ah, so yours is the other magical presence I have sensed," Ramla said to the younger man. "I am relieved to know there are others with such abilities who do not lean toward the dark side of their powers."

"Aye, I am Danhoul Calhoun," he said, offering his hand. "And sure, there are many more beings that choose to use their abilities for malevolent purposes."

"This is Ramla, Danhoul. He seems to know much of magic."

Danhoul and Alainn listened as the man continued with his ominous warnings.

"You must keep clear of the evil-doers, White Witch, for they long to learn more of your powers and will attempt to make them their own."

The young soldier nodded his head.

"Perhaps you would be best advised to keep your magic at bay for a time, White Witch. All will be keeping an ever watchful eye on you for a time."

"I'm not certain that is the best advisement," the younger man said. "I understand there will be many beings watching Alainn, but if she does not practice and hone her magical skills, they will be unpredictable and of little benefit in protecting her."

"So what is it I am to do then?" she asked, confused. "Do I keep my powers hidden? Do I practice them so that they might assist me? Morag, a valued healer and the woman who raised me, often warned me to keep my abilities a secret, that I should not reveal them or develop them lest I become unable to control them. Yet the Glade Witch, who I have recently learned is my mother, always insisted I should use my magic and learn from it."

"There are few certainties with magic, White Witch," Ramla said solemnly.

"Sure, the old healer did what she thought best for you, Alainn," said Danhoul. "She wanted to keep you safe from those would misunderstand you or persecute you. But these abilities are part of you and sure there is a reason why you possess them. If you do not learn exactly what you can achieve by way of your magic, if you do not practice and test it, you may never know the full extent of your powers and the limitations. How will it benefit you should you be forced to use it to protect yourself or those you care for?"

The large man nodded in agreement.

"It is surely wise to call upon your powers only when alone or in the company of those you can trust entirely," he said. "Use them only during daylight, unless it is necessary to protect yourself," he warned.

"An oak grove offers protection," said Danhoul.

"Aye, and there are herbs and spells that offer magical protection as well," Alainn added.

"And if you find means to enter the fairy glade without passing through the Unseelie Court, you shall receive protection from all within there as well. Outside of the glade when you are using magic, it may be wise to have one of us nearby for we may be able to assist you in detecting if a malevolent being is near. But, do not dare to enter the spirit world as you did this day!"

"But I felt as though I was being summoned to the spirit world by Morag, there is a subject of grave importance she wishes to discuss with me."

"Then she must come to you, White Witch."

"She cannot, surely something prevents it."

"Aye, it is a dark spirit or an evil entity," Danhoul stated.

"You know of this, Danhoul?"

"Aye, and of the dark being within the castle's dungeon."

Although Alainn was grateful to be in the company of those who also laid claim to magical abilities, with so many warnings and so few certainties, even surrounded by the healing light, she now felt little relief.

"What do you know regarding ending or undoing a curse?" she asked.

"Was it a curse born of a potion?" the big man asked in a deep voice.

"No."

"A purposeful spell chanted at midnight under a full moon?"

"It was cast after darkness, and I have no notion the time of night or phase of moon, but no, it was not a spell given mediation or thoughtfulness."

"So it was one spoken in fury and anger, a curse uttered in retribution for a wrongdoing done to the person who issued the curse?" Danhoul queried.

"Aye, precisely that!"

"Ah, the most difficult type of curse to reverse or undo."

"To reverse it would cause the conditions of the curse to fall upon the one who issued the curse," said Ramla.

"Well the issuer was my mother and that would indicate her line would die out, an option I am not so very fond of," Alainn said dryly.

"Not a useful end."

"And there is no means to simply undo the curse?" Alainn's voice portrayed little hope in a solution.

"Does the person who was cursed yet live, White Witch?"

"No, he met his death many years ago."

"'Tis unlikely then," the young Irish soldier relayed. "And is the end of the O'Brien line the only stipulation of the curse? Are there other conditions that might be met to alleviate it?"

"Aye, if I am accepted as nobility by the O'Briens. If I regain all that was taken away by them."

"Then, I sense you should not be without hope. It is truth you are a daughter of a noble man. What proof is needed so that the O'Briens will believe it so?"

"Morag's spirit attempts to assist me with this, but cannot come to me. Her presence is blocked somehow, and the only other proof, a piece of metal with the druid family crest, apparently lies within the dungeon walls."

"Protected by a dark being."

"Aye, it is surely so."

"We will do what we can to assist you, White Witch. I will attempt to calm the dark entities with my magic," the older man assured her.

"And I will be attempt to discover what I might from the spirits, and why your Morag is unable to come to you," Danhoul offered.

"And what might I do?" Alainn asked, perplexed.

"There are many who hold much love in their hearts for you. They long to keep you safe and wish you only happiness. Allow them to care for you and assist you. Surround yourself with those who lighten your soul and lift your spirits. Use your magic wisely; learn about it and from it. We will soon be in touch with you to inform you what we have discovered and to alert should we sense any immediate peril."

She nodded her head, though unconvinced, feeling overwhelmed with the many uncertainties.

"And cheer up, Alainn!" Danhoul jested.

"I am to remain cheerful when I am apparently pursued by many dark evil entities who wish to seek my powers, when Morag's spirit cannot contact me even though she attempts to speak to me of something dire I need learn, when I am to employ my magic in degrees I have never attempted so that it may benefit me in my greatest time of need so long as no malevolent beings witness me so doing, when I must prove beyond a doubt I am a noble to end a curse that will otherwise claim the life of the unborn child I carry?"

"You did not inform us of that topic, White Witch."

"You kept that information quiet, Alainn."

"Aye."

They both looked at her so intently she blew her breath out with a huff and crossed her arms.

"You both possess unusual supernatural abilities and the gift of second sight! Perhaps I assumed you had discovered my condition. And 'tis not as though I simply announce that fact to anyone who cares to listen, especially when the father does not yet or may never learn it to be truth!"

"Danhoul Calhoun," announced Ramla, "I shall meet you this night, and we will combine our powers to see what might be done to assist the White Witch." The portal glowed and Ramla stepped through it.

"Alainn," Danhoul said, "I will walk you to the nearby clearing, for the woman who is your mother searches for you."

"Do you still believe I should simply be cheerful?"

"Aye well, a sunny disposition does tend to distance the dark souls," Danhoul replied, a hint of mirth in his blue-grey eyes.

"Then, I will attempt to be ever so joyful and mirthful," she sighed.

"'Tis not such a grand start," the young man coughed. Something in his mischievous smile was contagious. She felt the corners of her mouth turning up in spite of everything.

Chapter twenty-eight

Killian knocked upon the door to his aunt's bedchamber. She opened it a crack and peered out at her nephew.

"I have heard Alainn has returned? Is it so?" Killian asked, his face filled with concern. He noted how pale and drained his aunt appeared after their harrowing afternoon.

"Aye, she rests now. Father wishes her to attend the feast this evening. I am not certain that is the wisest of considerations, for she is undoubtedly weary. But he wants to present her as his granddaughter. He feels my husband will have no choice but to accept her as kin if the announcement is publicly offered. And then many of the requirements will have been made toward ending the curse. We must find the other portion of the amulet, for that will end all doubt that Alainn is of noble birth. Mara says only Alainn will be capable of finding it, for there was a protection spell placed upon it."

Killian had stood listening intently to his aunt's words.

"Does she appear well? I worry much for her."

"Then tell her of your concerns, Killian. You know she will not be bullied. If she is capable of abilities that allow her to be taken to another location in times of discord and uncertainty, we must all attempt to assist her, not to impose more tumultuousness upon her."

"Aye I know it, Aunt Siobhan, and I agree with you."

He held a package in his arms and passed it to his aunt as he spoke. "Please see to it, Alainn wears this tonight. I want her to have it, though perhaps you might not tell her it is from me. She seems very sore with me."

"She'll get past it, Killian. But, you must give her ample time. She's being made to contend with many issues at the moment."

"Aye well, of course I care about her feelings, but 'tis her safety that must first be addressed, and her bruised feelings later."

"Perhaps," Lady Siobhan simply stated as she watched her nephew leave.

* * *

"I see no need for such primping! I have never had maids attend to my gowns or my hair!"

"Aye, you are a natural beauty, of that there is no question, Alainn, but my nephew takes it for granted he is the only one for you. When every man in the hall has his eyes on you, it will surely force Killian's hand to take you for his bride."

"I do not want to force any such thing!"

"Your child needs a name and a father."

Alainn sighed heavily, for she was unaware the other woman had learned of her condition. She was donned in a lacy chemise and when she glanced at the long gown the handmaids were carrying in, she gasped aloud at the beauty of the garment. It was a combination of silk and velvet, and an array of many hues of blue. It had a front skirt panel and long flowing sleeves with shoulder ties of dark blue ribbons.

When she was finally stuffed into dress and the many ribbons were tied, she stood before the immense looking glass and felt her eyes well with tears. Never had she seen such a lovely gown. It fit perfectly. The velvet bodice hugged her breasts, but revealed little. The back was open half way down. Lady Siobhan did a minor adjustment so that the gown rested lower on her chest and her cleavage was evident.

"You look radiant! And your hair is magnificent in that manner. It suits you most well."

The lengthy tresses were swooped up and piled upon her head in a queenly fashion. Several long wispy curls had been left to trail down her neck and shoulders. Alainn had insisted the combs Killian had given her be placed in her hair, and the blue blended perfectly with her gown. Lady Siobhan dabbed a lovely feminine scent upon Alainn's neck. The two servants smiled warmly and nodded their obvious approval.

The knock at the door made Alainn jump for she was uncertain if she hoped it would be Killian or not. It was not. Her newly discovered grandfather smiled appraisingly at Alainn's appearance.

"You are a vision, Alainn O'Rorke!"

Her eyes grew wide at the usage of a name she had never known to be her own.

"I apologize for my behavior earlier this day. I did not wish to insult you or to be—"

"You must surely have gotten your temperament from your father," he chuckled. "Teige was a strong-willed young man. 'Tis another testament to the similarities between you and my son. He was a good man, but headstrong to be sure."

"He is not gone from this world, for he was not within the spirit world."

"Teige is not dead?" he whispered hoarsely.

"I cannot seem to locate him, for I have tried much this day. I have attempted to summon his spirit, but no, I do not believe him to be deceased."

"But, he would have come back to us. Sure even as angry and displeased as he was at me, he would not have held a grudge for all these years."

"Something prevents his return, but it is not within my power to yet see what it is."

The man reached within the pocket of his tunic and drew out an amulet with a fine silver chain. Alainn recognized the trinity knot, the triquetra symbol, from her original amulet. This one was smaller, more delicate and feminine, and on the back it bore the O'Rorke family crest. She was moved at the man's obvious acceptance of her.

"The castle blacksmith is a capable man," he said. "He fashioned it for us this very day, and it has been charmed for you. By my blood as your father's sire, by the blood of your mother and of Killian's."

"Why would Killian's blood be a required element in the protection charm?"

"He is your protector and surely the most important person in your life. He will be necessary to your safety and well-being."

"Sure he is thrilled to be a necessity in my life," she muttered softly under her breath.

Her grandfather placed the amulet around her neck and fastened the clasp. It grew warm as it touched her skin and began to glow.

"Do not remove this, child. It will keep you protected from evildoers, and from your own powers as well. It may limit your powers somewhat, but it is necessary. I ask you freely to not remove it, for I sense if I forbid it, you will resent me and perhaps rebel against me."

"I do not intend to be so difficult! 'Tis the way I am and have always been."

"'Tis an inherited family trait and part of who you are. I hope we will get to know one another better, for I suspect there is much we can learn from one other."

Lady Siobhan smiled at the two and felt moved to hug them. They were clutched together in a loving embrace when a loud knock came to the door of Lady Siobhan's bedchamber.

Alainn shuddered and turned, rasping, "Chieftain O'Brien!" when the door was violently flung open and he stalked inside the room uninvited.

"What in God's name is the meaning of this? A servant girl dressed to dine with nobility? What guise is this? And why did my wife and father-in-law see to it her wedding was prevented this day!"

"Calm down, Hugh!" Chieftain O'Rorke ordered.

"I'll calm down when I'm damn good and ready, and when my questions are answered!" he roared. But, the man could scarcely keep his eyes from the young woman who stood beside his wife, for she was the most beautiful creature he had ever seen. No queen in all the world could have looked more stunning and elegantly regal.

"She is my granddaughter, the daughter of my son Teige and the woman you know as Mara. She will be wed to a noble when the time comes."

Alainn braced herself as she watched to see how he would respond to this knowledge. For although she had admitted to Hugh O'Brien to being Mara's daughter even she had not previously known her actual paternity.

"It cannot be!"

"Of course it can, Hugh," his wife insisted. "Take a long look at her and you will see. She is like Teige and my dear sister, Shylie, and even liken to our son, Rory."

"My God, can it be true? Is she nobility? Is she truly the one to end the curse?"

"If she is acknowledged as nobility and allowed to live the life of a noble, accepted by all the O'Briens, then the curse will finally be ended!" Lady Siobhan exclaimed.

"What proof do you have, beyond the physical resemblances?"

"We have Mara's word."

"Which is worth nothing by my estimation!" The man glared at Alainn as he spoke.

"I know it within my bones!" the older man assured his son-in-law. "She had possession of my brother's amulet, given to Mara before Alainn was born."

"And you are certain it is your brother's amulet?"

"Most certain, though the family crest is missing."

"I will not accept her as a noble until the amulet is found, and even then she will be an illegitimate child, a product of an adulterous fornication."

Alainn glowered at the man but held her rage as she spoke to him. "Soon there will be evidence of my ancestry and of my legitimacy. I will bring you proof so that the curse will be ended forever."

"Aye well," he said gruffly, "I will await proof then before I pass judgment on my opinion of this matter."

"There is another matter of which I wish to speak with you. I would ask you to reconsider the acceptance of Killian's challenge. No good can come of kin fighting kin," Alainn asserted.

"It was my nephew who offered the challenge, and only he can rebuke it."

"But it was you who issued such unfair and unreasonable stipulations."

"I was never informed of the reasoning for the challenge. Perhaps you would care to enlighten me as to why Killian feels he must do battle with you, husband?" Lady Siobhan asked.

He was saved from answering by yet another knock at the door. This time it was Riley accompanied by his uncle, Hugh's brother, Sean. It seemed they both needed to speak with the chieftain. He quickly left to address their needs rather than to deal with his wife's uncomfortable inquiry.

***

Alainn stood between her grandfather and her aunt feeling more nervous and anxious than ever before in her life. Her grandfather had just publicly declared her to be his granddaughter. There had been stunned silence from the crowd for a time, then a muffled chorus of low voices in conversation. From down the long table, Rory smiled and raised his goblet. Riley would not meet her eyes, and Killian was nowhere to be seen. He had not come to the banquet hall and Alainn couldn't help noticing that Mary MacDonald was also absent. The feast had begun and still no sign of Killian was to be had.

Alainn picked at her food, feeling entirely out of place dining with nobility. Brigid smiled at Alainn from down the table and even her sister seemed most amiable, though their mother appeared riled by the news that the woman she thought of a lowly servant was now proclaimed nobility. When the meal was nearly concluded, Hugh O'Brien stood to address his guests and made a startling announcement of his own.

"I wish to address all of you and inform you of a rather unusual turn of events. Earlier this week I announced the betrothal of my two sons and of my nephew. There have been occurrences that have brought about some changes to the details. My brother Sean has requested he be allowed to wed the eldest McConnel, Iona. Since her father and my son, Riley are in agreement to this, and the alliance of the clans will remain unaffected, it will be so.

"My son Riley has requested he be wed to Mary MacDonald. Again all parties involved have agreed to the arrangement, so the betrothal is accepted. And my nephew Killian will remain unwed at this time, until a suitable match for him is found." He coughed and glanced briefly at Alainn as he spoke, but she avoided his eyes.

Once more the crowd buzzed with much discussion. Alainn glanced over at Sean O'Brien and saw how adoringly he looked at Iona. She appeared entirely pleased as well, and Alainn supposed her happier temperament could be attributed to her falling in love with Sean O'Brien, for love held great power over one's happiness and disposition.

After the meal was completed and many of the tables had been cleared for dancing, Alainn received numerous offers to dance by many lords and chieftains of varying ages. She politely refused most, accepting only a couple, and was very relieved when Rory saved her from dancing with a most obnoxious and entirely drunken young lord. Alainn felt comfortable for the first time that evening and she smiled at Rory as he led her in the dance most aptly.

"I thank you Rory for not treating me any differently than if it were any other day."

"No thanks is necessary, Alainn. Truly, I think of you no differently than before I knew you were my cousin. I would have not been surprised to learn you were my sister. I oft wondered if you were a product of one of my father's indiscretions, for always I have felt a connection to you."

"And my powers have not frightened you?"

"Aye well, they are somewhat unsettling to be sure, but it was those powers that allowed you to save my life so many years ago, so I will not question whatever abilities you possess or where they have come from."

"I would suggest you are alone on that count, for Riley looks at me as though I have sprouted another head, and Killian, well, I feel his absence speaks volumes as to how he's regarding me this night."

"Give him time, Alainn. Though he is strong and undoubtedly courageous, he is easily wounded. I am certain he will come round soon enough, for he loves you well."

"But, is love truly enough, Rory? I wonder if love can actually conquer all as I once believed."

"There, you worried unnecessarily after all, Alainn," Rory said, pointing. "Here comes Killian now. And he appears to be looking quite dashing."

Alainn's eyes found him immediately, and she blushed for Rory was most correct in his assessment of Killian's appearance this night. He wore a tunic of rich velvet, a dark green shade that complimented his eyes. His trews were of a matching color and fabric, and gold buttons adorned the area that covered his muscular thighs. His dark brown hair was tied back in a plait, which was an oddity. Alainn was uncertain she had ever seen his hair worn in such a fashion.

She noticed that Mary MacDonald had arrived as well, and she and Killian appeared engrossed in conversation. Perhaps, Killian was regretting his hasty decision to allow Riley to marry the pretty Scottish girl.

Alainn gazed intently at him, and his eyes turned toward her as if he felt her gaze. His eyes warmed immediately though he did not attempt to approach her. Her dance with Rory ended and he left her standing with their grandfather.

"Would you allow me this dance, Alainn, or is your heart set on saving the remaining dances for the man from whom you cannot take your eyes?"

"Am I that transparent?" she whispered, flustered. She placed her fingertips gently in her grandfather's hand, and they stepped into the dance floor and stood waiting in line, facing up the hall. The music began; it was a refined and stately dance. She smoothly followed her grandfather's lead, circling and meeting, moving between the couples, turning and honoring him with a curtsey. He took her hand and they turned in a circle together to exchange places with the couple next to them. He bowed and commented on how graceful she was as they continued the elegant dance.

Across the room Killian felt his heart flutter erratically in his chest as though he were a nervous, infatuated boy. He could scarcely pull his gaze from Alainn as she glided across the dance floor in the dress he had chosen for her. He felt entranced. He felt bewitched. He thought he might faint like a woman if he did not soon take a breath.

She had not come to him when he'd entered the room, but she had not turned away either. Alainn had been in a rare temper this afternoon when she'd vanished in a vaporous mist. Her powers were seemingly endless and so many new capabilities were beginning to develop within her. It was not that he couldn't accept her abilities, but he feared for her. He had finally accepted that she was his destiny; he would not lose her again.

Chapter twenty-nine

Killian placed his hand in the pocket of his tunic and felt the letter. He had gone searching for her earlier in the kitchen herb-chamber where she worked on her alchemist duties. She'd not been there. He'd questioned Cookson regarding the letter and the young man had retrieved the folded paper. It possessed many creases, for the man had carried it with him believing Alainn or Killian would one day ask him for it. He also told him Alainn had wept the entire time she'd written it.

Killian had read it so many times he knew the words by heart. The first time he'd read it, he'd gone to the dolmen; their secret spot, the location where they'd first made love. He could hear her sad voice as he'd read the poignant words in her bold yet feminine handwriting.

> *My only love,*
>
> *I must apologize for the anonymity of this letter, but I am hesitant to put to ink my thoughts. If you are reading this, then, in all likelihood, we will remain forever parted. Please know that is not how I would have it if my choices were less severe. I would never purposely cause you pain, for I love you more than one could ever love another, as though I've loved you all my life.*
>
> *My leaving is the best and kindest gesture I can do. I know you'll not believe it, and I can see the stubborn set of your jaw as you read these words, the anger in your captivating green eyes that I love so dearly, but there are truths that will surely*

make you think less of me. Events have transpired that will cause dangerous ramifications should you come to know of them. I will not risk your happiness; I will most definitely not risk your life.

Please know I regret none of what we shared, not from beginning to end. Only that it was made to end long before I would desire it.

I wish you happiness, my love. I wish you a life of plenty; of love and contentment, and a dozen bonny children to bounce upon your knee. You will be a good and loving father, and I believe within my heart it will be a certainty; you will be a father of healthy, beautiful babes. I only regret we will not share that dream together.

I must close now, for I think I could go on forever, prolonging my farewell to you. Please do not attempt to search for me. I will not be found until long after you are wed to your betrothed. This is my gift to you: a life without the consternation and difficulty that accompanies me.

Know that I will love you all the rest of my life, and that if I could have been your wife, I would have lived my perfect day for all eternity. My plight is greater, my love, for I have been forced to make the decision for us both. I feel my heart breaking, and there is no hope of mending it.

Be happy, and all that I have sacrificed will be worth it.

Love, your L.

The letter had left him in a torrent of emotions. It was evident Alainn loved him, but once again she had taken it upon herself to make decisions for both of them. And he was riddled with guilt, for he had not been there to console her, not for the loss of Morag, the discovery that her whole identity was a falsehood, an attempted rape. None of it! He'd been off fetching a woman he had no intention of marrying because his uncle had demanded it.

Niall believed they must wed soon to protect Alainn from a type of enemy that chilled Killian to the bone. For once, he would make a decision for the two of them, and she would abide by it. He would see to it!

Killian was making his way to Alainn when a messenger hurried through the great hall to the chieftain. The matter was clearly of great importance.

"There is news from England!" his uncle called out to the guests. "The English Queen, Anne Boleyn, has been executed," the crowd gasped, "by manner of beheading. King Henry has apparently already taken a new wife. If he is half as shrewd in his dealings with the Irish as with his own, we will be made to suffer greatly, I fear."

The noise in the great hall rose as everyone spoke at once. Killian scanned the crowd for Alainn. She stood across the room, a look of profound sadness on her lovely face. She turned abruptly and left, and for a moment he thought he'd lost her, until he saw the flowing skirts of the blue gown disappear up the stairs to the south solar.

He found her near the parapet, looking out at the waxing moon.

"Oh, Killian," she murmured.

"You mourn for the loss of an English queen you have never known?"

"I mourn for the loss of a love so great he risked the ridicule of his kin, his country, his subjects, his church, and the entire world. He defied the Roman Catholic Church and all that is holy to have her, and then he cast her away. What utter sadness she must have felt to believe he loved her only to discover she was being replaced by another. And her daughter is so young; she will never know her mother. Perhaps your uncle is correct, Killian. Perhaps love is fleeting."

"Are you telling me you no longer love me, Alainn? Have your feelings toward me changed?"

"You know me better than that, Killian."

"Sometimes, I am uncertain, Alainn."

"You needn't feel you must be here with me. Though my mood is not joyful, I'm not about to throw myself over the edge of the parapet."

"I didn't suppose you would."

"Then why are you here if not to keep me safe?"

"I must speak with you. 'Tis important."

She turned to meet his gaze, and tears glistened on her cheeks. She stood there, so fragile in the soft blue gown, and he thought there could be no lovelier or more ravishing woman anywhere on earth, yet he made no attempt to draw closer or speak.

"What is it you wish to speak of, Killian?"

He cleared his throat nervously.

"I spoke with Mary this afternoon. We are no longer betrothed, and she was quite agreeable to a marriage with Riley. I have also spoken to the commoner's priest. He has agreed to marry you and me later this night."

Alainn's eyes widened, clearly taken back by his words.

"Mere hours ago you did not believe you could couple your fate with mine. What has changed your mind so drastically?"

"Your grandfather believes you must be kept safe."

"So 'tis only obligation that has spurred this declaration of intent to marry me?"

"No, that is not the whole of it, and you know it well enough. I will marry you this night. The priest will be expecting us at twilight. I thought it best that no one else attend for I have no desire to have my uncle learn of the marriage until after it has been done, though I think part of me will be most pleased that my marriage will rile him. When the missing portion of the amulet is found, he will accept the marriage, for it will prove even to him that you are nobility. The curse will surely be lifted then."

Alainn felt her temper flare.

"So 'tis to end the curse, and to rile your uncle that you would wed me!"

"If the curse is ended, it will be well worth our being joined. Wouldn't you agree?"

"I will not wed you this night, Killian O'Brien, or any other," she snapped, stamping her foot. "I will not!"

"Of course you'll marry me! 'Tis high time we made our union honorable and holy, and not simply secretive and lustful."

His presumptuous attitude proved to anger her further.

"You'd best rethink your decision regarding your marriage to Mary MacDonald, for I would never marry a man who lacks romance and charm!"

"Oh, so ye think I've no charm then, do ye!"

"None whatsoever! As a boy of ten and two you told me my eyes were strange, called me stupid, threatened to throw me in the dungeon and have me burned at the stake, and I think you've no more charm now than you did back then! You may know well enough how to cater to the needs of a woman's body, but you've fallen more than a wee bit short of knowing how to treat a woman's heart."

"Aye well," he snarled, "I've had a good deal more experience with women's bodies, I suspect!"

"Aye, and you can go back to your lecherous ways for all I care! I'll not be cheated out of a proper romantic proposal simply because I've already shared your bed, Killian O'Brien. So you can tell the priest he'll not be needed this night."

Killian rubbed his hands over his face. "This not is how I envisioned my proposal would go."

"Proposal? I don't recall any such thing. You might as well have ordered me to wed you for it would have sounded as tender and heartfelt as your bloody attempt at proposing!"

"You needn't sound so entirely bitchy about it."

"Now I'm a bitch then? Is that what you're saying?"

"You're a bitch a good deal of the time, Alainn. But, I've known that for a time, and it hasn't swayed my feelings for you."

"Your eloquence truly has no end, Milord!" she spat, as she spun around and headed back toward the stairwell. She met Rory at the top of the steps, and by the look on his face, he had heard the entire exchange.

He simply stepped out of her way, and she fled down the stairs.

"Christ, that woman could cause a saint to commit murder!" Killian roared. He formed a fist and struck the stone wall, then cursed himself for his stupidity.

"I've not much experience in dealing with women," declared Rory, watching as Killian nursed his bleeding knuckles, "and because Brigid was chosen for me I had no need to formally propose, but I would estimate that was the most pitiful attempt at proposing to a woman that I have ever heard tell of."

"So you take her side now that you know her to be your cousin!"

"You may as well have ordered her to marry you and sent the guards in. There was no question posed to her. And you spoke not of love or affection, or even need."

"Alainn knows well enough of my love for her."

"So, you do not intend to tell her so because you think she knows? You cannot know her as well as you think you do, Killian."

Footsteps echoed up the stairwell and Killian turned to see what other fresh hell was coming his way. Riley and his grandfather stepped out into the evening air, his cousin wearing a huge smirk upon his face.

"What is so cursed funny that you grin like the cat that swallowed the first bird?" Killian raged.

"I had to come find out what you did to make Alainn look as though she was about to pitch a fit. Do tell us then, what did you do?"

"I proposed marriage," he hissed between gritted teeth.

"You've clearly lost your touch, cousin."

Killian simply growled in response.

"Women are dreadfully romantic creatures, one and all," offered Niall O'Rorke. "And my granddaughter has fairy blood runnin' through her veins, as well. Fairies are fanciful, whimsical creatures, lovers of beauty and romance to a fault. I'd not want to be in your shoes if you've pushed her when you should have wooed her."

"I think we are far beyond the stage of wooing, Niall."

"Ah, lad, that is where you are mistaken. Women are never through with being wooed, and if I can offer you any advice after having been happily married for so many decades, 'tis to become a romantic yourself. Show her and tell her you love and need her a dozen times a day if that is what it takes to keep her content. For with all the powers she possesses, it will be in times of distance and discontent with you that she will be tempted to the dark side of her powers."

"I think I've enough on my mind without needin' to worry about some dark side of Alainn's abilities. I can't seem to even get the woman to consider marryin' me."

"Does she hold a grudge then?" the old man quizzed.

Killian did not answer, but Riley chuckled and offered his opinion.

"Let's just say Killian won't be samplin' any honey for a time unless he looks elsewhere."

"Aye, you might as well prepare for a lengthy time of discord," Rory agreed.

"I'd best go find her," Killian grumbled, "for I've a lot of groveling to do." It looked as though he had a rough night ahead of him.

Chapter Thirty

Their eyes met briefly across the great hall as she danced with her partner across the floor. He didn't miss the fact she was flirting openly with one of the men he was to meet in a challenge in two days time, a McLennan from the north, and one of the biggest, strongest men in the tournament. He was also a noted womanizer, and Alainn was batting her eyelashes prettily at him. When Killian cut in, sliding smoothly into the man's spot to replace him as he turned, McLennan seemed less than pleased. But, as the crowd laughed and cheered the move, he bowed out and blew a kiss as he left.

"You know, he's the man that may end my life with a battle axe on the day after tomorrow."

"Aye, I was giving him pointers!" she snapped, doing her best to avoid his eyes.

He sighed. "Allow me to apologize, Alainn."

"For being a buffoon and a horse's arse?"

"Aye."

"And horridly insensitive?"

"Aye!"

She made the mistake of looking into his eyes and felt herself mesmerized by the deep green pools. He slowly drew nearer to her so that their bodies were nearly touching as they moved through the steps of the dance.

"None of that, Killian O'Brien. I am quite furious with you at the moment, and I won't allow you to cloud my judgment by arousing me."

"So you're roused by me then, Alainn, but not enough to want to marry me?" With that, he lowered his lips to place a gentle kiss upon them, but she turned away to make a small circle on her own as the dance instructed. He quickly turned on himself, out of time, nearly bumping into his neighbor only to find Alainn stepping away on a double, hand in hand with another man. The crowd cheered again, but Killian only growled and stalked off to find some drink.

He placed his hand on the pouch attached to his belt, making certain the ring was still inside. When the dance ended he looked for her but could not locate her. His aunt stood watching him, a sympathetic expression on her face. He approached her.

"You've been talking to the O'Rorke or your sons then?" he groused.

"Aye, sorry I am that the proposal did not go as you'd hoped. Sure, she's as confused as you are, Killian. She's betwixt and between, can't go back to what she was, yet does not feel as though she belongs in our world. But you have always been a part of her world, Killian, even if you were from different classes. Your love spanned that, and it will surely survive whatever has you at odds."

"Should I give her time, Aunt Siobhan? Should I press her? Once I knew so well what made her happy, now I am unsure."

"You dwell too much on it, Killian. Don't think with your mind, but follow your heart. Sure, that is the way you won her; it will hold her as well."

***

Alainn had spent the last dreary moments talking with Mary MacDonald who was bubbling about how delighted she was to be promised to Riley. When he had come to find Mary for a dance, Alainn was surprised to see him smile at her.

"You've got my cousin by the ballocks you know," he laughingly whispered, "You might loosen your grip a little!"

"Aye well, I intend to do so, eventually," she said, returning the grin, so relieved she was that Riley was speaking to her after what had transpired in the grove. But, in truth, she was nearly exhausted and felt the need to inhale the cool air and be distanced from the large, noisy crowd. She sought out Lady Siobhan to bid her good night.

"Sure I am weary, Lady Siobhan, I request permission to take leave now."

"Alainn, please, I insist you call me Aunt Siobhan, and most certainly you need not request permission if you wish to end this surely trying night. I am hoping to go soon myself. You must share my bedchamber this night until we find a suitable chamber."

Alainn's face registered uncertainty.

"I mean you no disrespect, Lady…Aunt Siobhan, but I had hoped to spend this night at Cook's cottage with his family, with my friend Molly."

"Aye, I see you need the familiarity of your friends' home this night."

She embraced the younger woman with warmth and affection. Alainn was greatly relieved at how understanding and insightful her aunt was, and prayed she was still welcome at the cottage. After a quiet night's rest, perhaps her mind would not feel so entirely muddled.

Chapter thirty-one

Alainn hadn't yet changed out of her formal dress, but she'd loosened her hair and allowed herself to relax for the first time that day. She had just settled in with a hot herbal drink, while Margaret and Molly sipped some mead, when soft melodious music drifted in through the open kitchen window. It was a slow melancholy ballad, and she felt herself growing sleepy as she listened. Occasionally an off note was hit, and she pondered who might be fiddling at this time of the night, especially so close to Cook's cottage.

When Cook came home from the castle, the music had been going on for some time. He entered, wearing a broad smile.

"What has you so bemused this night, my love?" Margaret asked as she greeted her husband with a loving embrace.

"We've a private musician serenading our cottage this night, Margaret, and not entirely well, I might add."

"Who is it, Da?" Molly asked excitedly.

"Someone not wanting to romance me or mine, I'd wager." He nodded his head toward Alainn, who had been watching him with half-lidded eyes as she sat sleepily sipping her drink. She jerked upright, nearly spilling the hot liquid.

"'Tis Killian who fiddles?" she asked in a puzzled tone, for she'd never known him to play before.

"Aye, and he tells me he'll keep up all night if you don't go speak with him. I'd rather he didn't waken the children or set the dogs in the entire village to howling, so I'd be much obliged if you would go talk to the lad. He's lookin' more than a wee bit sheepish, yet utterly determined, I'd say."

Alainn sighed deeply, but made no attempt to move. Molly linked their hands.

"I'll go talk to him for you, Alainn, for I'd like to give him a piece of my mind."

"'Tis none of your concern, Molly," her mother scolded, "Alainn will deal with this in her own way and the sooner the better, I'd suggest." Margaret grimaced in response to a particularly unpleasant, high-pitched note.

The baby inside her kicked forcefully, and Alainn laughed softly.

"Sure, the babe does not like his father's music any more than the rest of us. He's protesting most earnestly!"

Cook and Margaret chuckled.

"Might I go speak with your man if you won't?" Molly quizzed.

"Aye, if you don't mention the child, you may talk to Killian for as long as you like."

"Do you plan to tell him at all, or are you just going to present him with a child when the curse is ended and the baby is born?"

"No, I will tell him this night. I have already decided it shall be tonight, but I must sit here for a time and summon my courage for I am uncertain how he will react to my keeping it from him for such a long time."

* * *

Killian looked up hopefully when the door to the cottage opened, but when the moonlight fell on curly red locks, he exhaled deeply and kept on with his less than perfect playing. The girl leaned against the stone wall.

"You're not very good."

"Alainn has always told me how quiet and polite you are."

"Perhaps she's not such a good judge of character."

"Am I to conclude Alainn has said some rather unflattering things about me, then?"

"No, she gets in a temper about you at times, but she does not malign you." Molly listened silently for a bit, a pained look on her face. "She cries herself to sleep more times than naught, and sure 'tis you she weeps for."

"I would not see her sad, Molly. I would do anythin' to see her happy for the rest of her life." His furrowed brow and sad green eyes startled the young girl.

"You're entirely sincere about that, aren't you?"

"Aye, I am."

"Then, what happened this night to make Alainn so unhappy?"

"She's still displeased? Well, I did not think my offer of marriage was something that would cause her such grief, but apparently I was a bit of an arse about the askin'."

"You've asked her to be your wife?"

"Aye I have, but in a purely unromantic and cold manner, and I'd like the chance to redeem myself, but I can hardly manage it if I can't look her in the eyes. I'm no singer, so I couldn't sing to her, or a poet either, not like your new beau."

Killian noticed, even in the moonlight, that Molly's cheeks became as bright red as her hair. In her embarrassment, she returned to her shy, meek self and seemed uncertain what to say. He spoke instead.

"Do you think you've any pull with her? Could you talk her into comin' out to have a word with me? I promised your father I'd not wake up all the children by barging inside."

"I cannot imagine how they've slept through the hellish fiddling," she jested and went back inside. After a moment, her head popped out. "She'll be out straightaway so think of somethin' hopelessly romantic that she'll be unable to resist!"

"I'll do my best, lass."

* * *

Alainn stepped outside, still wearing the blue gown, her hair hanging loose and lustrous down to her waist. A soft, cream-colored shawl wrapped her shoulders, and she was barefoot. She walked toward him and stopped only a short distance away. She looked radiant.

"I didn't know you played, Killian."

"Aye, not very well. My father taught me years ago, but I haven't touched a fiddle in all the time he's been gone. He used to play for my mother when she was sore at him, said he could melt her heart with the lovely Celtic tunes. I thought it couldn't hurt to give it a try. My father was a romantic man; I should have paid closer attention."

"You're not unromantic, Killian. And I fear I treated you harshly this night. My temper must make me appear a spoiled child at times."

He stopped playing and gently placed his hand to her cheek. "No, you were right to be cross with me, and you have every right to a romantic proposal. I tend to barge ahead and take control. An admirable trait during battle, but not so praiseworthy when dealing with the woman I love."

His hand tenderly caressed her cheek, and he noticed how her eyes sparkled in the moonlight. He was not a man prone to nervousness and had always been at ease with Alainn, but he found his heart beating rapidly and his mind racing.

"Just speak from your heart, Killian. 'Tis me, the one you have confided in for so long. I promise not to be prone to prickliness for another second of this night."

He chuckled softly at that and wrapped his arms around her. She returned the affection, and for a moment, they just held each other.

"Alainn, you know I love you." He paused, unsure how to express all that he felt for her, the degree of love and affection, respect and burning desire in something as plain and mundane as words. So, he said simply, "I want to spend forever with you." She looked up into his eyes. "I would be honored if you would allow me the privilege of bein' your husband. Lainna, tell me you'll agree to be buried with my kin. Will you be my wife?"

"Oh, Killian, my only love. How I love you! And I want more than anything to be yours forever, for our lives to be joined for all the rest of our time on this earth. But, I am uncertain I can laden you with all that comes with loving me."

"Whatever hardships or uncertainty that may come with loving you are better a thousand times than living apart from you."

"But, there is much about me I don't even know. These powers I possess seem to take on a life of their own at times, and new ones present themselves at a rapid rate. 'Tis not as though I won't oft bring you concern or uncertainty."

"Our lives are never a certainty, Alainn. No matter how carefully we plan or how calculated we are in charting out our lives, it seldom turns out as we thought it might. I did not plan to fall in love with a witch, but I have, and I'm head over heels in love with you.

"It won't always be sunny days, and we won't always see eye to eye. We'll have arguments and there'll be bickering, but that is part of what we share. I won't expect you to obey me. Well, not entirely at any rate!" he chuckled. "You've captured my heart. In truth, I would rather spend all my life in a miserable dispute with you than have a blissful relationship with a meek and obedient woman. I cannot bear the thought of ever being parted from you, Lainna."

He allowed his lips to brush against hers ever so briefly before he spoke again.

"So, will you marry me then, Alainn?" He placed his hand inside the pouch and retrieved a ring. It caught and twinkled in the moonlight. "'Twas my mother's wedding ring. She had promised it to my brother to give to his wife when they were wed, since he was the eldest son. After he died, I thought she would be in agreement that I give it to the woman I love. 'Tis the main reason I wanted to go back to my father's castle after we were in Galway. I needed to retrieve the ring so that I could give it to you."

It was a dainty feminine silver band with an inscription. By the moonlight, she read the words: *To Lainna, my only love. From your husband, K. O'B.*

"You had it inscribed before you asked me, Killian. What if I'd said no?"

"I had it etched this day, 'tis why I missed the feast. And well, you're correct I suppose in telling me I'm presumptuous, but wait, you're saying aye!" He beamed from ear to ear.

"Aye, Killian, I will be proud and happy, and elated to be your wife. But, first there is something I must tell you, another secret I have kept from you.

Chapter Thirty-Two

"Perhaps you might wish to sit down!" she warned.

"Alainn, you're causin' me great anxiety. Would ye just get on with the tellin' woman? I'm a man. I doubt I'll be overtaken with the vapors upon hearin' the news."

She took a deep breath, and opened her mouth, but the right words wouldn't come out. "You are going to be thoroughly vexed with me for keeping this from you for so long."

"I'm already becomin' thoroughly vexed, Alainn; will you not just spit it out, then?"

She took his large, strong hand and placed it to her stomach at precisely the same time the child within her issued a swift and sturdy kick. Killian's eyes grew wide and he did lean back against the stone wall, but held tight to her hand.

"Aye, Killian O'Brien," she said softly. "I carry your child, conceived the first time we were together. You've strong seed."

He leaned against the wall, feeling weak, quietly contemplating all her news would imply. Finally, he noticed the troubled look in her serious blue eyes.

"Are you well, Alainn?"

"I suffered with the queasy stomach for a time, but it is much improved. I am more weary than usual, but I don't feel unwell. And your son is already active, Killian. He will be a strong, healthy child."

"You know he is a boy child, and that he is well? Christ, Alainn, what of the curse? How long do we have to end the bloody spell?"

"Less than six moons, I would estimate."

Killian placed his hand to her belly and was rewarded with a barrage of steady thumps.

"Is that usual to feel such strong movements so early on?"

"Every woman is different, it is perhaps a bit early, but I have always been a bit unusual, haven't I now?"

"Aye, but only in a lovely way. Sure we must be wed then and with haste. The priest is still in agreement to perform the ceremony. I told him I was not certain it would be this night, but hoped it would be."

She glanced up at the moon. "Aye, the moon is waxing. 'Tis a sign of good luck to be wed during the waxing moon. And it is a marriage ceremony by a priest, you request?"

"That is not to your liking, Alainn?" He bristled slightly.

"I have been raised a Christian, Killian. I would have it no other way, but I thought, with the uncertainty of all I possess, a handfasting might be more to your liking."

"Ballocks! I'll not settle for a handfasting. When I wed, it will be for life, Alainn, not simply a year and a day. Most people who choose a handfasting are either uncertain they will be compatible in life, or in their marriage bed. While our life together may very well not remain ever-smooth, I think we are most compatible, and since we have already shared a bed and found it most agreeable, I insist we enter into a marriage for a lifetime."

"Most agreeable?" she giggled.

"'Twas the only word I could think of that would not put me in an immediate state of arousal. Is it safe for the child for us to be together in that manner?" He made a displeased sound and then cursed out loud. "By God's bones, Alainn! I took you so roughly the other night. I would never have…if I'd known I would have been gentler…you should have told me!"

"'Tis perfectly natural for a man and woman to continue a healthy physical relationship well into the woman's term, sometimes right to the end, though I fear I may look less than attractive at that point, and I am told a couple must become a wee bit creative in finding a way to complete the joining."

"Enough, Alainn, enough talk of physical joining or I'll have my way with you here and now, for I think I have never seen you lookin' as beautiful as you do right now. And Riley was correct, the rogue! Your breasts have blossomed."

"You discuss my breasts with your cousin, with my cousin!"

"Well, not as a rule. It was he who brought up the subject."

Her eyes narrowed, and Killian sensed her hackles being raised.

"We must be off to the abbey. I picked some wildflowers, and Mary made you a lovely bouquet."

"Mary knew of your plans for us to wed?"

"Aye, when I spoke to her about wanting to be released from my betrothal to her, she said she would agree, but on the condition that I take you as my bride as soon as it could be arranged."

She started off for the cottage and he caught her hand. "I should collect my slippers and brush my hair," she explained.

"'Tis perfect as it is, Alainn."

"Well, I must fetch my combs, for they should be worn at our wedding. And I will return the ring so that you might slip it on my hand during the ceremony. And I must fashion a ring for you."

"I doubt there is time for that, Alainn."

"Aye, there's time, for 'tis with my magic I will create a ring for you."

She glanced around to see what might be used to create the ring, and her eyes fell upon the amulet around Killian's neck. Though she did not remove it, she held it tight in her hand and whispered words in an ancient language. A small portion of the metal snapped off in her hand. She did the same thing with the amulet she wore around her neck.

After setting the two tiny pieces of metal upon a stone, they burst into flame. She mixed them together with a twig from a nearby tree, waved her hand above it, and blew softly. Tiny snowflakes fell upon the metal, cooling it. Alainn then twisted the metal to form a perfect Celtic knot. She placed it to her lips and spoke a chant that Killian did not know or recognize. With that, Alainn slipped it over the third finger on his right hand. He was not surprised to find it fit perfectly.

"You have no aversion to wearing a ring, Killian? Not all men want to alert other women that they are taken."

"I shall be proud to wear it, Alainn."

When she ran back into the cottage to fetch her combs and slippers, she found a lovely wreath of ribbons, wildflowers, and sprigs of shamrocks lying on her bed. Molly had fashioned it for the ceremony. She placed it on Alainn's head.

"You look beautiful, Alainn," Molly said in a choked voice, and the rest of Cook's family agreed.

"Sorry, I am that we have kept you up half the night, and that we will have no guests in attendance. After our marriage has been made public, which should be in just a few days, we will have a banquet and invite all of you who are so dear to us."

"When the chieftain learns of this, what consequences will befall the two of you?" Cook asked worriedly. Killian answered from the doorway.

"He will have no choice but to accept our marriage, for now that we know Alainn is of noble lineage, he cannot dispute our being wed." Killian sounded so confident, Alainn wanted to believe it would be so. "But I'd as soon wait till after the challenge before he learns of it, no need to add fuel to the flames when we will soon meet head to head, and sword to sword."

Alainn cast him a wary glance, and he regretted speaking of the upcoming challenge. She gathered her articles and joined Killian at the door.

"Would you wait outside for a moment, Alainn? I'd like to have a word with Cook."

She nodded and stepped outside where he joined her shortly. He took her hand and smiled at her with a warmth and affection that soon made her forget the pending duel. He scooped her up into his arms in his usual effortless manner, and she noted how strong he was. When she was with him often, she seemed to forget what a tall, muscular man he had become. He set her back on her feet and led her on a path not connected to the village church. She raised an eyebrow.

"We'll pass by the loveliest scenery tonight," he said simply.

"Killian, what are you about? Haven't you kept the priest waiting long enough?"

"In truth, it was not me who kept him waitin' but you, and sure the man will wait a minute longer while I spend a few quiet moments with the woman who will soon be my bride."

"But, could we not spend those moments after we are wed...in activities that don't include walking or wearing so many garments?" She gazed at him seductively from under her long lashes; his manhood stiffened in response.

"Aye, you've a point there, Lainna," he groaned. "But, half the pleasure is in the anticipatin' of it."

"Killian O'Brien, are you avoiding the ceremony after makin' such a grand event of proposing?"

"I'm certainly not avoidin' bein' wed to you, Lainna, my love."

"Shall I read your mind?"

"Can you?"

She closed her eyes and concentrated, then shook her head.

"'Tis a jumble of scattered pieces. 'Twill be most unfortunate if I cannot know my husband's thoughts."

"Well then, you'll not know when I'm thinkin' of beatin' you, will you?"

"That may not be the best way to get me to the altar."

He stopped to kiss her, deeply and sensually, his lips lingering on hers as he lifted his head.

"What are you up to, Killian?" she asked in a husky voice.

"You're awfully suspicious for a woman is to be my wife."

"That still remains to be seen."

"And you've a temper. Can I not have a wee bit of merriment? You always accuse me of bein' too serious."

"Have you cold feet, Killian?"

"Perhaps we should wait to marry until dawn breaks, for 'tis your favorite time of day."

"Among my favorite times," she replied suspiciously.

"Then let's head off to the abbey. We'll get there in time for a ceremony at dawn."

When they entered the church, the priest smiled broadly and opened his arms wide in welcome. Alainn was startled to find Lady Siobhan stepping out from within an adjoining room.

"Alainn," she bubbled, "I am so happy for you, for both of you!" She clasped Alainn's hand and pulled her close. "Come with me. I'll help you dress for the ceremony."

"But, I am wearing a gown; 'tis the one Killian chose for me. And how did you know we were to be married? I thought t'was secret."

Killian and his aunt exchanged a knowing look.

"He has been planning this most of the day, wanting every detail to be perfect for you. But he was so intent on preparations, he almost failed to gain your pledge."

"Killian?"

He led her to a corner of the foyer and spoke quietly.

"Go with your aunt, Alainn. She never had a daughter and has missed out sorely. She loves you dearly and wants to assist with this."

"What gown does she wish for me to wear?" she asked, as Killian smiled in relief.

"'Twas the garment she wore on her wedding day. I've not seen it, but I believe 'tis a traditional druid dress."

"A white dress?"

"Aye, most certainly."

"But, white indicates purity and is to be worn by virtuous women. 'Tis hardly the case when I carry your child."

His eyes filled with unquestionable love and pride. "You were virginal when you came to me, Lainna. And I will be grateful forever you chose me to be the first and only man to share such a love. Wear the white dress, for I know it'll suit you well."

"But you chose this one for me."

"Aye, and you wore it all evening and all night, come to it. You wore it for the proposal, so it's served its purpose well."

"Have I told you how very fortunate I am to have you?" she whispered, as the priest and their aunt looked at them with some impatience, as though there may never be a wedding.

He pushed Alainn toward his aunt, and Lady Siobhan pulled her into the room to the side of the entrance way. Mara stood in the room, smiling uncertainly.

"Your mother was made to miss much of your life. I thought it fitting she be here to see your wed," explained Lady Siobhan.

Alainn nodded and attempted a smile. Her mother gently took her hand, and Alainn had to resist the urge to pull away for deep down she still felt a deep sense of betrayal toward the woman who had given her away so many years before. She attempted to calm those dismal emotions and allow only joy within her heart.

"Be happy with your man, Alainn. Have the life your father and I were not allowed together."

"Aye, I'll be happy every day that we are together."

Her mother wore a dress that must surely belong to Lady Siobhan, and she was pleased they no longer harbored a deep animosity for one another.

When Lady Siobhan presented the long white gown, Alainn gasped in awe of its beauty. The soft shimmering fabric was slightly yellowed with age, which only added to the loveliness. Its boned-fitted bodice had flowing white sleeves embroidered with soft pink flowers. Many pink ribbons laced the back from nape to hollow. They helped Alainn into the treasured gown, stepped back, and sighed.

"It fits you as though it was fashioned for you, Alainn," her mother said.

Lady Siobhan lightly placed her hand to Alainn's abdomen.

"How can you carry a child when your stomach remains so firm and your waist so slender? And your mother tells me you are past your third month." She sent a worried glance to the dark-haired woman by her side.

"Aye," whispered Mara, "pray your husband and his kin accept my daughter, so that the wee babe will be without peril."

"Where is your husband, Lady Siobhan?" Alainn dared ask.

"Please, you must call me, Aunt Siobhan. And you needn't be concerned with where my husband is for he is passed out in his bedchamber."

"You gave him a potion?" Alainn asked in disbelief.

"Aye, I am not without knowledge of herbs, myself. I thought you and Killian deserved a wedding without his wrathful ways lending discord to the mirth. He has caused enough trouble for the two of you."

Her aunt gathered two portions of hair at Alainn's temples, braided them and tied it with a pink ribbon. Her mother then placed Molly's flowered wreath upon her head. The two women fussed over her until Alainn was primped to their satisfaction.

"Sure you are the loveliest girl in all of Ireland, the loveliest bride there's ever been!" Mara gushed. "I named you most aptly for you are lovely, pure beauty, my Alainn!"

"Your mother's correct, but I'd say yer the loveliest girl in all the world, Alainn. Killian always has had a way of attractin' the pretty girls, but he's won the heart of the most beautiful lady in the land, with no doubt!"

"The two of you make me blush with your kind flattery, biased though it may well be."

Alainn only then noticed the sprig that lay upon the small table by the door. She picked it up and inhaled the aromatic scent of thyme. Sure, Morag had left a sign she was happy she would wed her only love. Alainn tucked it inside the sleeve of her dress so as to have Morag with her on this special day.

A knock was heard upon the door, and Lady Siobhan opened it. Her father peeked in and when his eyes fell upon his granddaughter, he shook his head softly.

"Yer an enchantment, granddaughter, a fetching, fanciful sight liken only to tales of the fairies, I should say."

"Well, she is from the line of fairies," her mother said proudly.

"And druids as well," the man reminded the witch.

"And she's inherited the great beauty of both." Lady Siobhan beamed at the girl.

"Enough of this, you'll drive me to tears, and I appear most dreadful when I weep!"

"You've a young man waitin' outside the door, and he's becomin' more nervous by the second, Alainn. Might I escort you to him?" The elderly man offered his arm.

She gave him her hand and placed a gentle kiss upon his leathery cheek.

Chapter thirty-three

When they stepped through the door, Killian looked up and his green eyes filled with wonderment. Overcome with bashfulness, he thrust towards her a bouquet of lovely wildflowers tied with a plaid ribbon.

"'Tis a Scottish wish of happiness from Mary," he mumbled.

"You look incredibly handsome," she whispered, taking his arm. He led her to the back door of the chapel, and they stepped outside. It was a good thing he was holding her close for her legs felt suddenly weak.

There were surely a hundred people gathered outside. Flowers were strewn all the way to where the priest stood, and in the distance, mist covered her beloved green hills as the sun rose, gold and pink, warm and promising. The music of a dozen harps and pipes filled the air with the joyous sound of a Celtic love song, and the songs from the many birds in the surrounding trees added to the magical moment.

"I want you to remember this day as everything you would have it be," said Killian. "And when I wed the most beautiful woman ever created, I need to declare it to more than just the priest. I want to tell the entire world of my joy and good fortune. And we are on holy land being wed by a priest, so in truth we are both getting what we desire."

"Aye, we are!" she whispered.

"Walk with me, Lainna, my only love, the first steps of our life together, forever entwined."

"And I accused you of being unromantic, Killian. What a horrid woman, I am."

He laughed at that and pulled her closer. "Aye, you're utterly horrid!" he teased. She tilted her chin to meet his eyes and breathed in sharply for she could not have appeared more beautiful or angelic. Her hair shone in the morning sunlight, and her deep blue eyes pooled with unshed tears of happiness.

A soft breeze blew against her cheeks and played with her hair. Alainn smiled radiantly as she passed all those dear to her: Molly, Cook, Margaret and Cookson, Rory and Brigid, Riley and Mary. Alainn thought every person who had ever meant something to her in her life was surely here, all but Morag. But, the thought had barely formed itself when she momentarily gazed off toward the castle churchyard and saw the old woman's spectral figure standing and smiling at her. A small sob escaped Alainn's lips, and she waved lovingly to the old healer.

The ceremony was simple and traditional, performed partially in Gaelic and Latin as was customary. Tears spilled down her cheeks as she said her vows to the man she so loved, and she noticed tears glistening in his eyes as well. He reached out and wiped her tears away with his thumb. Killian spoke his vows to her in a deep, unwavering voice and slid his mother's ring onto her right hand as was the custom.

The priest declared them wed to a cheering crowd, and when they sealed the ritual with a most passionate kiss, they roared and clapped their hands. Soon they were overtaken by the embraces of many well-wishers. Rory and Riley almost tackled her in their joint hug as though she had always been a part of their family, and Molly and Mary kissed her cheeks and cried.

"Thanks be to the two of you, my oldest friend and my newest, for the flowers and for your friendship."

When they walked toward the gate in the churchyard, Alainn spied the old farrier standing there, holding the reins of Killian's horse. He smiled as though apologizing to the young woman for their past.

The steed's neck was draped with a wreath of wild flowers, and his mane had been braided.

"He's very pretty," Alainn complimented, and though Killian did not appear entirely in agreement that his stalwart steed had been adorned so entirely, he laughed.

The priest ran up after them, a crowd following close behind.

"It is customary to bless the marriage bed, have you a bed in mind?"

Killian at that moment wanted to exclaim that any bed would do as long as it was nearby, but he answered the man civilly. "We'll have our bed at my father's castle blessed by the priest there, when soon we make the journey."

"Aye, fine then, that'll do."

"But, where are you going to spend your wedding night, or day, as it were?" Rory asked.

Killian looked at Mara, and she came forward. She spoke quietly so that only her daughter and Killian could hear, but it was Killian at whom she looked.

"It has been arranged, they will be expecting you. You have three days, by our time, ten days in the fairy glade by my estimation. 'Tis all my limited powers could allow."

"We are off to the glade?" Alainn's eyes shone happily though not without some trepidation, considering her recent conversation with Ramla and Danhoul.

"Aye, your husband asked me if I would see to it."

"But, I was certain you couldn't enter the glade, Mara…Mother."

The woman's own startling blue eyes filled with tears, and she clasped her daughter tightly to her. "I called the fairies out, and as of late the Unseelie Court does not seem as interested in me, so perhaps I am mostly forgiven for my past deeds."

"Thank you, the both of you," Alainn whispered.

"Aye well, you deserve a magical honeymoon, Lainna. And we'll make do with ten days until we can arrange the journey to our castle."

It was the first time Killian had referred to the castle as something other than his father's. Finally now, he seemed ready and willing to move forward and become chieftain.

"Time is of a different measure in the glade. Surely we don't have ten days?" Alainn asked.

"I've a feeling the sun will be overshadowed by dark clouds soon enough," her mother answered, peered up to the sky. "The rain will set in for days and the completion of the tournament and the challenge will need to be postponed once more."

Alainn smiled, realizing her mother's powers were returning.

"But, surely your uncle will question your absence from the castle for such a lengthy time, Killian."

"Don't worry about anythin', Alainn. And no mention of him will be made for the entire time we are in the glade. Are we in agreement?"

"Aye, in complete agreement."

"Don't you fret about my husband," Lady Siobhan said, pulling a vial from the pocket of her gown. "He'll be occupied and rendered harmless for some time."

Killian lifted Alainn upon the horse and mounted behind her.

"Be happy, the two of you!" Rory yelled as they started off.

"And keep your man satisfied, cousin!" Riley called out to Alainn.

"Aye, I intend to!" she laughed. His arms encircled her lovingly as the horse trotted off toward the glade. The wind caught her hair as she inhaled the fresh morning air, and she knew she had never felt such complete happiness.

Chapter Thirty-Four

When they reached the thick briars surrounding the fairy glade, Killian dismounted.

"Animals are allowed within the glade," she said.

"Aye, but I intend to carry my new bride over the threshold."

He pulled her gently from the beast and slid her slowly down his body until she stood on her feet. Then, he lowered his lips to hers in a deep and thorough kiss that left her dizzy. Swinging her up into his arms, he stepped forward and clucked his tongue for the horse to follow.

At the hedge, Alainn whispered the words, and Killian listened intently for future regard. Both of their amulets began to glow and warm their skin.

"There will be more to see this time, Killian, and sure you'll be allowed to see more. I should warn you, fairies adore brides and love, romance and weddings."

"I've heard they've been known to steal brides away because of their great beauty, and sure there's never been a more beautiful bride than mine. Will you be safe?"

"They'll not steal me away, Killian O'Brien," she reassured him, "for they'd be stealin' one of their own."

"If you say so, Alainn O'Brien."

"I am at that, an O'Brien," she mused.

"Forever more," he said and stepped to the portal.

He paused. The sound of pounding horse hooves fast approached. They glanced back to see the chieftain's captain galloping toward them.

"The chieftain has disappeared!" he shouted. "I was keeping watch on the man, myself, so you could marry without incident. He woke in his chambers, completely enraged; I have never seen the man so unreasonably furious. He consumed more of the potions you advised against, Alainn, and I tried to calm him down, even attempted to subdue him by physical restraint. He has an unusual strength I have never witnessed before, certainly not in a man of his condition or advancing age. He threw me against the castle wall as though I were a feather and charged out of the chamber like a demon possessed." Mac rubbed the large lump on his head and regarded the young couple with deep consternation. "I have many men searching for him, for I dinna ken where he would have gone in such a state."

"Aye, we are well grateful to you for that, Mac."

"Fare thee well then the both of you, and I give you my good wishes on your nuptials," he said almost as an afterthought as he turned his horse back toward the castle and sped off.

"Should we go back then?" Alainn asked quietly.

Though his brow was furrowed with deep consideration, Killian shook his head.

"No, 'tis our wedding day and sure we will be safer within the glade. Mac and his army will do what they can to find and contain my uncle until he returns to himself."

"But will your mind be with me in the glade or with the uncertainty of your uncle's disposition and the safety of his family?"

He opened his mouth to respond when Danhoul Calhoun came running toward them from around the nearest bend in the briar bushes.

"You must come with me now!" he urged in a breathless voice.

They followed him without question to a location not far from the portal. Lying upon the ground was Ramla, his garment soaked a deep red. A pool of blood covered the ground near him, and a large knife protruded from his chest. Alainn knelt beside him and noted his skin remained warm and rigidity had not yet begun to set in. When she looked more closely at the weapon, she saw it almost pulsed with an eerie greenish glow, as though it exuded wickedness.

"A cursed blade," Alainn whispered dishearteningly to Danhoul.

"Aye, 'tis what I suspected as well," Danhoul soberly agreed.

"Who is this man?" Killian demanded, gesturing to the dead man. "And what does this musician or soldier, or whoever in hell he may be, have to do with any of this?"

"This is Danhoul Calhoun. He possesses magical abilities, as did Ramla, this man recently killed. They were helping me in learning what dark forces were attempting to seek knowledge of my abilities." Her voice held much regret as she continued to look upon the body of the large man. "Sure it was because of me Ramla was killed."

"Do you know who might have done this to him?"

"I was on the other side of the glade near the alternate portal," said Danhoul. "I thought perhaps to find another way inside. We were to meet back here, and that is when I found him like this. I saw your chieftain's priest lurking near the edge of the stone close, earlier this day. He had the oddest look about him, and his aura was unusually dark."

"His aura always has been dark, even since I was a child and first able to recognize auras, but recently it has grown more sinister to be certain. I have attempted to avoid the man entirely since my return from Galway."

"You believe the priest murdered this man?"

"'Tis a possibility," said Danhoul.

"Aye, the priest believes I should be put to death because of my powers. If he learned of Ramla's supernatural abilities, he would have been spurred to end his life."

"And you did not think to inform me of any of this?" Killian asked, trying to contain his growing anger and trepidation.

"I thought we had quite sufficient quandaries to confront."

"You may be safest within the fairy glade," Danhoul suggested.

"But what of your safety, Danhoul? If Ramla's life was ended simply because he was enlisted to assist me, then your life is endangered as well."

"Someone must search for the killer."

"And do you not believe yourself to be in danger?" Killian asked.

"In truth, I have faced danger and uncertainty much of my life. I will not be dissuaded because danger is a possibility."

Killian looked at Alainn with resignation, and she feared what he was about to say.

"I must help the man, my love, for sure you are both in peril because of the supernatural abilities you possess. And your mother must be warned, as well."

"What is it you suggest we do, then?"

"Perhaps if you go to the glade, surely the fairies and benevolent creatures within will see to your safety."

"'Tis not how I envisioned our wedding night," she lamented.

He held her close, his heart thumping loudly with fear and uncertainty. A booming crack of thunder made them all jump. The sky blackened and more thunder beat the air, which began to shriek with a cold wind, setting the nearby briar bushes to humming. The entire thick hedge began to glow, looking as though it might burst into flame, and all three dove to the side as a beam of light shot down from the skies liken to a bolt of lightning. A bright glow surrounded them and they shielded their eyes.

Chapter thirty-five

A haughty but exquisite woman stood before them, clad in heavy battle armor and possessing a golden sword and elaborately adorned shield. She exuded arrogance as she scanned the group before her.

"You will come with me now, woman," she ordered and held her hand out toward Alainn.

"I will certainly do no such thing!" she answered abruptly.

The woman huffed loudly and impatiently.

"You will come with me now. This is not a subject for debate," she said and drew nearer to Alainn.

"You will not touch her!" Killian warned as his hand went to the hilt of his sword.

The peculiar woman rolled her eyes in fury. She merely swept her sword lightly to the side, and Killian's weapon was cast off into the bushes thought it hadn't been touched. He grabbed his knife, and the woman smiled, looking at Killian seemingly for the first time.

"Ah there is a most definite grandness about men! Sure you are a handsome, brawny thing, and clearly most brave to defend your woman."

"She is my wife," he proudly stated. "And who by God's blood are you!"

Alainn felt consumed with jealousy as the other female openly and seductively admired her husband's attractive face and muscular body. When she stepped forward to touch his thick dark hair, Alainn held out her hands and the woman's own sizable sword flung from its sheath and sped off to sink itself deeply in the trunk of a nearby tree. The woman looked at Alainn with interest. Her shield was then torn from her hand and landed at her feet.

"The power to move inanimate objects is not a remarkable ability," she sneered condescendingly. "In truth, little ability is required to accomplish it."

"I will not be spurred to reveal all my powers!" Alainn countered.

Danhoul spoke to Alainn with his mind.

"She will take your defiant words as a challenge."

"I will not be pulled into her challenge, not if that is what her intention may be."

The female looked at Alainn with small smile upon her face.

"So you possess the gift of telepathy. Slightly more difficult! Impress me further, young one!"

Alainn glared at Danhoul. "Are you assisting her in this challenge?"

He held his hands up before him and shook his head.

"I will not fall into this entrapment, not for sport!" Alainn shouted angrily.

"We shall see," the woman smirked. With that, she glanced at Killian's sword that lay upon the ground and sent it flying toward Alainn. She jumped out of the weapon's path without using her powers.

"Oh you're a stubborn sort, are you?" the woman murmured.

This time she sent both the sword and her shield toward Killian. Alainn held out her hands and both objects were hurled high up into the air to land half a field away."

"Now we are getting somewhere," the unusual woman said, clapping her hands together to applaud her abilities. "To be capable of stopping a moving object is far less common."

In the distance, they could hear a loud barking growing louder, soon accompanied by a frantic whinnying. And into the clearing raced Alainn's beloved Irish Wolfhound, the black mare she had healed as a child, and the horse Killian had recently given her from the stables.

"The ability to control animals," the woman listed.

"I did not call these animals to me!"

"Even better. They protect you. And what of flora?"

"I have no notion of what you speak," she said with increasing annoyance.

The woman caused nearby trees to bend over nearly to the ground. Alainn glanced down at a large patch of stinging nettles, willing them ripped from the ground by their roots and soaring towards the woman. She pushed them effortlessly out of the way, but grinned widely at Alainn's amusing feat.

When Alainn heard a sizeable tree snap and begin toppling toward them, she closed her eyes and a gale force wind sent it in the opposite direction. It came crashing down in the bluff.

"You control the weather!" This time, the woman appeared taken aback. "By the gods! Such unusual powers. You did not inform me her abilities were so mighty or developed, Danhoul."

"'Tis not as though Alainn has had occasion to reveal her powers to me."

"You know this woman?" Killian accused.

Danhoul bowed his head toward the woman.

"Aine," he began, "a dramatically grand entrance, as always."

"Aine?" Killian gasped. "Aine, the Celtic Goddess?"

"Aine, the fairy princess and protector of women?" Alainn inquired further.

"Aye," Danhoul affirmed.

"You are actually real, not simply myth?" Killian's mouth gaped open. Alainn too, looked on in awe.

"You find my existence so difficult to believe when you are apparently wed to a mortal woman with god-like powers never before witnessed?"

Killian did not respond, but Alainn asked a most specific question, "If you are truly, Aine, you are then my—"

"—great-grandmother," the woman finished. "I told you there is an irresistible grandness about men. I succumbed to my attraction once many years ago and mated with a human male. Thus we created your grandmother, Ainna. I much regretted the need to give her away shortly after her birth."

"She was a tweenling, and your own daughter!" Alainn accused.

"Ah, you judge me woman, but you know little of what is required of a goddess, a fairy princess, the protector of women."

"And with all your many powers, with being a goddess," sneered Alainn, "you could not even protect you own daughter from dying in childbed?"

"And this god of yours, the one worshipped by so many, this god of Christianity, is he so different in that regard? Did he not allow his son to suffer an end even more cruel?"

"Aye, but for a purpose, to save human kind!" Killian shouted.

"Perhaps you are correct," she said simply. "I will not debate that topic this day."

"Why are you here?" Alainn demanded.

"I am taking you with me. Did I not make that point quite clear earlier?"

"I would as soon be taken to the Unseelie Court," Alainn sniped.

"I assure you, you would not!" she glared and looked at Danhoul in exasperation. "Is she always so difficult?"

"She is of your line."

"Perhaps that explains much."

"Listen well, Alainn. Danhoul is one of your guardians, as is your new husband. One is magical, one mortal. One has a soul connection; one has captured your heart. Both are necessary to keep you safe and out of harm's way so that you may live to fulfill your predetermined destiny."

"You might meet with less resistance if you applied tact," suggested Danhoul.

"I have no time for such trivial human necessities."

"Aye well, Alainn is not typical of most humans."

"There is truth in your words, young Danhoul. But alas, there is naught to be done. She must accompany me for she is much in need of protection. A third guardian will watch over her when we enter the realm of the gods."

"A third guardian? Do you speak of Lugh?" Danhoul asked in a disapproving tone.

"Aye, he is the god chosen for this task."

The expression on Danhoul's face was sour.

"I will not go with you, no matter what the reasoning!" cried Alainn. "This is our wedding day. You cannot take me from my husband on our wedding day!"

The clear blue eyes of the female before them filled with something close to regret, but it was short-lived.

"Sorry I am on that count, but heed my warnings, to fall prey to darkness would be far less appealing to you!"

Alainn looked hopelessly at Killian. He grabbed her and held her tight.

"We cannot be parted on this our day that was to be the happiest of days," she whispered as tears rolled down her cheeks. His green eyes were tormented with sadness.

"Go, Lainna!" Killian urged, "Go with her to where you shall be well protected."

He bent over and tenderly allowed this one moment to hold his trembling wife, placing a gentle kiss upon her lips. Then he unclasped her hands and pulled her toward the goddess, his heart aching so much he did not know how he would survive. Alainn cast him a look of fear.

Aine reached into her pocket, retrieved a dusty substance, and blew it toward Alainn, who immediately sent it back to the woman.

"Do not fight me on this, woman! It is for your own safety. Humans must be protected when entering the realm of gods." She tossed another handful in the air before her, cloaking Alainn. She gasped in surprise, then crumpled senseless to the ground.

"What have you done to her!" Killian cried in a ragged voice.

"She will remain unharmed, Killian O'Brien."

Danhoul touched his arm in reassurance.

"She will be well, Killian, and safe. Though Aine's methods are less than pleasing, she is to be trusted."

The horses stood calmly by Danhoul, and Wolf sat quietly at Killian's side. Aine gently moved her hand, and though unconscious, Alainn slowly rose, pausing suspended in midair. A pulsing beam began to grow, soon encircling the women with a brilliant light. It flashed once and soared upward. The women were gone.

"Alainn!" Killian screamed jumping to his feet. "Alainn!" He stood helplessly, eyes searching the heavens, his heart pounding with panic at seeing his cherished love whisked away to a realm he could scarcely believe existed.

Danhoul remained standing, quietly watching the broken man. Then a speck of dust caught his interest, and a hazy spectral figure appeared before them. At first her appearance was nearly vaporous, but within moments she formed the shape of a young woman with long pale hair and empty eyes. She spoke to them in a voice that quivered eerily in the mid-day air.

"You are to follow me. The spirit of the old healer, Morag, has sent me to you."

"Why did Morag not come to us herself?" challenged Killian.

"Something prevents her." She paused as if listening. "I am told to make haste."

"But, what proof do we have she is truly doing Morag's bidding and not that of a darker spirit?

She opened her hands to show a tiny sprig. She closed her hands again, and he was startled to find it suddenly in his own palm. Stunned, he placed the sprig to his nose and inhaled the strong aroma of thyme. How often had he noticed that scent upon the old healer? It soothed him as nothing else could.

The woman began to drift away, so the men quickly mounted the horses and started after her, Wolf racing at Killian's side.

"Who are you spirit?" asked Danhoul, trying to keep up with the grueling pace.

She turned to face them, and Killian saw that the eyes were no longer spectral and vacant, but an achingly familiar shade of blue.

"I am Ainna, daughter of Aine, mother of Mara, grandmother of Alainn."

Killian was suddenly filled with hope, and her next ghostly words seemed to echo within his very heart. "Old Morag has the means to end this curse and save the futures of many. But you will both be required to put aside fear to assist her in this difficult quest. Keep faith, and you will learn what must be done to prove beyond a doubt your beloved witch is The Chieftain's Daughter."

Book Three in
The Irish Witch Series – *The Chieftain's Daughter*,
is expected to be available the summer of 2016

Printed in Canada